I

To my beautiful, first born Son, soon to be 18 years old.

You drive me insane, you leave crummies everwhere and you have terrible taste in music, but boy, I love you so so much!

I wish you a lifetime of happiness as you become an adult. Happy Birthday Tiki xxx

Best wishes
Love,
Emma Lee Rogerson
x x x

EMMA LEE-JOHNSON

FESTIVE FLINGS

FUN, FETISHES AND FROLICKING

FESTIVE
FLINGS

Synopsis:
Jamie Knowles is facing a Christmas all alone after her childhood sweetheart dumped her for another woman. Until she realises, for the first time in her adult life, she is very single and ready to mingle. She may be ready to find something new, but has the man of her dreams always been right in front of her?

Jamie's older sister, Billie, is married with children, but both she and her husband can feel the spark fading. In order to save their marriage, they decide to spice things back up both in and out of the bedroom as a Christmas present to one another.

Jamie's work colleague and friend, Tim, has a particular taste in women. In the past he has worried about his friends' reactions. When he meets a woman, one who ticks all his boxes, can they both be brave enough to take what they want?

Are you ready for fun, fetishes, frolicking and a few Festive Flings?

FESTIVE FLINGS
SUGGESTED PLAYLIST

1. ALL ALONE ON CHRISTMAS- DARLENE LOVE
2. ALL I WANT FOR CHRISTMAS- MARIAH CAREY
3. ONE MORE SLEEP- LEONA LEWIS
4. IT'S THE MOST WONDERFUL TIME OF THE
   YEAR- ANDY WILLIAMS
5. DRIVING HOME FOR CHRISTMAS- CHRIS REA
6. SANTA BABY- EARTHA KITT
7. WHITE CHRISTMAS- BING CROSBY
8. BLUE CHRISTMAS- ELVIS PRESLEY
9. THE POWER OF LOVE- FRANKIE GOES TO
   HOLLYWOOD
10. DIG A PONY- THE BEATLES
11. EMPIRE STATE OF MIND- ALICIA KEYS

EMMA LEE-JOHNSON

CHAPTER ONE

~ Jamie ~

My legs turn to jelly as his hot, wet tongue caresses my folds expertly, sending jolts of pleasure directly from my womanly core to every nerve ending throughout my body. Fuck, he is good.

As he plunges his darting tongue deep inside me, I am engulfed by the building tension that is brewing and overflowing within me. I want his tongue, his fingers and more importantly his thick, long cock, and I want them right now.

He leisurely laps up my slit until he grazes over my swollen bud, and as he flicks his tongue out, my hips buck involuntarily, searching for more of his delightful touch. His lips clamp down on my clit, the feeling so intense that it causes me to shout out.

Then, all too suddenly, it stops. I thrust my wanting, weeping hole up, trying desperately to reconnect, begging with my frantic reactions for release, for more.

Beep. Beep. Beep. Beep. Beep.

As my early morning alarm clock startles me awake, my hand is

2

down my pants and I am frustrated as hell.

It's the third time this week I have had one of these dreams, and they are becoming more vivid and realistic each time. I seriously need to get laid. And fast.

After showering and dressing in my skirt and blouse, I pick up my mail, and notice both my sister and I have received identical handwritten envelopes. I set hers, along with the rest of her mail, on the lamp table before I set off to work.

I work in London's elite business and financial district and the roads are busy every morning, so I opt for public transport. By taking the tube to Canary Wharf, I arrive at my office ten minutes early, giving me enough time to get myself a cup of coffee and open my personal mail.

The heavy parchment envelope with silver hearts on the corners captures my attention once again. Despite its pretty outward appearance, my insides seem to constrict and then turn to ice water as I read the contents.

Staring in horror, I reread the invitation. This cannot be real. I am invited to the wedding of Carl and Francesca on Christmas Eve. The very same Carl who had been my boyfriend for six years. Then, four months ago, I returned from a training course early and found him in our bed with the aforementioned Francesca.

Six years we were together and never in that time had he mentioned marriage or weddings or even an engagement. What makes Francesca so special? Deep down, I know what truly haunts me as I question: why wasn't I special enough?

A note with my name scrawled across it falls to my desk as I continue to stare at the invitation in disbelief; it must have also been included in the envelope.

Dear Jamie,
I hope there are no hard feelings.
I wanted you to know that I never meant to hurt you.
I just couldn't help falling in love with Fran.
I would love it if you could come to my wedding, for old times' sake.
You could bring a friend if you don't have a date.
Love, Carl x

I hate the insinuation that I won't have a date. I don't, but he doesn't need to know or presume that. In the four months since I split from the man I thought I would spend eternity with, I have been celibate.

I think I have been in a state of shock, if I am completely honest. Carl's betrayal hit me hard. I felt like such a fool because I had no idea that he was being unfaithful. I thought we were in a good place. I thought he loved me as much as I loved him. He cheated on me and I am the one left with a broken heart with a side of shattered self-confidence.

The first person to call is my big sister Billie, who's obviously opened her envelope as well. "Did you just get an invite off that cheeky bastard? I can't believe he's getting married to this other woman, Jay. I won't go if you don't feel comfortable –"

Cutting her off mid-rant, just as I usually do when I don't want her to know I am hurt, I try to play it off. "Bill, it's fine. I'm happy for him, honestly, I am." I almost believe my lies too, as I recite to myself: I am fine, I am great, I've never been better. "Look, I've got to go, my boss just walked in."

My sister whistles down the phone. "You know, sis, the best way to get over a man is to get under another one, and your Mr. Matthews could make any girl forget her own name, never mind her ex's."

My sister has been salivating over my boss; Owen Matthews, ever since I introduced them at my birthday night out just before I found out about Carl. The tall, handsome, rich and successful Canadian evidently made a lasting impression on my sister. "Goodbye, Billie, and for goodness sake, remember you are happily married," I chastise her before hanging up.

I stuff the note and invitation into the top drawer of my desk, plastering a welcoming smile on my face and take my boss' coffee through to him.

If I can just get through today, I will be okay. I just need to paint a face on for the world for the rest of the day and then at 5p.m., I can go home and lick my wounds. Just nine hours. I can do this.

"Jamie, what happened, eh?" My boss, Mr. Owen Matthews, looks concerned. "You are as white as a sheet. Are you sick?" I shake my head. I need this job; I need my wages so I can keep my apartment. I remind myself that everything is great, I am fine.

"I'm just a bit tired, Mr. Matthews. Nothing a good night's sleep won't cure." I smile at him, but from his enquiring look I know he doesn't believe this is the reason for my dour presentation. However, he lets it slide and accepts his coffee.

Taking a seat, I give him the rundown of his day and he tells me everything he needs me to do.

By the time our morning meeting is finished, I am falling apart, the kind of crumbling that can only be solved by a good cry in the toilets. My life is a mess. I am twenty-four years old and for the first time in my adult life, I am single.

Wait a minute. I am single.

Suddenly, I realise the world is my oyster. All along, I've been looking at this as a bad thing, but it doesn't have to be. I am single and I am ready to have some fun. Carl has moved on; it's time I do too.

Carl and I were together for all my adult life. I have never really been on other dates. I have never slept with another man and the prospect is both scary and exhilarating.

For the first couple of months after our split, I had no sexual desire whatsoever. Nothing. It is as though Carl ripped that out along with my heart and soul. However, pent-up sexual frustration has slowly started to show up, and I have had to invest in a couple of toys to assist me. But God, I miss the feel of flesh on flesh, the heady feeling of being one with another person.

It's time to get back in the saddle. I am ready to start again, but first I want to have a little fun.

Christmas Eve is about six weeks away. Surely, by then, I can be over Carl, and maybe even have a true date for his wedding. The city is full of men, and it's time I stopped crying over just one.

~ Billie ~

While running around my kitchen trying to locate a lunch box, I shout to my children to hurry up or they'll be late for school. Oscar stomps in, annoyed that he has to go to school in the first place. At seven years old, he is already developing an attitude.

Chloe, my little girl, not quite five years old yet, skips towards me with no shoes or coat on.

Once again, I'm going to be late.

In the morning rush hour traffic, I drive the children to the breakfast club attached to their school and make my way to work.

Even traffic can't sour my mood for long, though, since I have the 'Best Job in the World': I'm actually thinking of trademarking it.

I own and run my own tearoom, Tables & Fables Book Café. Fortunately enough for me, my husband, Jonty, inherited the building from his grandparents,so I set up here with very little costs. It is in the popular borough of Greenwich, near to the market and the Thames. Because the area is steeped in history and culture, including a few tourist attractions around it, I get quite a decent footfall.

My tearoom combines two of my favourite things: books and cake. People come here to read and write and chill out, and I provide the best refreshments known to man.

We have an Open Mic Night on Thursdays and Saturdays where people can recite their poetry or read excerpts of their work, while songwriters can sing their latest pieces of brilliance. We have short plays when scriptwriters have a breakthrough, and my current favourite is stand-up comedy night.

After getting married and becoming a mother, I gave up my job, but I quickly grew tired of being the doting mother and wife and began looking for something more I could do. Then, inspiration struck. I wanted to offer afternoon teas and specialty coffees and make cakes like I had dreamt of as a little girl.

Jonty was not impressed. "You are not going to earn much doing that, Bilbo. It'll be hard work for buttons." Eventually, though, I got what I wanted, because Jonty could never, ever refuse me. I know his weaknesses, and I worked and worked on him until he eventually gave in. Oh, the days when a blow job could get me my heart's desires!

A scant few weeks later, my handsome husband took me to view the rundown building that he had inherited and told me if I could make a tearoom out of it, it was all mine. That is how Tables & Fables was born. The more I thought about what I wanted from the space, the more my vision developed. I could see creative types writing and reading while eating my homemade signature bakes and drinking the specialty teas or themed coffees.

Now, Tables & Fables is well-established. We have solid cherry bookshelves filled with old classics and more modern literary greats, some of which have been penned right here.

My food is well known and liked. I now have a team that helps to create and make the freshly baked items together with a merchandise line. We also offer tourist experience days and a takeaway service.

It will never be a multimillion-pound business, not when the chains who shall not be named keep popping up coffee shops all around me, but I have something they don't. I have a complete package and an array of services that they can never compete with.

Today marks six weeks until Christmas and it's time to decorate the place for the festive season. My menu will completely change over in a couple of days to festive afternoon teas and themed hot chocolate and lattes.

It truly is a magical time. However, I find that lately I am more excited about work and my tearoom than my marriage and sex life. How sad is that?

I am madly in love with Jonty. He is sexy, handsome, and giving, but it feels like something is missing lately. We seem to be drifting apart, and I don't like it. I love my husband, but things have become stagnant and old between us. We used to have fire between us. Now, it's like wet fireworks. Our spark is fading fast.

Letting myself into the building, I notice my sister, Jamie, has left my mail on the lamp table. Jamie moved into the apartment above the café after splitting with her boyfriend. At first, she wouldn't tell me the full details, but I finally discovered that he cheated on her in her own bed, and when I did, I moved her here. Although she was hesitant to accept my help, I set her up as best as I could. She deserves better than that piece of shit.

Looking at the fancy parchment in my hand, I can hardly believe what I am reading. Why is it that the bad guys always get the happy ending?

I will never forgive Carl for what he did to my sister. She suffered greatly, not just because of the breakup, but from the humiliation of everyone knowing why they broke up, too.

My sister looked shell-shocked for a couple of months. She lost weight, her pallor was grey, and the spark extinguished from her eyes and smile. She is just starting to live again, and I don't want this to knock the stuffing out of her.

The fact that we have to remain polite and cordial with Carl despite him acting like an immoral ass-wipe is infuriating, but our fathers have been business partners for over thirty years. Hence, the invitation.

As soon as I can, I call Jamie, but she is doing her best 'I'm not bothered in the slightest' impression and refuses to talk about it. I just wish she would find some happiness for herself, whether that be as a single woman or with a partner. I might suggest she set up an online dating profile; I'm sure she could have a lot of fun if she was open to that.

I pull up the shutters for the start of a new day and I welcome the array of sounds and smells that blend and create the atmosphere of my workplace; the coffee machine hisses and spits, the dishwasher is already in full swing and the delicious smells wafting from the kitchen set my tummy rumbling.

Christmas is just the best; I love this time of year. If I can get Jonty and I back to how we used to be, everything will be perfect. I decide to bite the bullet and talk to him about it tonight. Hopefully, this time tomorrow, I will be walking like John Wayne after a night to remember with my sexy husband.

~ Tim ~

Absent-mindedly, I scroll through my phone looking back on the pictures from last weekend. I had a blast. A night out with my friends, and I ended up with a gorgeous girl called Lauren when the club closed.

My friends and her friends had teamed up– we were downing shots, playing beer pong and dancing around and against one another. My friend Jason pulled a tall, leggy blonde and begged me to take on her friend.

"Go on, Tim, take one for the team. Please, mate. Take the bag of beef and I promise I will return the favour next time."

The bag of beef. I fucking hate that phrase. The bag of beef is what my friends call the stragglers at the end of the night. The leftovers, the girls you picked up in the takeaway shop or the taxi queue because they were ugly or desperate or both.

In this case, the girl in question was a bag of beef by proxy. She was the girl who would inadvertently cock block because her friend wouldn't leave her on her own.

"You said that last time, Jason. Which one is she?" Jason was blind drunk by this time and struggling to find the girl he planned on taking home, never mind the one he wanted to unload on me.

"Jason, is this your friend?" The leggy blond enquired, looking me over and assessing if I was good enough for her friend.

"Yes, Eryn, this is my best mate, Tim, he's going to keep your friend company while we go for a talk. What's her name again?" Eryn stretched out her hand and grabbed a redheaded beauty by the wrist and pulled her towards us.

My breath caught in my throat as I laid eyes on her: average height, dark red wavy hair, with the most beguiling green eyes I have ever seen. When she smiled at me, her cheeks dimpled, and I just wanted to poke my finger playfully into them. She was gorgeous.

"Lauren, this is Tim. Tim, meet Lauren and look after her." As they walked away, Jason turned back and mimed thank you to me.

"Hi, Lauren, so shall we get chips or pizza?" I asked her, hoping to break the ice, but she scowled at me.

"You think because I'm fat that I'll want food at this ungodly hour?" She challenged me. I looked her up and down in surprise. Yes, she is curvy, but fat? She isn't fat.

"Actually, I asked because I am starving. I didn't call you fat." I tried to smile to soften my chastisement, but she tutted at me and shook her head.

"I know you just got lumbered with me, don't pretend. I'm fat and you're fit. Fact. Let's just get our chips and get a taxi."

Geez, she had a complex. But I liked the way that she didn't back down and the way she had been blunt in confronting me. I didn't like the way she viewed herself; I couldn't believe she thought herself fat when she was stunning.

We walked in companionable silence towards the chip shop. At one point, it became overcrowded, so I held her hand so I wouldn't lose her, but she tried to snatch her hand away. "I don't want to lose you," I told her honestly, and she surprised me by allowing me to hold her hand. I noticed that her eyes seemed to soften, which made her look younger and more vulnerable. She certainly appeared less hostile. She was perfect.

"Will you judge me if I get curry sauce on my chips?" I asked her and she smiled again, flashing those adorable dimples.

"I won't say a word… as long as you don't judge me for getting gravy on mine. So you're Northern, right?" And that was when I knew: she was something special, some*one* special.

"Tim? Tim! Earth to Tim." Shit, I am daydreaming again. My colleague and friend, Jamie, is trying to get my attention.

"Sorry, Jamie, I was just thinking." She chances a peek at my phone, but I lock the screen before she can see anything.

"Could you set me up on a date with one of your friends, please? I'd like to get back out onto the market." I am shocked she's asking me; she has met my friends and knows they can be complete dicks at times.

"Nah, you don't want to go out with one of those idiots, Jamie. They'd buy you dinner to get in your knickers and then never call you again."

She raises her eyebrows at me. "Maybe that's exactly what I'm looking for."

There is a new determination in my friend's eyes. Since she broke up with her boyfriend, she has been nursing a shattered heart, but she looks set on moving forward now.

"Any preferences?" I jokingly ask her, like she is ordering from a catalogue. I mean height, hair and eye colour, religion... that sort of thing.

"Well-endowed with excellent stamina, please."

I think my chin hits my desk. Who is this woman and what the fuck has she done with Jamie?

"Yes, ma'am. If you're sure?"

"I'm sure, Tim. It's time I started having some fun."

As she walks back to her office, I catch my boss, Owen Matthews, watching her walk away from the doorway of his own office. I wonder how much he overheard.

"What's up with Jamie?" He asks me when she closes the door to her office.

"She asked me to set her up on a date with one of my friends. It looks like she is ready to get back out there. She must be finally getting over Carl, the cheating asshole." There is a flicker of something in his eyes, but he quickly covers it up and asks me about a spreadsheet for his presentation next week.

"Tim, please remind Jamie she needs to book accommodations for the both of us for this pitch; we will probably spend two nights there. Oh, sorry, I also forgot to ask her if she wants to drive or be driven, too." I give him my assurance I will pass on his message and he returns to his office.

My thoughts quickly revisit my night with Lauren. I ensured she got home safely, even going in the taxi with her.

"Do you want to come in for coffee? That's not a euphemism, by the way. Just coffee." She looked rather flustered as she made the offer and I have to admit she also looked cute as hell.

"Okay, but only if I get a biscuit too." She laughed at that, and it honestly felt surreal to be invited in for coffee by this alluring woman.

I had literally sat down when my phone started ringing. Jason. Oh, fuck off, Jason.

"Tim, I need you to come and get me now. That Eryn is a fucking looney tune. She threw me out of her apartment, and now I can't find my wallet. Will you come and get me please, mate." I groaned down the phone. "Oh, come on, Tim, don't tell me you're screwing the beached whale. You have no standards, mate."

"Fuck off, Jason. You're a grown man; find your own way home." I turned off my phone; Jason's comments irritated me. He didn't give a shit about anything except himself. A second later, Lauren's phone started to ring, too. Eryn was calling her and when she answered all I could hear was wailing.

Lauren spoke to her friend for a few minutes and then returned back to me. "It seems your friend puked up all over mine as they were… you know."

We both looked at each other before we burst out laughing. "That's Jason for you. He's a complete mess; your friend has probably got off easy."

She shook her head. "So, are you as bad as your friend?" I shook my head no, and I felt myself leaning towards her, wanting to kiss her plump, pink lips. "You don't have to do this, Tim."

When I heard that, I shifted closer to her and wrapped my arm around her shoulder. "Aww but, Lauren, I really, really want to kiss you so much."

As our lips touched, she let out an involuntary gasp. I wanted more. So much more, but I also didn't want this to be a one-night thing.

"Can I get your number? So I can call you? Maybe we could go and get chips again some time."

My heart skipped a beat when she said yes.

So here I am, looking at her profile picture and considering what the hell I should text this beautiful woman.

"Tim! TIM! Why are you so distracted? Did Mr. Matthews leave any messages for me?" Jamie stands next to me with her hands on her hips. She looks so funny when she is mad, her cheeks are pink, her blue eyes are wide and her bobbed blond hair sways as she wobbles her head in outrage at me.

"Stop shouting, Jamie, or I'll set you up with Jason." She gasps in shock at me. She met Jason and has made her thoughts about him clear. He is a dirty dog and she doesn't like him.

"You wouldn't! Fine, I'll sign up to the dating app that Billie sent me instead. There is more than one way to skin a cat." She winks at me and, for a fleeting moment, my old pal Jamie is back, the one before her break-up. Cheeky, cheery and fun. I missed her. I hope by the time Christmas comes, she'll have moved on and we can look forward to a better new year.

CHAPTER TWO

~ **Owen** ~

Walking back into my office, I shut the door firmly behind me. The blinds are already closed on my side window so no one can see me. I want to rip this tie off and the stupid stuffy suit. I am constricted and I want to be free. Agitation and restlessness fill me until I reach the inevitable conclusion: I have to do something. Now.

It all starts and ends with Jamie. She is acting weird and I want to find out why. However, any questions I ask are rebuked and if I ask Tim again, he is going to become suspicious.

Tim's words repeat over and over again in my head: 'It looks like she is ready to get back out there. She must be finally getting over Carl'. But what if he's wrong? I don't want to miss my chance but I don't want to scare her away either.

I have been in love with Jamie, my personal assistant, for what feels like the longest time. She is sweet and cute and feisty and sexy. It tormented me when she had a boyfriend, but she seemed content enough and so, I let it go.

However, when she was left brokenhearted by the creep who was foolish enough to let her go, I began to realise that if I could be patient and give her time to heal, we might have a chance.

But now, panic rushes through me at the idea that she asked Tim to set her up. She still doesn't know I exist, or at least not as anything other than Mr. Matthews, her boss. I want that to change, I just don't know how to make the change.

Thinking back, I recall when it first came to my attention that my feelings for Jamie were more than platonic boss-employee. My cheeks flush in embarrassment whenever I think of it.

~*~ *Flashback* ~*~

~~~ **Two Years Ago** ~~~

I'm at the office Christmas party in The Savoy in London. The management have gone all out and not only are we all treated to dinner, drinks, music and dancing but they paid for our accommodation too.

I brought my girlfriend, Georgia, with me. Georgia is gorgeous. Long, black hair, dark eyes, tan skin and a body that should be outlawed. However, she is a bit dull. I like a woman with brains, who can challenge me, but so far, Georgia is just arm candy. She is wearing a revealing red dress that plunges at the front and just covers her ass. Red high-heeled shoes adorn her feet and I will beg her to wear them for me when I fuck her later. She looks immaculate, flawless even, but the beauty only guises the dull, it will always resurface.

The sex is amazing though, and the thought of spending Christmas alone isn't a nice prospect, so I am going through the motions. We will have a nice Christmas but then I am ending it.

Georgia pulls me up to our room after the main course. "I'm your dessert, Sir!" she tells me, and I am not going to refuse. I am feeling frustrated, uptight. I don't know why. Georgia has taken to calling me 'Sir' every time she feels frisky. It's a bit weird. I bet she had a thing for a teacher when still a schoolgirl.

I swipe us into the room and undress, but Georgia catches my attention. She places both hands on the desk and leans forward.

"I have been naughty, Sir! You're going to have to spank me!" Well, that's new. She's never asked to be spanked before. I am up for trying some new things. I like to think that even if I am a bit vanilla, I'm open to some experimentation.

I take the bait and play along. "What did you do, Georgia?" She giggles back at me, still leaning over the desk, wiggling her round, plump ass at me.

"Take a look, Sir!" She wiggles her ass at me again and lifts her skirt a tiny bit more so I can see her bare and shaven pussy lips glistening from between her legs.

"What are you doing to me, Georgia? For fuck's sake, have you had no panties on all night, eh?" She laughs again.

"Oh, that's not all, Sir. I am ready to come, I have been edging all night." She told me about this edging thing a couple of weeks ago. It seems like torture to me, but she really enjoys it. It involves me bringing her close to orgasm and then stopping, and then repeating again and again and when she finally does cum, it is like an explosion.

"How have you been edging all night?" Visions of her in the public bathroom frigging herself off play out in my mind and it isn't a pleasant thought.

"Come and feel, Owen, come and see my toy." She looks back playfully over her shoulder as she slips her hand down between her legs. I walk towards her, unsure of what I may find. "Hold your hand out here, Sir, and watch me cum."

18

I follow her instructions and watch her, she's a screamer when she cums. She starts to vigorously rub her clit, and all of a sudden a silver ball pops out of her hole. "What the fuck is that?" But she doesn't answer me, she starts to wail as she finally cums.

"Oh my god, I'm squirting, Owen, I'm squirting! Fuck me hard now, from behind, please, Owen, I am having the most intense orgasm ever."

Lining my cock up to her wet entrance, I thrust into her. She's warm and ready but when she thrusts back onto me, screaming my name as she bangs her hands on the desk and throws her head back, my once solid-as-a-rock cock becomes flaccid. This doesn't do it for me.

"What's wrong? Why are you going soft inside me?" She pulls away and my limp cock slops against my leg and balls.

Sitting on the edge of the bed, I try to explain what is going on. "I'm sorry, I'm just distracted. I'm not into all the kinky stuff, Gee." This isn't her fault, we just want different things. She deserves someone who will appreciate her and embrace the same things she wants.

"Can we just talk, Owen? Let's just be upfront and honest for ten minutes. I know this isn't going to work out. We want different things and that's okay. I'm enjoying having fun with you, but I know you're in love with her."

She raises her eyebrows as she regards me, but I have no idea what she is talking about.

"I've suspected for a while now but tonight confirmed it for me. The way you look at her, the way she makes you laugh and smile. The broodiness when her boyfriend walked in. How long have you been in love with her?"

Looking up at her, I am completely dumbfounded. I do not know who she is referring to. "Who am I in love with? I have no idea what you are talking about, Georgia."

"Oh my God! You really don't know, do you? All this time, I thought you were failing at hiding it from me, but you haven't even realised it yourself yet. You're in love with Jamie, your personal assistant."

Laughing at her, I disagree firmly. "No, I'm not. Besides, she has a boyfriend."

However, Georgia stands firm and challenges me. "Look, I just want to have some fun. I realise this isn't serious or long-lasting between us, but can we carry on having fun until the new year? She has a boyfriend, and it doesn't look like they are going to be breaking up anytime soon, so why be alone?"

I stay with Georgia until the new year, and we have plenty of fun. However, once I return to work after the holidays, I know she is right. I have fallen in love with my young personal assistant who already has a boyfriend.

A year passes by, and it's the Christmas party again. This time Carl doesn't turn up at all. Hopeful that things are fizzling out between them, I relax into the night and festivities, until I overhear Jamie talking to one of her friends in accounts. "I think Carl will propose this year. He's been kind of secretive and I found a receipt for a jewellery shop in his car."

My heart plummets into my shoes and all over Christmas and New Year. I wait in sick anticipation for an announcement on social media or a group text, but nothing comes. When we return to work in the new year, I continually give her jobs that involve showing her hands so I can catch a glimpse of a possible engagement ring, but there is no ring and no further mention of it.

Another six or seven months pass by and I am startled when Jamie's sister calls to tell me that her sister needs a short sabbatical. She found Carl in bed with another woman and is devastated.

I hate that he broke her heart and that she is hurting. However, I begin to believe this is meant to be, it is fate. That relationship has to fall apart so a better one can come together. I cannot stop wishing that it's a relationship with me.

I visit Jamie in her new apartment in Greenwich, bringing her flowers,chocolates and a card from everyone in the office, but she looks completely stunned. I want to wrap her in my arms and give her all the words of comfort and love that I can muster, but I have to settle for a whispered 'there, there' and a kind pat on her shoulder.

~*~ End of Flashback ~*~

Jamie needed time and space, I knew she wouldn't be ready to start something else for a while. Stepping back to allow her to process and get over the imbecile who trampled all over her delicate heart was hard. Finally, it looks like it is time to make my move before someone else does. Standing by and watching another man treating her as less than she deserved, tormented me once before. I don't want to do it again.

So, how do I get Jamie to notice me? She still insists on calling me Mr. Matthews for fuck's sake. Will I always be just her boss, or will I ever be able to see me as something more?

Jamie is all I want in a woman; I wish for more with her. Honestly, I believe she could be 'the one' because I want everything with her. Now, I just have to be brave enough to show her I want her and only her.

~ Billie ~

The Café is jam packed and I work hard all day, hardly getting a chance to sit down or have a cup of tea. My back aches and my feet throb.

Dana, one of the lovely baristas here, helps me with the Christmas decorations. The place looks amazing. Between the red, green, gold and white decorations, the twinkling lights and the freestanding Santas and Gonks, it looks inviting, classy and festive, just as I envisioned it.

"I've brought you a reindeer cupcake to try and I have a snowman snowball we can share. Here is your gingerbread latte. Merry Christmas!" Dana says to me as she returns to the table. We are testing a couple of the Christmas offerings before we lock up for the day. "The cupcakes you saved for the children are in a box on the counter too."

"Thank you, sweetie. I think with the flavoured hot chocolates, the gingerbread Santas and the festive sandwich selection, we have a superb Christmas menu." I left a box on the lamp table for Jamie too. She could do with cheering up, and nothing cheers you up like chocolate cake does.

Tonight, is one of the nights we close early. There is no open mic or other event this evening and I am glad in a way. I've been feeling on edge for a couple of hours. I am going to talk to Jonty and finally address the issues we are facing.

Greenwich isn't too busy today, there is no market on, and the colder weather is keeping people at home. I am able to get in my car and hit the road within a few minutes, which is highly unusual.

As I make my way home, I turn on the radio and smile when a favourite Christmas pop song plays cheerily, I sing along to the catchy lyrics.

The children are already at home with our childminder. I wave Kerryn goodbye, relieving her from her duties so I can spend time with my babies.

"Did you bring some cakes, Mummy?" Chloe asks me impatiently. My little girl has been eagerly waiting for the Christmas menu to be launched. She keeps asking for the delights I brought home last year. The stocking sugar cookies and Santa belly cupcakes were a roaring success last year, but I wanted to keep things fresh and had decided early on that I would try and do similar items but with slightly differing concepts.

"I have got both you and your brother a reindeer chocolate cupcake for after your dinner. But first, where are my hugs and kisses?" I tease her. "Is Daddy home yet?" She shakes her head vigorously before jumping into my arms.

"Thank you, Mummy!" she shouts, giving me a warm, sticky kiss. God, I love this little girl. Ever since last Christmas when she became aware of my job, she tells everyone that she is going to run a tearoom just like me, much to Jonty's horror. He wants her to become a barrister, not a barista. However, if that is what makes my baby happy, that is exactly what she will do.

I sneak into the lounge where Oscar is playing FIFA on his game console. My son loves football. If he isn't watching it, he's playing it, or collecting cards for it, or talking about it, or gaming it. He has buckets of drive and ambition. He frequently reminds me of his father. Well, not so much now, but prior to having children, Jonty was passionate and zealous. I want that version of Jonty back; I miss him fiercely.

"Hey, sunshine, I'm home." Oscar grunts in reply. "Oscar?" I try to get his attention and fail. "Right, one more game and then turn it off, mister. Come and talk to your family like a normal human."

He glances at me fleetingly. "Okay, sorry just let me finish this match and then I'll come and talk to you."

When I return to Chloe in the kitchen, my phone beeps with a message from Jonty.

Jonty:
Be home in twenty minutes... starving!

After putting the pasta bake and fish into the oven, I freshen up, wanting to look appealing for my talk with my husband. All I want is to feel the heat and desire in him. For him to look at me, *really* look at me, and find me attractive.

Looking in the mirror while brushing my long blond hair, I assess the damage. I don't think I look too bad. A bit more worn than I used to be: age and life will do that.

After a quick spritz of perfume, I return downstairs and ask the children to help set the table while I lay the food out in the middle..

Jonty arrives just as we are about to sit down. "Something smells delicious," he shouts to us before coming into the dining room.

Chloe runs to him first, leaving the seat she has just sat in. "Daddy!" she shouts and he laughs as he picks her up before placing her back into her seat.

Oscar holds out his fist and father and son fist bump. "Dad, you'll never guess what player I got in my ultimate team."

My words of greeting are lost in a haze of excited children, and it's not the first time I realise Jonty doesn't even notice me.

I serve the dinner in silence, feeling conflicted and embarrassed. Am I jealous of my own children? Of course, I love their relationship with their father, and it's great that we are all so close. Is it wrong for me to want a bit of my husband's love, affection and time? I am fading like a wallflower, when I was once his centrepiece.

"You're quiet, Bilbo, is everything okay?" I manage a tight smile, but I am annoyed that these are the first words my husband has said to me. Goddamn it, where is the love and the passion? There was once a time when Jonty couldn't keep his eyes and hands off me.

After dinner is another blur of washing up, bath and story time, a quick game of FIFA and under the bed monster checking. When we finally get to our bedroom, we both flop onto the bed exhausted.

However, tonight I am not accepting 'I'm tired' or 'it's late.' We are in serious danger right now if we don't talk.

"Jonty... do you still love me?" I blurt out. I don't mean to start off with that but the words leave before I could stop them.

"You know I do, where did that come from?" He turns onto his side and looks at me with concern in his eyes.

The very same steel-grey eyes he once couldn't keep off me, the eyes that used to light up at the mere mention of me, or at the promise of what was to come.

"Evidently, I don't know you do, or I wouldn't have asked. I'm worried about us. Things are quickly getting stale and old between us, and I think we need to do something now before we start to lose our connection." He looks back at me with shock, but I can see he is protectively going to defend himself.

"Is this about sex? I'm just tired, Bill. It's been a long day; it's another long day tomorrow. I just want to get in my comfies and chill out. I want to chill out with you."

"Yes, this is about sex. It's about everything. I miss how things were before the children." As I say the words, I am filled with surprise that I'm actually saying them out loud. We had agreed we wouldn't mention our time before the children, because it wouldn't be wise to continue with that lifestyle once children were involved.

"You miss the swinging? The threesomes? The sex parties? The kinky stuff? We agreed once the children came we would go vanilla so it would never affect them, Bill. I miss that stuff too, but we can't go back to that time."

"Why not? Would us doing some kink really affect the children? Can't we find a way to have a bit of what we used to enjoy? I miss us, Jonty, we are fading away and quickly at that ! We need to rekindle that fire and keep it burning or we aren't going to last."

I look down at my husband, his eyes are dark and filled with the passion I have ached to see. I can see the evidence of his excitement, the tent in his pants confirms he still wants that stuff too.

But will he give in to his desire and take the plunge with me again?

~ Jonty ~

There are many events that are imprinted in my mind, events that have shaped the man I am today. The death of my father when I was fourteen years old, graduating from the University of Cambridge with a first-class honours degree, the birth of my children, marrying my beautiful Billie. But the one event that pales all of them in comparison is the day I met my future wife for the very first time. I can't help my mind wandering back to the day I met her and our subsequent courtship and first year of marriage.

~*~ Flashback ~*~

~~~ Twelve Years Ago ~~~

As I enter the restaurant, I pull my friend Marcus back by the arm. "Promise me she isn't a weirdo," I say to him.

Marcus laughs as he replies, "Honestly, she's a stunner, dark haired, stacked and great in the sack, apparently."

As a favour to my friend, I am going on a blind date. His new girlfriend begged him to bring a friend for one of hers and Marcus roped me into going with him on the proviso that he foots the whole bill.

Marcus gives his name to the maître d' who tells us that the ladies have already arrived. As we approach the table, the beautiful brunette stands and greets Marcus and then Marcus introduces me. "Jonty, this is Michelle." We shake hands and make small talk while we wait for her friend to return from the bathroom.

"There she is!" Marcus exclaims, and as I turn in my seat to finally meet my friend's new girlfriend, my breath catches in my throat.

She is an angel; she walks towards us with the light shining behind her giving her an ethereal appearance. Her blue eyes twinkle with mischief and merriment. She has shoulder-length blonde hair, she is tall and slim with long legs and curves in all the right places. She is exquisite, absolute perfection. She is also my friend's new girlfriend.

"Billie, this is my friend Jonty. Jonty, meet Billie, the girl I have told you all about." My tongue feels double its usual size as I try to greet her. This is going to be a long night.

About an hour later, Marcus asks me to join him at the bar. "I'm guessing you don't fancy her then? She is putting it on a plate for you, Jonty. Don't you want to have a bit of fun, no strings?"

"How serious are you about Billie?" I ask him bluntly, pleading with him to be as honest as possible.

"We're just having some fun... why? Do you like her? Is that why you've been acting funny?" he asks, excitement growing on his face. He looks happy and not at all offended, so I tell him the truth.

"I'm going to marry that girl. She's the one."

~~~ Ten Years Ago ~~~

It took me a year to persuade Billie to marry me. She confided in me that she had wild oats to sow before she settled down and was reluctant to make a bigger commitment to me until she had done all the things she wanted to. It, therefore, took another year to make it down the aisle.

I tell her we will sow those oats together. In our first year together as husband and wife, we try many things. We honestly admit to each other after a fantastic first year of marriage exploring our sexuality that we both want more, and we want it as a couple.

She says I am crazy and I confirm I am. I am completely and utterly crazy about her.

I have always been fascinated by all things kinky. Fortunately, I did partake in a few threesomes before I met Billie. With my experience to guide us, I take my love by the hand and slowly introduce her to all the things she wants to experience before she fully settles down.

The first threesome we have is with another woman, at Billie's insistence. I make her tell me in explicit detail what she wants, and her face reddens as she explains that she wants to know what it is like to sleep with another woman, to taste her and fuck her with her fingers and mouth. She wants me to watch her as she pleasures another woman, and to help her pleasure that woman too.

We arrange a suitable woman through an agency. She is vetted, tested, and we paid for her discretion. Billie wants a petite brunette and as long as Billie is happy, that works for me.

Ruby is a 30-year-old escort who specialises in kink. She is indeed petite, straight up and down but pretty enough and Billie really likes her. We book a hotel room and ask Ruby for her services for the whole night.

Before we start, I sit both women down with a drink so we can agree on the boundaries. Billie vocalises exactly what she wants because she wants this to be done properly.

"You two can do anything apart from full sex, agreed?" she requests and I agree straight away.

I sit leisurely in a high-backed armchair and watch as my wife kisses another woman. Where Billie is tall, Ruby is short, Billie is fair haired, and Ruby is dark. They are like yin and yang, a superb mingle for me to see.

Ruby, being the more experienced party, slowly undresses Billie, who turns back to me, her eyes reaching mine searchingly. "Go on, sexy, it's okay." I encourage her and give my permission, so she knows this is all good.

Billie smiles back radiantly at me and tells Ruby to stop. Billie takes control, she undresses Ruby, slowly unbuttoning her blouse and kissing her neck and clavicle. I watch in lust as Billie licks up the other woman's chest. She looks amazing; she is made for this.

Billie then removes Ruby's bra with a lot more elegance and grace than my best efforts. As Ruby's small tits spring free, Billie lets out a groan of lust before palming the little swollen bee stings and suckling the perfect pink peaks.

Billie looks over at me again. Her eyes are full of want and desire; she looks fucking hot. "Hmmm, Jonty, she tastes so good. Come and have a try."

I don't need to be invited twice.

I join my wife and our new friend and revel in her delight. Whatever Billie does to Ruby, I mirror back to Billie. As Billie's hands move south, she gently pulls down Ruby's skirt to reveal lacy panties and stockings and so I do the same to Billie. I slide my hand between her legs, and I can feel the heat and wetness already building from within her.

"You like that, don't you, baby? Tell me what you want to do next." Billie bites her lip and points to the bed. "Take off your panties and get on the bed please, Ruby," I instruct her on Billie's behalf.

I slip the rest of my own clothes off and fist my cock. Billie is now completely naked. She climbs on the bed and then hovers over Ruby. I watch in fascination as Billie uses her hands and tongue to explore every millimetre of Ruby's body.

My breathing is erratic. My engorged cock becomes even harder, the veins popping out, as I watch my beautiful wife lick out the writhing woman on the bed.

As Billie licks down Ruby's pussy lips, I think I'm going to cum. "Are you enjoying the show, Jonty? Do you want to get closer and really see what I am doing here?" Fuck yeah, I do.

I sit on the edge of the bed and watch Billie as she uses her tongue and lips to pleasure Ruby. She finds Ruby's clit and sucks on it, scraping her teeth over it before plunging her tongue into her wanting hole. I am so fucking hot for her right now.

"*Do you want to taste, Jonty? She tastes so good, and I will share.*" *She wipes her mouth with the back of her hand. I can see Ruby's juices still glistening on her face.*

"*I want to taste you, Bill. I want to lick you out while you lick Ruby. I want you to eat her until she cums in your face and you cum in mine.*"

Billie's eyes darken with desire. "*Yes, I want that, but first I want to watch you so I can see how you eat Ruby.*"

I quickly ask Ruby's permission, eager to please her and meet my wife's demands. "*Yes, please, make me cum, you're both teasing me now and I'm so close.*" *I roll my tongue over Ruby's clit, causing her to squirm and moan. Billie pulls me back.*

"*Show me how. How did you make her feel good?*" *I show her the tongue movement I used, first on her hand so she can watch and then I repeat it on Ruby, who bucks her hips, begging for more.*

"*She's close, Bill. Do you want the honours?*" *She quickly nods and shifts so her ass is in the air as she laps at Ruby's clit while also sliding two fingers inside her pumping in and out and swirling them about in circular motions.*

"*Yes, you dirty little bitch, make her cum, fuck her with your fingers.*" *I encourage her, knowing she loves my dirty words and it'll help her on her way to fulfilment too.*

"*Yes, like that, like that, owwwww, YES!*" *Ruby shouts as waves of pleasure flood her body.*

After making Ruby cum, Billie looks back at me in triumph.

"*Now it's our turn to make you feel good, Bilbo.*"

We use Ruby's services a few more times, and each time becomes lewder and more salacious until, finally, Billie requests that a man joins us instead next time.

It won't be my first time; I have participated in a lot of experimentation with both men and women. However, this is the first time I will share the love of my life with another man, and it does worry me slightly how that will affect me. I have never loved anyone the way I love my wife. Therefore, I am willing to try because I want to experience all these things with Billie and, ultimately, I want to fulfil every fantasy Billie has.

After a few years of wild oat sowing, we both become restless for a family, so we have one final blow out year of indulgence before agreeing to put all this in the past for the security of our family unit.

~*~ End of Flashback ~*~

For about a year now, I have been hiding that I have those feelings again. I want more from our sex life. I want the bondage, the threesomes and the rest of the kinky stuff, but I can't say anything about my change of heart. We made an agreement, and I have no right going back on my word. I don't want Billie to ever think that she isn't enough for me; I am still crazy about her.

"Can't we have a bit of what we like without it interfering at home?" Billie asks me seriously and it's a good question. At the time, it seemed inevitable that we couldn't carry on with what we were doing in case it spilled into our home life. However, now we are here, we have a better understanding of how to navigate through this safely and discreetly.

"Do you really want this, Bill? I do, and if you're willing too, then we can talk about ground rules and boundaries."

Her face lights up and it confirms that she wants this just like I do. "I want this, too. I love you, Jonty St. James. I am so excited about all the fun we can have this Christmas."

For the first time in a long time, I am filled with lust and desire. I can't wait for some festive fun too.

CHAPTER THREE

~ Owen ~

It's 4:40 p.m. and our day at work finishes at 5 p.m. I summon Jamie to my office so I can ask her out before I miss my opportunity.

As she walks in, I shift uncomfortably in my seat. I'm getting hard for her already; I'm as bad as a teenager. She looks good enough to eat, and God knows how I would make a meal out of eating her.

I'm not sure why but she looks a bit different. She carries her bag and coat with her and looks ready to leave.

"Are you wearing make-up?" I blurt out and her face turns crimson in embarrassment.

"Oh my God, does it look awful? I managed to get myself a date tonight straight from work and I have been trying to make myself look nice, but the lights are terrible in the staff toilets." She takes out a small compact from a pocket in her bag and examines her face in it, and I feel like I'm going to be sick.

I'm already too late. After all this time, I am going to miss my chance. I am definitely going to lose her now. Not that she's mine to lose, but I want her to be mine.

"No, it looks great! Sorry, you just look different." I stumble over my words, but I continue talking anyway. "A date? What's brought all this on, eh? I thought you were concentrating on yourself for the time being." I try to keep my voice level, but panic is building inside me and I hear it as the words come out of my mouth.

"This is what brought it on. It's time to move on. If Carl gets to move on and be happy then I deserve that, too... don't I?" A card and a letter fall on my desk. I only have to read the first few words to understand: that fucker invited her to his wedding!

Rage bubbles up in my stomach, pushing out the panic. Who the fuck does he think he is, messing about with Jamie again? She has been to hell and back getting over him, and now he callously throws this at her, too. My hands clench into fists, wanting to punch his face in.

"Of course, you deserve to be happy. Just be careful, Jamie. There are some weirdos out there, and I would hate anything bad to happen to you."

She looks stunned that I would be concerned. "Thank you, Mr. Matthews. I promise I will be careful."

Mr. Matthews! How do I change that?

"Jamie? Can I just talk to you, not as your boss, Mr. Matthews, but as Owen, just for a minute?" I wait for her to agree before I continue. "So you're really ready to start dating again?"

When she nods yes, I know I have to ask her. I have to, I can't leave it to chance any longer.

"If this date doesn't work out, then how about we go out sometime?"

Her look of complete bewilderment confirms that she really has no idea how much I like her. Her lovely eyes are wide, and her cheeks have turned pink. She is so beautiful, and now I will finally know if there will ever be a future for us.

"You'd like to go out with me, Mr... I mean, Owen?" Jamie is gorgeously gobsmacked; she really has absolutely no idea of how amazing she is.

"I'd love the chance to get to know each other outside of the office. Obviously, if your date turns out to be your future husband then we'll pretend this conversation didn't happen. But if he's not..."

She still looks stunned. "I didn't think someone like you would be interested in someone like me. I will think about it. I don't want things to become awkward between us if it goes wrong; we would still have to work together."

"You have my number, but can you put it under Owen, please?" When she smiles at me, the smile goes all the way to her eyes and turns my insides to jelly.

"Ok, I will change it to Owen." She opens the office door and as she leaves, she turns back, all professional once again, and calls out, "Goodnight, Mr. Matthews. See you tomorrow."

My heart gives a leap; fuck, she is insanely sexy. I can only imagine what it would be like between us in bed. It has annoyed the shit out of me for almost two years that she calls me Mr. Matthews. Now I'm having all sorts of visions of her naked in the middle of my bed beckoning me to her by calling, "Mr. Matthews... Mr. Matthews".

Shit, I'm in deep here and I don't know how I will make it through the night not knowing how her date is going with some other man.

I should have made my move earlier, but goddammit, she moved fast once she made the decision to start dating again.

I should have asked her where she is going, who this guy is and where she met him.

Casting my mind around for a solution, I finally hit on one: Tim! Tim might know. I'm at his desk in record time.

"Tim... can I have a word before you leave?" I ignore his look of annoyance; he obviously has stuff he would rather do, but this is important.

"I'll make it quick... Do you know who Jamie is going on a date with?"

Tim looks surprised by my question. "She's got a date already? She literally downloaded the app this afternoon." He looks bashful, but I don't have the time and patience to dissect the reasons why.

"She wouldn't do anything silly, right? She will have told someone where she is going and who she's going with? You know she's never dated anyone except for Carl." I am hoping my questions portray me as a concerned boss rather than a creepy stalker, but Jamie's safety is more important than office gossip.

"Oh, shit! I didn't even think. She's been so wound up about something today. She asked me to set her up, and I threatened her with Jason when she annoyed me. So she told me to shove it because she would find her own date. I'll call her now. We'll find her."

My heart is pounding. She was right there in front of me, and I was too busy being jealous to think to question her about who she was going out with.

Tim gets his phone and tries calling her, but she doesn't answer. My stomach turns and fills with knots of anxiety. "I'll check her socials, hold on." He scrolls through the different platforms before shouting, "Bingo! She checked in at The Ivy; it's just down the road. Come on."

I run after Tim who leads us down the stairs, out of the building and down the road. "It's on the next block," he shouts back and we both slow down as we approach the restaurant.

I hear Jamie before I see her. She is shouting angrily at someone. "You dirty, twisted, little pervert. If I ever see you again, I will chop off your bollocks and make you eat them. You make me sick." She almost runs into us as she turns to leave.

"Woah, Jamie, what's going on?" Tim holds her arms to steady her as he asks the question.

Jamie recoils at the sight of us. "What are you two doing here? Did you follow me? Are there any decent men in this fucking city? Leave me alone!"

She runs away, flagging a hackney cab and speeding out of our view, and I have never felt so desperately heartbroken as I do watching her go. I've definitely messed up my chances now.

~ Jamie ~

This day just keeps getting worse. It's hard to believe how much of an idiot I am. How many times must I fall for all the bullshit men feed me before I realise that there are no good ones; they are all bastards.

As I cry in the taxi home, the driver tries to talk to me twice before I tell him to fuck off and leave me alone. I set up the date all by myself, and I had been proud that I had been able to not only do it by myself but do it so fast.

The man I 'met' said his name was Harry, he looked gorgeous, the body of a Greek god and devastatingly handsome. I had already decided I was going to sleep with him, so that Carl was no longer the last and only person I've ever had sex with.

When I arrived at the bar, I couldn't see Harry anywhere, so I bought myself a drink and waited for him to arrive when a man in his fifties approached me.

"You look even better in real life, love." I gave him a tight smile and carried on waiting for Harry. "Are you going to give me a kiss, then? I've come all this way to see you and you act like the cat's got your tongue."

"I'm waiting for someone," I told him impatiently. He laughed at me, so I frowned back at him. What the fuck was his problem?

"Jamie, it's me, it's Harry. Now, are you taking me back to your apartment to fuck me senseless or what?"

How could I have been so stupid and reckless? I am an idiot, and even Tim and Mr. Matthews know it now, too. I completely humiliated myself and I never want to leave my bed ever again.

Picking up the box Billie must have left for me, I let myself into my apartment where my cat, Smokey, greets me. It is cold and dark in this place I call home, and I have never felt so alone.

~ Billie ~

My talk with Jonty is going better than I expected. He is hard and excited just from talking about the fun we will have if we allow our boundaries to widen again. For the past year, our sex life has been so monotonous, and I know if I'm honest there has been more than once I imagined him fucking another partner. All three of us together or Jonty watching me screwing someone else. The possibilities are endless.

Jonty has always been sexy. I was 22 years old when we met, and he was almost 30. Some of the things I found most attractive were that he was older, more experienced, and definitely more open to new adventures than anyone I had ever met.

Now, Jonty is 41 years old; he has aged well. He is a distinguished silver fox. He is still toned and fit and even more handsome, like a good aged wine. I am looking forward to reigniting the flame between us.

We make love after our talk, and it is hard, fast and ferocious between us. There is more passion and enthusiasm in this single act than I have felt in a long time. It is so hot and it sets my soul alight. I want more; I need more. I want it all with him, and now I know he wants it too.

He agrees to us looking into a third party, and my insides churn in desire and need. We enjoyed many threesomes in the past. I enjoyed the times we had with another female, but I quickly grew bored of that. I want a variety of girls and a second man to join our bed again, and Jonty is willing to facilitate that.

The memory of the first time I slept with two men at the same time comes rushing back and I have to squeeze my knees together to ease the throbbing in my core.

~*~ Flashback ~*~

~~~ Nine and a Half Years Ago ~~~

We picked him from a catalogue. His name is Romeo, apparently, and he is young, dark-skinned, tall, toned and hung like a donkey. I lick my lips as I sit facing him, and notice that he looks up my skirt when I uncross my legs. I like that. A rush of excitement runs through me. I am desired, I feel sexy and dirty, and it thrills me.

"Okay, ground rules. I am happy for you two to engage in everything you desire apart from kissing on the lips. Is that clear?" Romeo quickly agrees but I frown. He's happy for another man to fuck me but not kiss me?

"Billie, your ground rules, honey. What are your ground rules for Romeo and me?" I frown at him and his incessant bloody ground rules.

"Why no kissing? I like kissing, Jonty." It's important to me; it's part of the sensual excitement.

"Just not on the lips please, Bill. If you want to kiss on the mouth, kiss me." He asks so little of me that I relent, but it sincerely bothers me because I don't understand. I kissed Ruby and it didn't bother him, why wouldn't kissing Romeo be the same?

I am completely dominated all night. As Romeo fucks me hard and deep with his huge cock, I suck Jonty's. Later that night, Jonty asks me if I trust him.

"I want both Romeo and I to be inside you at the same time... do you want that?" Yearning fills me like lava in the pit of my stomach. We have tried and enjoyed anal, but double penetration is next level. Yes, I unquestionably want it.

I am just unsure of the mechanics, but I put my full trust in Jonty, as I have many times before, and he never lets me down.

As Romeo lies on his back, I climb on to his cock, and slide down it. It fills me and stretches me and hits places nothing else ever has. I grind against him and on him, lifting myself all the way to the end before dropping my full weight back down on him. Then, I feel Jonty behind me. He already has lube on his fingers while he plays with my puckered rosebud. I am full to capacity but as Jonty stretches me in preparation, the lava in my tummy starts to bubble, I am going to explode.

"I'm going to take this really slowly, Bill, I don't want to hurt you, baby. Tell me if it hurts. Do you promise?" I nod my agreement.

There is pain, but not overly much and I like the way the pain mingles with the pleasure, it makes everything feel more intense. I have never felt such fullness, or pleasure so intense. I have never been as fulfilled as I feel being fucked by my husband and our friend. As the three of us move as one, all of us moaning and groaning in delight, nothing has ever felt so right. Jonty gently rubs circles on my clit, and I am already so far gone that I cum like never before, all within a couple of minutes.

Jonty chuckles in my ear as I pant and moan my way through my prolonged orgasm. "Yes, baby! Tell me how much you love this."

"That is the best orgasm I have ever had. Now, I want both of you to cum inside me."

They both quickly find a rhythm that works for them and as they move inside of me I just crave to be kissed. I want that intimacy. I have to wait for Jonty to finish before I can have it.

I loved every minute of it. It takes me three days to recover, and we almost immediately begin to plan our next session.

Later, when I ask Jonty about the kissing on the lips, he tells me that is the most intimate act in his eyes. I am his Billie and all my kisses belong to him. I don't understand it, but I accept it. I ask why he let *me kiss Ruby, and he just shrugs and says it is different, that kissing a woman is different from kissing another man.*

He has been so willing and giving with everything else, it is a small sacrifice for me to make him happy.

~*~ End of Flashback ~*~

I have a lot of hope for this weekend. Jonty suggested we go dogging to slowly ease ourselves back into the scene. Dogging is when we go watching or having sex in a public place. It's usually under the cover of darkness. Jonty had been part of the exhibitionist scene for a long time before I met him. We had done it before the children and the plan was to just watch this time and test our own resolve and boundaries before jumping to something bigger.

Dogging is awesome because of the spontaneity of it. You could literally watch anyone fucking, someone else might join them, you can also be invited to get up close and personal or you can just stand in the background and jerk off with their permission. I get such a high from watching others acting out their salacious acts, but an even bigger high from being watched by complete strangers who fantasise about fucking me too.

Jonty is making all the arrangements. I just have to ask Jamie if she would mind babysitting overnight one day this weekend.

As I drive into work the day after my heart-to-heart with Jonty, I sing along with Mariah, and grin at the other motorists. Happiness and fulfilment flow through my veins and it simply rejuvenates me to be looking forward to the next few weeks.

When I get to Tables & Fables, I instantly know that Jamie hasn't left the building yet. The door chain has been left on and I now have to open up the front of the Café so I can get in. She must have slept in. I try to call her but her voicemail instantly kicks in.

"For fuck's sake, Jamie!" I mutter to myself as I trudge around the front of the shop. By the time I have the shutters up, Dana and Moira, the baker, have also arrived for work.

"Open up for me, please, Dana, while I go and kick my sister's ass." I bound off up the stairs and open her front door with my emergency key.

"Jamie, wake up; you've slept in." I wait for her to reply but she doesn't. Now, I am seriously worried about her. After her break-up with Carl, she was depressed for a while. I hope getting that invitation yesterday hasn't set her back.

"Jamie, you little bitch, get up now. I had to walk all the way around to the front of the café, because you left the chain on the door. You're late for work."

"Go away!" She shouts from her bedroom, and while I'm relieved she isn't dead, I'll kick her butt for scaring me.

"What's up with you? Can I come in?" Silence follows for a while before she answers me.

"Just leave me alone, Billie. I never want to leave this room. I'm such a stupid dick." I can hear the crying in her voice and my heart breaks for her. I had hoped she had moved on enough for her not to be heartbroken once again. I guess she isn't as far along as I thought.

"I'm coming in." I open the door and the fucking cat jumps at me, claws out and hackles raised. "Get off me you smelly fucker!" I screech, and through her tears, Jamie starts howling with laughter. The cat runs off, hissing and wailing as it does, and I stand looking at my sister in astonishment.

"Oh my goodness, Bill, I was feeling so down and sad but that has made my day. That was the funniest thing I've seen in ages." She starts laughing again and even though her feral shit machine has scratched my head and plucked my beautiful scarf, I end up laughing along with her.

"What happened Jim-Jam, why aren't you at work?" Jamie covers her head with her quilt and groans. I wish she'd put on the Christmas bedding I bought her.

"Aww, don't make me tell you. I'm so embarrassed, Billie. I think I will have to resign from my job," she explains in a wail of pain.

"You've got to be kidding me; you've just watched a cat attack me. Come on, tell me what happened, and we'll sort it out."

She tells me her sorry tale, and I am ready to go and choke this Harry. My sister is still a bit green when it comes to the matters of the world. She is sweet and naïve, and some people will take advantage of that. I am ten years older than her and have always been overprotective.

"So what does this have to do with you leaving your job?" She groans again, her cheeks turning pink.

"They followed me. And they saw and heard everything, and I shouted at them for following me. Now, I feel too embarrassed to face them." Tears form in her eyes again.

"Who saw?"

"Tim and Mr. Matthews… I mean Owen did. He asked me out, and I said I would think about it. He's not going to want to go out with me now, is he?"

"Who asked you out? Jamie, I have no idea what is going on."

She tuts at me. "Mr. Matthews… Owen, he asked me out just before my date with the fake guy. But now he'll think I'm crazy as well as an idiot for believing that a sexy guy could really want to date me in the first place."

This is great news. I have long thought that Mr. Matthews would be a good match for my sister. He seems to have his shit together and he is hot. Put it this way: I wouldn't say no to him joining us. I mean I would have to now, if he and Jamie hook up, because that would be weird, but Mr. Matthews has got it going on.

"Well, he's going to start thinking you're a lazy bitch if you don't turn up for work. Jamie, look, things happen and yes, it's embarrassing, but you get back up, dust yourself off and try again." I open her wardrobe and pick out a killer suit for her to wear. "This seriously isn't worth staying in bed over or giving up your job for. And if you don't go out on a date with that boss of yours because of this, I think you need your head examined!"

I leave her and go back to work where thoughts of Jamie and her misdemeanour are quickly replaced by thoughts of my weekend with Jonty.

I can't wait to make more dirty memories.

~ Tim ~

Overwhelming guilt fills me as Jamie runs away from us. It didn't even cross my mind that my actions may embarrass her. I didn't mean to undermine her ability to think for herself or defend herself. Mr. Matthews seemed really concerned, and I guess, I got carried away. On reflection, it's evident that I crossed a line by tracking her through her social media account when I couldn't reach her by phone. In the moment, it seemed the most logical thing to do. It is only I realise how condescending that is.

Mr. Matthews loses his shit when Jamie runs away and gets into the taxi. I have never seen him lose his composure before.

"I've messed that up now, haven't I eh?" he asks me as he rubs his hands over his face and into his hair.

"Do you fancy *Jamie*?" I ask him, my voice dripping with shock. I had no idea; I just presume everyone sees Jamie as I do; like she is my kid sister.

He doesn't answer me and I don't want to push because he looks distraught. How have I managed to get myself caught up in the middle of this?

We walk in silence back to our office; I don't know what to suggest. The woman on the front desk shouts over to us.

"Where did you two run off to? We were just saying you looked like Batman and Robin." There is no prize for guessing which one I am.

We step into the elevator and my boss looks desperately sad. I am overcome with a need to at least try and comfort him. "Don't worry, Mr. Matthews, we will speak to Jamie in the morning and apologise. I will explain that we got the wrong end of the stick. Once she calms down, she will be okay." He gives me a small nod but I don't know what good it has done, if any.

I check my phone as soon as I get back to my desk and I am disappointed when there is no reply from Lauren to the text I sent about an hour ago. Maybe she is at work or maybe she isn't interested. I don't know, but I know I'll be checking my phone all night, hoping she replies to me.

The next morning, I arrive at work and Jamie isn't in. She is always earlier than me. I sent her an apology last night, but she hasn't replied. When 8 a.m. comes and goes and she is still a no-show, I go into Mr. Matthews' office to discuss it.

"She is probably taking her flexi day, Tim. She is owed quite a few for all the ones she's missed." Mr. Matthews avoids eye contact with me, deeply engrossed in his spreadsheet. He is back to being all business and proper and so I don't mention anything about him being heartbroken the night before.

Unable to concentrate on my work as thoughts of Lauren and her nonexistent reply continue to taunt me. And Jamie and her absence is starting to weigh on my conscience.

At 11:30 Jamie walks into the office. She looks fierce in a power suit with her lips painted red and her hair dramatically twisted on top of her head. A shiver of anxiety runs through me.

"Is Mr. Matthews free?" she asks me and I can't answer her verbally, the words are stuck in my throat, so I nod my head. "Good. I want a word with both of you. Now."

As she marches towards Mr. Matthews' office, the man himself opens the door. "Jamie! I... I."

Jamie is taking no prisoners today. "A word in private, if you please, Mr. Matthews." He simply steps to the side granting her access to his office.

I take a seat on the other side of Mr. Matthews' desk as he also takes his seat. Jamie stands, looking out the window for a moment before addressing us.

"I don't know where the hell you both get off thinking you can check up on me and follow me. It is unacceptable. I am not your damsel in distress; I am a grown woman. I am perfectly capable of making my own mistakes and taking care of myself, no matter how stupid those mistakes seem to you. I don't interfere with your private life. Do not interfere with mine."

Both Mr. Matthews and I sit frozen. I have never seen Jamie so annoyed but also so much in control.

"I am sorry, Jamie; this was all my fault, I overstepped the boundaries and I promise it will never happen again. I am sincerely sorry for bringing Tim in on this." Mr. Matthews concedes, and it shocks me, especially knowing how rattled he was about it yesterday.

"Yes, I am sorry too. We got over involved when we should have known you had it covered."

Jamie gives us both a stiff nod. I don't think she was expecting us to apologise so quickly. To be honest, I didn't think we would either but the transformation in Jamie has me quaking like a little boy in the head mistresses' office.

"Okay, thank you. We'll say no more about it. Tim, could I have a word with Mr. Matthews in private, please." As I leave the office, I take pity on Mr. Matthews who looks like he wants the ground to swallow him up.

When I return to my desk. I finally have a reply from Lauren.

Sorry, Tim. Had to go to Ireland and visit my family. My granny has passed away. Maybe we could catch up when I get back? Take care. Lx

I have never felt so disappointed.

~ Jamie ~

After Billie's pep talk, I decide to front this whole ordeal out. So, I made a mistake, so what? I am going to give a piece of my mind to Tim and Mr. Matthews for following me. I know they were concerned but it bothers me that they think I need rescuing. Would Tim have acted the same way if it had been Mr Matthews going on a date? I am not in need of saving or rescuing. I am strong, capable and Goddamn it, I can do this!

With my rejuvenated self-confidence spurring me on, I dress to impress. I need people to start taking me seriously. Tim says I'm like his little sister and everyone else seems to think I'm helpless and weak. Since my breakup with Carl, I have been hiding behind their misconstrued opinion of me. Well, fuck that! I am strong and I can do whatever I want. I don't need anyone's permission or approval.

Billie sends me off to work with a bacon sandwich and a cappuccino to go. "You are Jamie Knowles, and you are awesome!" she shouts after me as I leave the café and make my way to the tube station.

The tube is less crowded now because rush hour is over, and I even manage to get a seat. Maybe I'll start coming in to work at this time every day, I muse to myself.

When I walk onto our floor, I almost lose my nerve, but I have come all this way. I need to do this. Tim looks sheepishly at me, so I bite the bullet and summon him to Mr Matthews' office. They both apologise a lot faster than I anticipate and they both look contrite.

After I ask Tim to leave, my stomach starts to turn. I need to talk to Owen. I just don't know if Owen will want to talk to me.

"I'm not sure if mixing business with pleasure is a good idea. We both saw last night how quickly things could get out of hand. I think it's best we remain work colleagues and... friends?" As the words spill out of my mouth, I realise they are not coming out as I intended them to. I had wanted to give Owen an out, a chance to rescind his offer to take me out, but it sounds like I am telling him I am not interested.

I am just about to correct myself when he replies to me. "Yes, you are quite right, it would be silly of us to jeopardise our working relationship and friendship. I completely agree with you." He holds out his hand for me to shake, smiling as he does it. "Friends and work colleagues, eh?" and so I accept his handshake and repeat the words.

"Friends and work colleagues." However, I feel bereft. He took the out I offered and I don't blame him. I just can't explain or understand why I felt so disappointed.

I hadn't even thought of Owen as anything other than my boss, Mr Matthews, until last night. I hadn't taken in his handsome good looks or his fine physique, his charming personality or his generous nature. He certainly is a decent man and a good catch for the lucky woman who ends up with him... it just looks likely to not be me now that I have chased him away.

When I walk out of Mr Matthews' office, Tim looks glum. "What's up? I thought you'd be happy now we've cleared the air. I got your texts by the way. Thank you, they were cute."

"I met a girl over the weekend, but she just blew me off. Do you still want me to set you up on a date? How about you set me up with one of your friends and I'll bring someone for you? We could try a double date."

Fresh off the back of my humiliation yesterday and Owen's rejection today, what have I got to lose?

"Yes, sure, okay... but not Jason." Tim laughs at my stipulation.

"Not Jason. I promise I wouldn't inflict him on my worst enemy. How about tomorrow night, straight from work, we go for dinner. It's bound to be busy and fun, it's the Christmas light turn on."

It sounds like fun, so I agree. When I return to my office, I call one of my single friends, Iris. She is a beauty, and I am sure her and Tim will hit it off.

And who knows, maybe he'll set me up with Mr Right... or even Mr Right-Now.

~ Owen ~

I know I have messed up my chance with Jamie when she looks at me outside the restaurant. The look in her eyes as she screams at me haunts me all night. Anger, repulsion and hurt is etched all over her face and in turn I am ashamed for contributing to those feelings.

I never want to be the reason she feels that way. I only ever want her to be happy. So when she says that she thinks mixing business and pleasure is a bad idea, I quickly agree so she doesn't know how hurt I am by her rejection. I would rather be her friend than not have her in my life. It is a bitter pill to swallow; I had felt so close and now, I know, I have no chance of making something with her.

Tim tries to speak to me a couple of times about it all, but I shut him down. I am just about keeping it together, but if I start talking about how I feel about her, I don't think I will ever stop. I need to accept it will never happen, and that belief is reinforced when I step out of my office to overhear Jamie and Tim agreeing to set each other up on a date for tomorrow night.

"Can you two get some work done, please!" I shout sharply before going back into my own office. I am acting like a right scrooge, green is not a good colour on me, but I am jealous. I want her but

I can't have her.

I call one of my old hook ups. Maybe being with someone else will help me move on. All I know is I can't stand feeling like this. I arrange to take Suzy for drinks tomorrow night. It'll keep my mind off things and hopefully I will have some fun.

Around 4 p.m., Jamie comes into my office to give me the rundown for the trip to Copenhagen next week. Her hair has come loose from the severe bun from earlier, she looks adorable.

"There is a massive block right in the middle of your trip, Mr. Matthews, where you have no appointments, but I couldn't get them moved so it will be three nights, not two."

"That's no problem, it's beautiful this time of year. I'll find something to do." She gives me a brilliant smile back.

"You've been before? Did you visit the palaces? It'll be my first time, I am hoping I get time to go to the Christmas markets at Tivoli Gardens, I've heard they are the best in the world." I smile at her enthusiasm and at the joy she finds in something so simple.

"They are pretty spectacular. I'm sure you'll get plenty of time to go and explore."

I could offer to show her around, to take her to all the places I knew she would enjoy but I need to put space between us so I can move on.

"I will be taking my flexi-time tomorrow afternoon. I have plans with a friend and I want to leave early, so I will need you to lock up as you leave."

She stands up, and I can't help but admire the suit she is wearing. It fits her perfectly and makes her look strong and confident.

"No problem, Mr. Matthews. Enjoy your time with your friend." She seems to float out of my office, and I can do nothing but watch her leave.

The following day, I groan when she walks in and I see she has made an extra effort for her date. She laughs and jokes with the others in the office, and I internally scream for the clock to hurry up. At 1 p.m., I am leaving to pick up Suzy, but the minutes start to feel like hours.

Finally, when one o'clock arrives, I practically rush out. Jamie shouts goodbye to me and reminds me to have a good weekend.

Hopefully, I will be balls deep in Suzy in a few short hours and Jamie will be a distant memory.

EMMA LEE-JOHNSON

CHAPTER FOUR

~ Tim ~

I set Jamie up with an old friend of mine called Conor. He reminds me he isn't looking for anything serious, but I don't think Jamie will mind. We have reservations at the Italian Kitchen in Oxford Circus, and with our window table, we should be able to see the big reveal when the Christmas lights are officially switched on.

Jamie's friend Iris is nice enough. She is medium height with brown hair that falls in waves down her back, and she has a very slim and slight figure. She isn't my usual type, but she seems likeable. I am looking forward to seeing Jamie and Conor together and therefore, one date with Iris will be okay.

Jamie seems excited until we approach the restaurant and her nerves kick in.

"Tim, what was I thinking? I can't do this! I am a wreck. What if he doesn't show up or he doesn't like me? What will I talk about?" I drag her into the restaurant before she can change her mind. Thankfully, Conor is already inside waiting for us.

"You must be Jamie? Tim has told me a lot about you. What can I get you to drink?" Conor is charming. I watch as Jamie relaxes in his company, and I take pleasure in knowing I am helping Jamie move on from her dickhead ex, Carl.

This isn't going to be some big love affair. I can tell the chemistry isn't there between them, but this date serves to boost Jamie's confidence in dating. If they can have a bit of fun in the process, all the better.

We share a bottle of wine, and the banter between the four of us is brilliant. When the Christmas lights are officially switched on outside, we cheer. After we have finished eating, we walk hand in hand with our dates, soaking in the festive atmosphere and cheer.

"Come back to mine," Iris persuades me, looking at me seductively through her eyelashes and wetting her lips with her tongue. It is an open invitation for extra fun, and so we say goodnight to Jamie and Conor and head back to her place.

As I walk into her apartment, she presses her lithe body into mine, her dress is off in one swift movement and by the time we have our first proper kiss she is already naked. Within minutes she is on her knees in front of me, she frantically whips my cock out of my jeans and slowly wraps her tongue around my hard head. I groan in appreciation as she licks all the way down to the base and then all the way back up before taking me fully into her mouth. She works wonders with her tongue, her warm mouth is inviting and sends tingles of satisfaction right down into my balls, which she is now grabbing and holding.

"Slow down, sweetheart, or I'm gonna cum right down your

throat," I warn her, but that seems to encourage her all the more and after a couple more minutes, I shoot my hot load. However, to my great shame, something weird happens in those moments just before I do. Her face seems so clear in front of my eyes, but it isn't Iris' face.

It is Lauren's.

It freaks me out a bit, but I feel bad running out on Iris after she has just given me a pretty decent blow job, so I stay and reciprocate. As I run my hands over her thin body, I don't feel desire. Not like I did for Lauren. Iris' bony hips and skinny legs leave me scared in case I break her. I long for the soft, plump body I know Lauren had hidden under the clothes she didn't remove.

My thoughts about Lauren fill me with guilt about Iris, who is lying next to me. I want her to feel good and satisfied, and so I fuck her with my fingers, bringing her to orgasm before thanking her for a lovely time and leaving.

I walk a couple of miles to try and clear my head. I really like Lauren. I know she isn't the conventional 'pretty girl' but to me, she is perfect. It is frustrating and confusing that she seems to be avoiding me. She was so unsure of herself and vulnerable that night we kissed and part of me just wants to go and knock on her door and tell her how I feel. Knowing that I sound weird and overbearing, I stay away and hope with all my might that she will eventually agree to see me again.

Until then, I think I'm best keeping my cock to myself.

~ Jamie ~

After Iris and Tim leave, Conor invites me back to his place. At first, I am a little unsure. I have never had a one night stand before and I don't envision anything more than tonight happening with Conor. He is nice enough, but the spark isn't there between us.

"Come to mine, we can have a bit of mutual fun, nothing heavy. It's been such a good night, I can't think of a better way to end it."

So, with anticipation building up inside my body, I agree. A bit of fun is what I have been looking for, and no-strings-attached sounds like a good option.

"Okay, I'll come back with you. But look, I don't do this kind of thing; I'm not really sure what I am doing." He takes hold of my hand and tells me to relax and to trust him and that he will take care of me.

Carl and I had quite an active sex life until that last year, so I am not a shrinking violet, but he is still the only person who has carnal knowledge of me. I hate that he is the only man I have ever been with.

The prospect of sharing someone else's bed is scary, but I have been feeling horny and unsatisfied, and Conor seems to know what he is doing. I am hopeful that he can satisfy the itch that has been bugging me.

As we walk along Oxford Road, we kiss until we manage to flag a taxi. Heading back to his house, things quickly get hot and heavy between us.

Heat rises within me, and the ache between my legs begins to burn and grow. Conor is a decent kisser, and as we trundle along in the taxi he deftly slips his hand up my skirt and into the side of my panties.

"I know you want this, Jamie; I can feel how hot and ready you are. What do you like?" I do want this, and the more he teases me, the more I want him.

The taxi pulls up outside a new development and Conor quickly pays. He shows me to his second-floor apartment, which is on the small side but modern and tidy.

He pulls me into his bedroom, and we undress each other in between hot kisses. I am so tightly wound up now that it wouldn't normally take me long to cum, but we don't seem to hit a good rhythm between us. Conor is decent enough, but the sex is off-kilter, unfamiliar and awkward.

I don't cum, but he does. And once he does, he thanks me for a good time and kisses me goodnight.

Once my Uber turns up, I let myself out of his apartment. Feeling cheap and deflated, I consider my evening. Although I don't regret what I did, this night has confirmed to me that I am not that sort of girl. One night stands are not for me. I have got that out of my system and I will no longer wonder what that would be like.

I wake up the next morning after another spicy dream with my hand down my pyjama pants, yet again. However, this time it wasn't a faceless man going down on me.

It was Mr. Matthews.

~ Owen ~

My driver takes me to Covent Garden to meet Suzy, but we hit traffic and I end up being ten minutes late.

I've known Suzy since we were at university together. We met shortly after I moved to England twelve years ago when I was offered a prestigious scholarship at Oxford University to study Professional Finance and Accounting. There has never been anything romantic between us, just the occasional friends with benefits situation that is mutually beneficial.

Suzy is thirty-one years old, a year older than me, and she is fit and smart. Tall with copper hair that has become shorter and shorter over the years, she has an almost elfin look about her now with her pixie haircut. She looks younger now than when we met. If there is a cosmetic surgery, she's had it, from Botox to collagen, lip and cheek fillers, dentistry, implants, liposuction. You name it, she's tried it. She could easily pass for 25 years old, especially with the clothes she wears.

Suzy looks good and she knows it, and that is only half the

reason why she is a good occasional fuck buddy. She doesn't ask too many questions and has no unrealistic expectations. It is strictly no strings, hedonistic fun.

Suzy knows me. She can read me like a book, and as soon as I walk into the bar, she is on to me.

"Owen Matthews, you have just rambled into this bar like a dog who has just been neutered. What's up with you?" she asks through her wide eyes and laughter. In reply, I shake my head at her before closing my eyes.

"Don't. Just don't. I called you because you'll help me forget why I'm walking about like a neutered dog." She smiles and nods knowingly. "What are we drinking?" I add, pointing to her almost empty glass.

"Gin. Like that, is it then?" she remarks with an arched eyebrow as she wets her lips with her little pink tongue.

I look her dead in the eyes. "It's exactly like that." She gives a little chuckle and downs her drink in one. We wait for the bartender to serve us and quickly drink those too before I suggest we leave already.

"Your place or mine?" she asks as she steps down from her bar stool. "Mine is nearer." I nod my agreement. I don't really care; I just want to fuck her, forget why I'm fucking her and most of all forget the blonde-haired angel who is causing my misery in the first place.

The good thing about Suzy is that she knows when to shut up. I don't want to talk about it. I just want to lose myself, and I can lose myself in Suzy for a short while.

As always, Suzy has pulled out all the stops. She is wearing a red lace Basque with matching panties and suspender belt. She strips off her outer clothes as soon as we are through the door.

"You look amazing. Have you been working out?" I ask her and she nods slowly as she runs her hands over her enlarged boobs, searching for her nipples first over the fabric, and then under the fabric when she slips her fingers under the edge of the material.

She pushes the material down, freeing her large, round breasts. She pinches the little peaks until they stand to attention, and then she lifts each one to her own mouth and sucks them.

All this stuff, I have seen before. The first time I almost came in my pants; that's how hot she is. However, I get the shock of my life when I get to Suzy's bedroom and I cannot perform. My cock, my usually proud as punch cock, refuses to cooperate and remains flaccid and limp.

Suzy sinks to her knees and sucks me expertly, but nothing she does will encourage the little fella to come out and play. I am completely fucked off now. Suzy bobs up and down for a couple of minutes until, eventually, I ask her to stop.

"Suze, it's not you, it's me. This just isn't happening today. My head is frazzled. I just can't switch it off."

Suzy is understanding because this has never happened to me before. "Of course it isn't me. Look at me, I look like a fucking goddess!" However, I don't like her way of overcoming the issue. "I am afraid, Owen, that you will have to stop running and start talking about whatever has you rattled, mate. I've never seen you like this."

Of anyone in the world, I know I can tell Suzy and she won't judge me. However, the thing that holds me back is admitting the finality of how things ended between Jamie and I. Part of me feels like it can't be the end, we haven't even tried yet and admitting that it wouldn't work is like breathing life into something I will give anything for.

"What's her name, then?" Suzy asks me as we both begin to replace the clothes we had removed for nothing.

From nowhere, I tell her all about Jamie, how I feel about her and for how long I have felt this way. I explain to Suzy how I am not ready to let go.

Suzy looks at me pensively. "My buddy is all grown up. Look at you! Now, serious talk time. Why the fuck didn't you fight for it? You gave in too fast, Owen. If it means something to you, then you have to fight for it."

I don't think it's as easy as Suzy makes it out to be. I can't force Jamie to like me back, and besides, I really want her to like me and go out with me because she wants this as much as I do. I don't just want today. I want forever.

"It's definitely what I want. I've never felt this way about anyone before. She's so cute, and she makes me happy." Once I realised I had fallen in love with Jamie, I would find myself just smiling away in her company. An inexplicable connection seems to flow between us, and yet at times I questioned... Is this just me? Can she feel this too?

Every morning she greets me with my coffee and a smile, and she always adds sugar and cream just as I like it. I don't even have to ask. That has become the happiest time of my day. Her little quirks, her very British ways at times, her feminine traits and the way she laughs. I've seen her weep for other people's woes, she feels so deeply and empathically that I just want to wrap her up in my arms to keep her safe. She leaves little post-it notes in my documents, encouraging me and reminding me that I am awesome and I can handle anything. She is perfect to me. Perfect for me. I just know it.

Suzy snaps me out of my wandering thoughts. "So, Mr. Matthews, are you going to fight for what you want or are you going to carry on looking like a puppy who had his paw stamped on?"

She's right, and the more I think about it, the clearer my mission becomes: if I don't want to be the proud owner of a limp dick, I'm going to have to help Jamie fall in love with me.

~ Jonty ~

It's Saturday afternoon and we are waiting for my wife's sister, Jamie, to come and watch the children overnight. Tonight, we are travelling to a place just outside of Bristol that apparently has an awesome dogging scene. We will be staying overnight in a nearby hotel, and both Billie and I are excited and eager to get going.

When the doorbell finally rings, it seems like we all run to answer the front door. The children are eager to see their favourite aunt, and, well, Billie and I can't wait to get out of here.

We drive to pick up the rental car first. Just in case. Part of the draw with dogging is the seedy nature of it and the risk of being caught. However, now that I am a partner in the practice the last thing I need is to be caught at something like this. That risk makes it even more exciting for me though.

On the drive out of London to Bristol, Billie and I talk about when we met and fell in love. "When did you know I would like all the same kinks as you, Jonty?"

The truth is I didn't. I had hoped she would be open to experiment, and I had been more than surprised at the levels she would go to. She was perfect for me in every way, in more ways than I ever envisioned.

One of the things that made me fall in love with Billie was her passion for literature. I was sick to the back teeth of these other girls who all came from the same mould. *'I love to read, my favourite is the Bronte sisters or Louisa May Alcott or Shakespeare. Blah blah blah.'* They all said what they thought I wanted to hear, but all I saw was sheep, the blind following the blind.

Billie was different from all the other girls. I asked her about her favourite books, and she told me about Terry Pratchett, CS Lewis and Tolkien. When she told me she was excited to be re-reading The Hobbit, as her kid sister was reading it in school, I knew. I knew I loved her.

"I prefer the Lord of the Rings personally, Bilbo." And that was how I got her pet name. Bilbo Baggins is the main character in The Hobbit and Billie became the main character in my life. She is my Bilbo.

When we arrive at the hotel, Billie whistles low; I have spared no expense. I have gone all out on the best suite in the best hotel Bristol has to offer.

Tonight will be dynamite between us, if past experience had taught me anything. I want this to be somewhere nice and special because it has been such a long time.

"Before we leave for our... excursion... I want your ground rules." I always insist each time that we lay out our rules and therefore, we both know what to expect and what is expected of us.

"Tonight, I don't want us to leave the car. I just want to watch and we can have fun with ourselves or each other." I kiss her and tell her I agree. Under the cloak of darkness, we make our way to the site I have been researching since Billie asked to put some of our old pastimes on the table.

"Are you ready for this, Bilbo?" My wife is already excited; I can tell as she nods enthusiastically. The outlines of her nipples are visible through her shirt; they are already hard and screaming to be touched. She is wearing a skirt tonight so I can touch her without too much restriction.

"As ready as ever, Jonty," she tells me, sending a shiver of desire through me. As we pull into the clearing, there are already two cars here and a small crowd is gathering. As we edge closer, we can clearly see a couple fucking on a car bonnet as the others watch and record. One man has a professional camera. There are a couple of single people and another couple all there for the same thing as us: to get kinky.

We are back!

~ Billie ~

The sight of the couple fucking on the bonnet is hot, but what is even hotter is the frenzy of people around them. The way they are not only enjoying the show, but encouraging the fornicating couple, praising them and taking photos as mementos of their act fuels the building ache between my legs.

As soon as we park up, Jonty turns off our headlights. That is the universal signal on the scene that means we don't want to be approached yet; we are just here to watch for now. We get the occasional wave from our curious peers, but that is it.

Every one of my nerve endings buzzes with an energy, a tension, I can feel my desire pooling in my knickers as my pussy clenches and releases my juices involuntarily. "I'm already on my way, Jonty. I don't think it'll take much for me to orgasm tonight." His excitement is evident not just in his pants but in his eyes too.

I love to watch the others' reactions and to be the one responsible for causing the reaction in others. But I also get off on just being in the background, soaking it all up.

"What are you going to do, Bill?" A thrill of excitement buzzes through me as I close my eyes and touch myself, starting with a nipple between my fingertips. As I roll it and squeeze it, I can hear my husband's breathing catch. Jonty loves to watch me, he loves me to be vocal about what I want, what I need and what I am going to do. I am stimulated by the visual, and Jonty loves the audio.

"I am going to strum myself right here in front of you until I cum, and when I cum, I want you to bite my nipples right through my shirt."

I slip my hands between my legs as I tell him what I am going to do, quickly spreading my pussy lips and finding my clit. I use little movements this time, just so the friction of the pad of my index finger grazes across the swollen bud of nerves. I am mostly shielded from the crowd, and they are far more interested in the couple on the bonnet who have invited a third party to join them.

As a second man joins the couple on display, I groan in pleasure; I want what they are doing. On hearing my groan, I feel Jonty's breath on my neck. "You want a threesome, too, don't you, Bill? You want another man to fuck you at the same time as me. You want him to fuck me too, don't you? Tell me..." He bites my earlobe and my orgasm blasts throughout my body spontaneously. It's a lot stronger and harder than any orgasm I have had recently.

"That's what I want; that's exactly what I want, Jonty," I shout as I cum and he bites my nipple like I instructed him. My body shudders in satisfaction as my juices run on my hands and down my thighs.

"Yes, Billie, cum for me. You look fucking delicious when you cum. When we get back to the hotel, I am going to fuck you all night long, in every position and every hole. You won't be able to walk when I am done." I moan for my husband; I want him now; I need him now.

"Please, I need you; fuck me here."

He shakes his head at me, grinning when he does.

"Oh no, you dirty girl, you can wait for that. Let me taste your fingers." I remove the fingers that I have just pleasured myself with from my folds and place them near his lips. He slurps up my honey, groaning in delight as he does. "Taste it, suck your fingers, sweetheart. You taste divine, sweet and salty and fresh."

After sucking my own juices off my fingers, Jonty and I share a deep kiss. The scene outside has changed. There is a voluptuous woman masturbating on another car bonnet, and several men stand around her stroking themselves while complimenting her.

I start to stroke Jonty's cock, which throbs in my hand. "What would you do, Billie, if you were in that crowd, and that woman was in front of you, like she is right now?"

I close my eyes and imagine I am standing in front of the woman. "I would kiss her, just nibble on her bottom lip, and ask if she would like some help. I would tell her how much I want to help her, and she would agree. I would go down on her, nipping at her pussy lips and spreading her wide and then starting at her hole I would lick slowly up to her clit. I would suck on it and swirl it around in my mouth. I would slide a finger inside her and curl it at the end and gently rock her back and forward until she cums on my face."

I speed up my strokes and hold him more firmly, using my other hand to hold his balls, and as I mention the woman coming in my face, Jonty starts to pump his load. I lick my hand clean and moan in delight when I taste his bitter essence. I did that. I did that, and he loved every second and that made it all the more enjoyable for me.

As we clean up, another car pulls up and Jonty says he wants to go and talk to the other doggers, who now sit about talking with one or two kissing around the perimeter. I tell him I'm staying put for the time being and I watch him confidently stride over to speak to the others while I adjust my skirt and blouse.

I watch my husband from afar and I've never felt as much in love with him as I do right now. He is tall and strong and handsome. He moves with such ease and grace, converses confidently with a wide variety of people from all walks of life. The Jonty I fell in love with all those years ago is right in front of my very eyes.

When he returns to the car, he looks jubilant and younger. "Things are dying down for the night, sweetheart. But I got talking with some of the others and there is a big night planned for next Saturday."

My insides spark with arousal. I need to be here next week. "I'll ask Jamie if she can have the children again. I'm sure she won't mind."

I haven't left the children overnight for two Saturdays in a row ever before, but I will make it up to them. Tonight has reignited a burning fire inside me and I have never felt more alive or in awe of the man I married.

~ Jamie ~

I arrive at my sister's house as agreed and Billie and Jonty are practically running out as soon as I get there. I did want to talk to Billie about last night. She has been encouraging me to play the field and enjoy myself for months and the first time I actually do get a bit of action, she runs off before I can tell her about it.

I absolutely adore my niece and nephew. Oscar was the first baby I ever held, and I remember falling in love with the screaming pink bundle. He would scream until someone held him and when I would lift him to me, he would still in my arms and look curiously into my eyes. He was so demanding as a newborn, but I adored him so much that he could do no wrong in my eyes.

I always felt more like their big sister than their aunt because until I moved in with Carl, I lived with Billie and Jonty.

The kids jump all over me when I walk in. I have missed them, and it seems they have missed me. Today marks five weeks until Christmas so we are going to make shortbread and decorate a gingerbread house. I have also brought my Arthur Christmas DVD with me to watch with them later.

Oscar is whiny because his football match has been called off due to the torrential rain we are experiencing and Chloe has a million and one questions for me, and each one is followed up with ten renditions of 'why'. By the time I get them settled with hot chocolates, blankets and our movie I am yawning my head off too.

I don't have time to think about Owen again until I climb into bed that night and then my mind buzzes with what could have been if I hadn't messed it up. What is he doing now and with who? The burning question for me though is why didn't he fight a bit harder when I said I wasn't sure if us going out was a good idea? Maybe he wasn't that keen on me to start with.

There is a part of me that resents him for opening up this can of worms because I hadn't thought of him in that way until he put the seed in my mind. Now, he is all I can think about. He probably isn't giving me a second thought and that annoys me so much. He had no right to ignite feelings for him inside me and then move on from me like I don't matter.

I am bloody miserable now thanks to Owen Matthews and the very least he could do is be miserable with me.

After trying and failing to get some sleep, I go back downstairs with my blanket and watch the Hallmark Christmas channel. There is film upon film of cheesy rom-coms where everyone lives happily ever after. This is what I thought my life was going to be like. I actually thought some man was going to come and sweep me off my feet. It's so sad I could cry.

Chloe wakes me up the next day. I must have fallen asleep on the sofa. "Auntie Jim-Jam, who is Owen?" Oh FUCK! What have I been saying in my sleep?

"Oh no one, sweetie-pie, what would you like for breakfast?" She has a massive grin on her face. She is up to something alright!

"I maked you breakfast... look." On the coffee table next to me is a disgusting mug of... well I don't know what it is, but Chloe looks exceptionally proud of herself. "I didn't know if you like tea or coffee or juice better... so I maked you a mix."

My niece looks so proud of her amazing concoction. I'm sure she is attempting to kill me.

EMMA LEE-JOHNSON

CHAPTER FIVE

~ Lauren ~

I am a mess. My granny passed away and I had to travel to her native Northern Ireland for the funeral. There wasn't a lot of time for me to prepare as it is customary for funerals to be planned and executed within two days of a person dying there. With the travelling and the obligatory family time I have completely lost five days. There is absolutely nothing to show for them at all. My work is behind and the diet I started on Monday has completely hit the wall.

When I arrive back in London on Friday evening, I am so exhausted that I just crawl straight into my bed and fall asleep. Every part of me aches, and I found it overwhelming constantly being in someone else's company for the past few days.

My mother milked this for all it was worth, and as usual she took any opportunity she could to ridicule and belittle me in front of her family in Ballymena. The comments about my weight and size, I am used to. Her criticism of me and my weight are constant, and I therefore would have been more surprised if she had been pleasant to me.

"Stand up straight, Lauren. Suck in your stomach, Lauren.

As you can see, Lauren likes cake too much. What do you weigh now, Lauren? Have you considered a gastric band?" She pointedly made these comments and others loudly in front of whoever would listen, making me feel even more embarrassed and ashamed than I already do.

Unfortunately, that was her being pleasant. Once she was filled with liquor, everything deteriorated even more. "You are such an embarrassment. Why didn't I get a pretty, petite daughter? I would have loved a daughter like your cousin, Niamh. She is so beautiful and slender. Aren't Auntie Kathryn and Auntie Christine's daughters beautiful, Lauren? Just look at their attractive figures. I bet they don't stuff their fat faces with biscuits."

Once she was through with her critical analysis of me and my shortcomings, I honestly felt like I had gone ten rounds with Mike Tyson. At least now she has returned to the coast with my father, and I won't have to see her until Christmas. I am trying my best to get out of that too. I just don't think my self-esteem can take another searing scolding from her and her vicious tongue.

When I wake up on Saturday morning, I decide to hit the ground running. I resume my weight loss programme by jumping straight back on my weight loss shakes, I exercise on my cross trainer for thirty minutes and then jump in the shower. My mother made no secret of the fact that she despised my shocking red hair and forced me to dye it back to a dark chestnut brown before we went to Northern Ireland. She told me it would be seen as sinful to attend a funeral looking like a common whore.

Later on, when her mocking turned cruel and vicious towards me, she said, "you looked like a pig in a wig with that red hair all curled out and your makeup on trying to look attractive. You looked ridiculous." Which had really stung because I know exactly who and what I am. I have tried to find my peace and accept that is who I am, and once I apply a bit of makeup and have my hair done, I don't see myself as such a loser.

Doing normal average things allows me to feel like a normal average woman who likes pretty things and likes to wear nice clothes, perfume and makeup. I tried to be a lot more reserved for the rest of the time I had to be with her after that particular comment. No matter how much I told myself I didn't care, the aching abyss right inside my chest assured me that not only did I care what she said but that I also craved her approval.

Now that I'm back home, after I dress casually and dry my boring brown hair, I make my way to my most favourite place in the world.

I love it in Greenwich; it is a little piece of heaven hidden in London. There are pubs, bars and restaurants, a brilliant market as well as other shops and outlets. However, the hidden gem, the piece de resistance if you like, is the Tables & Fables Book Café. This is where I like to spend most of my time, and where I like to put in the hours for my work.

Today, the little café is bustling with other readers, writers, and hungry Christmas shoppers in need of a rest and refreshments. It has changed in here since last week. The Christmas decorations are now up; there are beautiful and tasteful lights and ornaments about. The place looks wonderful, both festive and fun. It won't be hard to get into the Christmas spirit and draw inspiration here today.

When I get to the front of the line to place my order, Dana, the Barista, greets me. "Hey, Lol, we haven't seen you all week. Where have you been hiding?" I like Dana and the other girls at the café. They are kind and chatty and genuinely interested in me and my work. Billie, the owner, is one of my biggest fans and advocates. She always pushes and encourages me to display my work, to push myself and be proud of what I have achieved. I can't see Billie today, which is unusual. She and her children are usually the standard features of a weekend.

I explain about my Granny and the funeral, and Dana murmurs all the usual condolences and tells me my favourite table, which is tucked away at the back, is vacant and waiting for me. She will bring my mocha to me when it is done.

When I am sitting at my table, I take out my laptop and turn it on. I have neglected my baby for almost a week, and I am anxious to get back to it.

"How is the book coming along, Lol?" Dana asks when she brings my drink to the table. She looks over my shoulder, and notices the number of readers I have and whistles. So there you have it, my biggest secret and the greatest love of my life is the one I create in my books. To my friends and family, I am Lauren, the girl with a weight problem and an overfondness of biscuits. To my online fans and readers, I am Lol Outloud, an award-winning romance novelist.

"My readers will be after my head for leaving them hanging for almost a week without an update. Hopefully I won't have lost too many," I reply and although I say it in jest, there is a part of me that sincerely fears this: that one day my readers will realise I am no good or that they prefer someone else.

"Your readers love you and will understand. Family comes first. Give me a shout if you need anything else. Ooh, is this a new book? I've not seen this one before." She points to the book I have just placed on my table and I hold it up for her to see.

"It's not mine. It's a book by my writing hero, Melody Tyden, called Mismatched Mates. She recently had a new cover commissioned on it and I just had to get it, isn't it beautiful? You should read it; the story is wonderful, and Melody is one of the best writers I've come across. I can only dream of being as good as her in the future." I regard the new design of my old favourite story as I tell Dana about it. The pinks and blues really stand out. I will have to seek out her designer for my next book, too.

"I will be sure to order a copy. When will your new book be ready? Are you still aiming for the beginning of January?" I eagerly hold up my crossed fingers. Goodness, I hope so.

I open my Word document and re-read my last couple of chapters when I am instantly reminded of why I wrote this racy scene. It was because of Tim, the guy who was lumbered with me when my friend went home with his friend.

Tim, the guy with the beautiful kind eyes. Tall and lean with just a hint of muscle, who treated me with such care and gentleness. What could someone like him possibly see in someone like me?

He kissed me, the softest of kisses, and said that he really wanted to, but he didn't take it any further. It didn't take a genius to work out why. He could probably have his pick of the thin, beautiful girls with their confidence and self-assurance. I would be a fool to think I could hold his attention.

I just am not the type of girl men fall in love with. I am the fat, jolly friend, the bag holder, the taxi money keeper and the sensible one. My greatest loves are my books and writing, and that will probably be my only love affair.

No one will love and fancy me. I am hideous. A monster. A big, fat, ugly bloater. If my own mother can't love me, I have little chance of anyone else loving me. I hate that I don't know if this is me or my trauma talking. I always feel worse after spending time with my mother and her acid tongue. There are times when I am happy to be *me* and I can accept who and what I am but an hour with my mother shatters all my self-confidence and I'm left with self-loathing.

Tim sent a couple of texts to me, and at first, I could have been swept away by the romantic notion of it all, but the longer I left it, the more my doubts took over. He was just being kind; he was trying to prove a point that he wasn't shallow. Could he be doing it as a dare or was he trying to complete some sort of sexual bucket list?

I just can't leave myself open in case I get hurt, and I know I could because Tim has something, something no other man has. He is special and I could fall for him, and then what would I do?

Even though I should be writing, I can't stop myself from looking back over his texts. If only he would text again, and I could casually remark that I am back in London. Deep down, I know he won't text again. Why would he? We shared one kiss; one amazing kiss that will be etched in my memory for a long time to come.

I could text him. I actually try. I write the message out several times, and then instantly delete it, shaking my head at myself. I don't have the nerve. The doubts about myself and the whispers I had heard about myself at the funeral, strangers and cousins alike whispering about my large tummy and thundering thighs, have robbed me of every ounce of gumption I once had. I can't, he won't, we would never be. That's all I can think of now.

Before I have a chance to delete the latest attempt at a message, someone knocks into me, and my finger hits send by mistake. Frantically, I try to stop the text, but it's too late. After a couple of seconds, the little ping sounds and the notification MESSAGE SENT appears.

Oh my goodness, I just texted Tim. At first, I am filled with shame and embarrassment, but gradually, another feeling takes hold: hope. He might reply.

But he doesn't instantly reply. My stomach sinks again as reality sets in. Oh God, he isn't going to reply.

I am just about to actually get to work and start writing my next chapter when my phone pings.

MESSAGE RECEIVED.

~ Tim ~

When I get back home after the double date, I can't stop thinking about Lauren again. I have been infatuated before but nothing to this degree. I don't know what to do anymore.

I felt really shitty about Iris, who must be wondering what the hell she did wrong, but I almost felt like I was cheating on Lauren. It didn't feel right at all.

As Iris had sucked me off, I had been able to cum by imagining it was Lauren on her knees in front of me. All I could think about was her cute face, with her dimpled smile and the cleft in her chin, shining up at me as she took my full length into her mouth. I had imagined her little moan of delight as she tasted my essence. I envisioned the way her ample chest would sway as she moved her mouth over my cock.

I needed to seriously have a word with myself. Not only had I thought of Lauren while another woman had sucked me off, but I had tried to imagine it was her I was touching instead. And now I am rock hard solid thinking about her all over again.

I pull out my swollen cock and stroke it, gripping myself tighter and moving my hand with more urgency until after a couple of minutes, I spew my boiling hot load all over the back of my hand. I haven't cum like this in years. It feels incredible, and it's all down to how much I lust after her and how turned on she makes me feel.

The night I kissed her, I had been the same, with a massive stiffy that I struggled to hide from her. I haven't been like this since I was a teenager and I had little control over my urges. I had to jerk myself off when I got home that night, too, just to try and get my cock to calm down. Then straight after I had cum while fantasising about the lovely voluptuous and curvy Lauren, I instantly became hard again. She is the most alluringly and sexy woman I have ever had the pleasure to meet.

How can I get her to talk to me without coming across as creepy or chasing her off? I just need to get to know her more. I want to know her soul; I want her to know mine.

When I arrive at work, I speak to Jamie about last night. We both agree to a wall of silence regarding our respective nights, but in no uncertain terms would we be arranging a second date for each other. I also speak to Conor who says Jamie is a nice girl, but she seemed preoccupied and too tightly wound. He didn't think she was that interested in him and is quickly moving on to the next girl.

Saturday afternoon I decide to get dressed and go for a run when I get the message I have been praying for.

Lauren
Hi Tim, I hope you're good? I'm back in London now if you want to arrange to meet soon. I've been thinking about you… Lauren x

Well, there must be a God after all. I quickly text back; I don't want to leave anything to chance. I don't want to risk losing her interest again. I know exactly what I want, and it is now my mission to secure a future with Lauren.

Tim

Hey Lauren, I've been thinking of you too… a lot. I would love to meet up soon, are you free tonight? We could have dinner or watch a movie? Or just talk? Tim x

A nervous energy now overflows within me. I pray aloud: *please say yes. Please say yes.* I almost drop my phone in eagerness to read her reply. All I need is an indication that she feels the same way and that she is open to pursuing something more with me.

Lauren

Yes, I'm free. But I've had enough socialising this week. You could come to mine? Takeaway and talk? Lauren x

Jackpot! She's interested! She's giving me the chance I have been praying for. I could kick my heels with joy. Now, it's time for me to win Lauren's heart. I have never done this before, tried to win someone's heart, and I'm glad in a way that I haven't. I want the first time I give my heart and win someone else's to be with someone as special as her.

Tim

Sounds perfect, see you around 7pm? Can't wait! Tim xoxox

Lauren

7pm works for me, looking forward to seeing you xLx

I postpone my run for another time to give myself longer to get ready, because I want to make an effort for the lovely Lauren. I want to impress her. So after a shower and shave, I iron my nicest clothes – that I don self-consciously– and then, once ready, I head out to try and buy her some flowers.

I know that finding a decent bunch of flowers is going to be an issue at this time of the evening, but that doesn't stop me trying. Lauren deserves flowers, chocolates and all the nice things in the world. After looking for about ten minutes the large red and green plant catches my attention. Having managed to procure a lovely Poinsettia plant, or a Christmas Star as it is more commonly known, I pay for the plant before hailing a taxi to her apartment.

I arrive at her place at 6:55 p.m. It's raining again, and unconcerned that she'll know how eager I am, I buzz her apartment instead of waiting until 7 p.m. I am eager. I can't wait to spend time with her.

"You're early!" she shouts through the door at me. I can hear her unchaining the lock, and when she finally opens the door to me, she looks even more gorgeous than I remember.

"You look beautiful, Lauren. You've changed your hair!" I say to her with my voice full of awe and desire. As I hug her in greeting, the blood rushes to my groin, and I have to turn my pelvis away, so I don't jab her with my unruly cock and scare her away. A faint pink covers her cheeks, and my stomach flutters as though it's full of butterflies. She is so adorable. It's the dimples; they get me everytime!

I like her even more than I thought. I didn't think it would be possible to fancy her more than I did, but with her dark glossy hair in waves around her shoulders and her cute-as-hell smile complete with dimples, I am completely and utterly mesmerised by this intriguing woman.

She invites me in again, and it is reminiscent of coming *home*; it is familiar and comfortable because she is here.

"I'm so glad you texted me back, Lauren. I thought I had messed up my chance with you." I tell her as honestly as I can. I want there to be no miscommunications. I want this woman; I want her with every inch of my being. I want her like I've never wanted anyone ever before.

"I want to be honest, Tim. I nearly didn't text you. Someone knocked my hand before I could delete what I had written out. I didn't think you would still be interested. I am having a hard time believing you are actually here at all. But I'm relieved that moron did bump into me. I don't know if I would have had the courage to text you otherwise."

As I stand close to her, I brush her hair away from her face with one hand. "A happy accident then," I say before I brush my lips over hers. She tastes delicious, like cotton candy, her scent is like vanilla and marshmallows and I just want to devour every part of her. "I'm sorry, I couldn't wait any longer. I just really needed to kiss you."

I could groan in pent up agitation when she bites her lip as she looks away with the hint of a smile on her lips; my words and my kiss caused that reaction in her. I wonder again what other reactions I could extract from her.

I know she is having a hard time understanding how she affects me. I hate that she feels insecure about herself, and that forces her to question whether my interest is genuine and long-lasting. I will have to be patient and understanding and show her that my yearning for her will stand the test of time. I have never felt like this about anyone. I think I'm falling in love with her. I have always preferred a certain type of woman. Curvy, voluptuous and sweet. Lauren is the whole package and more. She is smart and funny and although she doesn't realise yet; she is hot as hell. I could lose myself in her eyes and her dimples when she smiles are simply mesmerising. It's not just about her physical appearance though, I have always been on the fence on the matter of 'soulmates', not that I didn't believe it, but I had no proof one way or the other. But when I met Lauren, it felt like 'recognition'. I didn't know her, but something in me recognised her. She is all the proof I need, she is my soulmate. I know this is something special, I know we could make this work if she can let me in.

"You're a really good kisser. I like you, Tim. Please don't mess with me. I want to believe this is real, that you could like me too. But I am so scared of being hurt." I look into her eyes as she opens up to me. She is putting herself out there. So I will too.

"I really, really like you, Lauren. I went on a double-blind date, and all I could think about was you. I wished she was you. I promise I am genuine. I promise I will not hurt you. Well not deliberately or intentionally at least. I am really falling for you."

She kisses me this time, and I groan in pleasure as her soft body presses against mine. My dick throbs from the contact. There is no hiding it now; she must know by now how kissing her makes me almost cum in my pants.

"Is that for me?" she shyly asks me, and for a moment I think she is asking about my aching cock that has a life of its own; as far as she is concerned, the bloody thing will not behave and continually tries to joust with the poor woman.

As the blood floods my face turning me as red as a tomato, I am about to admit it's all for her, but thankfully realise in the nick of time that she is not referring to my wayward cock, but to the Poinsettia I am still gripping on to.

"Yes. It's for you. I wanted to get you a bunch of flowers, but I quite liked this when I saw it." She smiles radiantly as I hand the plant to her. Her eyes glow, and I am so glad I got it; the look of joy and appreciation from Lauren made everything worthwhile. I would shower this woman with anything her heart desires to have her look at me like that again.

We settle in her living room with trashy Saturday night television and order takeaway Chinese food. We talk away with ease like we have known each other for years. It's such a simple night, but I never want it to end.

More simple nights with Lauren sound like a dream come dream. There is nothing I want more than sharing evening after evening with Lauren. Especially as I can no longer envision a future without her in it.

Fuck I am falling fast. But dear God, it feels so good.

~ **Owen** ~

The next few days go by in a flurry of panic and disarray. London has been hit by snowfall and on top of the torrential rain we had over the weekend the place was starting to resemble a giant ice rink. Sunday evening arrives, and the higher-ups at the company advise us to allow our employees to work from home where possible.

I have an excuse to call Jamie. My palms become sweaty, and my mouth suddenly feels wet and dry all at the same time. I hope there is a natural opening for me to talk to her casually.

I dial her number, and after a few rings it goes to voicemail. So, I leave a message asking her to ring me back. Around ten minutes later she calls me back.

"Hi, sorry about that, I was in the shower, Mr. Matthews... Owen... I'm not sure how to address you this way." She starts off. Fuck my name sounds lyrical from her lips. Now all I can think of is her naked in the shower, rubbing soap suds all over her body.

"Owen's fine. Are you able to work from home tomorrow? We have been told to ask people to work from home if they can because of the bad weather." My voice has an edge to it as I try and fail to keep it level. I will myself not to think of Jamie sitting naked with just a towel protecting her beautiful body from my gaze. When I speak to her, I sound as though I'm angry instead of horny and frustrated.

"And that makes you mad because?" she asks me with a hint of a laugh in her voice. I can't help but laugh in reply.

"Sorry, I'm truly sorry! I know I sounded mad then, but I'm not. I just have to spend my Sunday evening convincing you all that working from home is a good thing." No! Why did I say it like that? Why do words continue to fall from my big fat stupid mouth?

The hurt is evident in her voice when she replies to me. "I can work from home, Mr. Matthews. I'm sorry to have taken up your time."

"Jamie, wait! I'm so shit at this. I didn't mean it that way. How was your weekend, eh?"

She does a bit of a groan before answering. "Well my date wasn't exactly what I had in mind. And I have been looking after my sister's children since yesterday afternoon. She's just got back now. So nothing too eventful. How was your weekend?"

Torture. That's what I want to say. I spent most of it torturing myself over you. "Yeah, it's been okay. I met up with some old friends, and now I am mopping up for the bigwigs while they eat roast beef with their families." That gets a small laugh from her at least.

"Rough. Well, I can stay with my sister and work from her office, and then make my way straight to the airport on Tuesday. Unless that's cancelled too?"

"Copenhagen is still on for now. Unless that changes, I will see you on Tuesday at the airport." I am cursing myself internally for ending the conversation so abruptly. I hate talking on the phone, although evidently, I'm no better in person either.

This means so much to me that the thought of messing it up

is causing me to actually mess it up. Overthinking about it is magnifying every single action I take or dont take. I need to just relax and let Jamie see me for me, as Owen.

"See you Tuesday then. Goodnight, Owen."

When she ends the call, I shout into the air "Fuck!"

I am not making a good job of this at all. All day Monday, I brood and sulk. I miss her and the little things she does. Before the trip, no other opportunity presents itself to organically talk to Jamie about us in the way that I crave. The waiting is my torture.

Tuesday arrives and the city has started to thaw. I arrive at the airport with plenty of time to spare. I had offered to pick Jamie up, but she told me her brother-in-law was going to drive her.

I wait for her under the information boards. She should be here any moment now. Time continues to tick by with no sign of Jamie. She is cutting it close now. I try to call her, but it goes straight to voicemail again.

She best not miss this trip. Fuck the business side of things; fuck our jobs; I cannot wait another day to see her.

"Sir, it's time to make your way to the departure gates," the steward who checked me in tells me as she licks her lips and pushes her tits together giving me a view of her deep cleavage.

"Yeah, I know. I'm waiting for someone," I tell her impatiently. Can't she take the hint? I am not interested in her.

"On this flight? This flight is fully checked-in, sir." she tells me as she scans her hand held device to double check. My heart thumps even harder, how did I miss Jamie? She must have arrived here really early.

I rush through to the departure lounge, and my heart starts to beat again when I get a glimpse of Jamie at the makeup counter in duty-free. She is, as I should have guessed, trying to get the best deal on her makeup while she is here. Her arms are overflowing with other things, so I collect a basket and start to take them from her before she properly notices me.

She is startled when she finally realises it is me. "Owen? I mean Mr..."

"Don't, Jamie, just call me Owen. Please! What is all this stuff, eh? You know they have a duty-free outlet on the way home, right?" I take a stuffed frog backpack filled with lollipops, a tin truck stacked with KitKats and the largest Toblerone I've ever seen from her arms.

"It's for the kids... Well, the Toblerone is for me, and I'll fight anyone who tries to say otherwise. And Billie gave me a list as long as my arm of cosmetics she wants."

I grin at her as I dramatically pretend to sniff the Toblerone. I quite like Toblerone, too. "I swear to God, Owen, I will choke you if you touch my Toblerone." There is a glint in her eyes, a twinkle of mischief and laughter. God, I want to scratch beneath the surface and discover the little imp inside her.

It's not just the Toblerone I want to touch. There isn't a single millimetre of this alluring woman I dont want to explore, and as much as I want to fuck her senseless, I also want to make slow, sweet love to her, too. My body and mind are overloaded with the desire to kiss her everywhere, every single nerve. I am in love with her, and I am going to fight for her.

"Owen? Owen... they just announced the final call for our flight. We have to hurry." Shit, she caught me daydreaming yet again. She quickly pays for all her goods as I bag up everything and then grab her hand and pull her to the departure gate. We have to run for part of the way, and we look at each other, holding hands, running and laughing as we race to make our flight.

"Here they are now, you almost missed this flight, sir. You and your girlfriend have seats next to each other in business class. Straight down to the bottom, turn left, go through the curtain and a member of our crew will be there to assist. Have a safe flight."

I don't correct her assumption and Jamie doesn't either; I like the sound of it, but maybe Jamie is just trying to save time? It's not something worth correcting; it's not like we are going to see her again.

As soon as we are seated and buckled up, the pilot announces we are ready to leave, and the cabin crew give their safety demonstration. As the plane starts to move, Jamie grips my hand again. I forgot. She hates flying. It's another one of the things I found endearing about her.

"Did you manage to book an excursion to the palaces while we are there?" She looks at me with panic-filled wide eyes and shakes her head. "Jamie, just breathe. Everything is going to be okay. I've got you, babe."

Her eyes flash open. There is no hiding her surprise and, more pleasingly, her desire when I call her 'babe.' It just slipped out, I didnt even think about it, that is what I naturally want to call her. Though her reaction pleases me, it also confuses me. Could it be that she does want this after all? As soon as we are off this plane, and have some privacy, we are going to talk. I can't take this not knowing anymore.

"Can I get you some refreshments? Champagne, orange juice?" one of the crew asks, breaking our moment far too soon. I want to groan in frustration at her.

"Could I have a cup of tea, please. A drop of milk, no sugar, please." Jamie's husky voice breaks my pouting. She's being offered champagne and the works, and all she wants is a cup of tea. How cute is she?! She makes me smile so much.

"Yes, could we have tea, please. And some biscuits to dip in... right Jamie?" She gives me the most radiant smile, and hope starts to build up inside me. We have a chance; I just need to stoke this fire that is starting to burn slowly between us. It's so precarious that I don't want to suffocate it. I need to go slow so I don't chase her off again. I can do it slowly; I'll take 'slow' over a 'no-go' all day long.

The rest of the flight is uneventful, and the car and driver we have arranged is already waiting to take us to our accommodation.

As we enter the hotel lobby my heart sinks when we are greeted by the PA of the associate I am here to meet with. Her name is Saffi and she is looking at me suggestively. She is tall and slender with long blonde hair and big round, surgically enhanced boobs. She is around my age, and she is as forward as the last time we met. I hadn't given her a second thought since that last time, and I didn't think she would still be here. "Owen, it's so nice to see you. Maybe I'll see some more of you again later, big boy?" Shit. I look at Jamie who frowns and looks away, her cheeks are red in anger.

The last time I was here, two or three years ago, Saffi and I hooked up and had some fun for the duration of my visit. Now it looks like she is up for round two, and she has made no secret of it in front of Jamie. Jamie's expression is now closed off, and I wish I could tell what she is thinking.

"This is your PA? She may leave now; Mr. Hansen wants to speak to you alone for today." She waves her hand dismissively at Jamie, who she then looks up and down with an expression that would suggest she could smell something really bad. I know what the smell is – it's Saffi's attitude.

"I will check us both in and leave your luggage in your room, Mr. Matthews. I will leave the key at reception for you. If you don't need me, I think I will go and explore." The urge to run after her, to tell her there is nothing between Saffi and I, not now anyway, is overwhelming. However, Jamie refuses to meet my eye, and I have no plausible excuse to delay my meeting.

The bellboy wheels our bags away, and she follows behind him. Before she leaves, I say to her with a strangled voice, "Eh, Jamie? Have a nice time." My heart sinks when all the warmth and affection on her face from before is replaced with a tight smile.

She turns back to me and murmurs, "Yeah, you too."

EMMA LEE-JOHNSON

CHAPTER SIX

~ Jamie ~

As I step into the elevator with the bellboy, I get a last glimpse of Owen and the big-boobed bimbo whose laugh is as fake as her gravity defying tits. My stomach turns in envy and resentment. On the plane, it felt like Owen and I were starting to get somewhere. I was excited for where that could possibly go, and then she comes in and blasts it all apart.

I look like a boy in comparison to her, with her stupid, big, bouncy breasts wobbling about. Even I couldn't keep my eyes off them. How am I ever going to get Owen to notice me now, with my skinny frame and flat chest? Maybe I am fooling myself. How could I ever keep his interest? He is rich, successful, accomplished and he is oh-so-sexy and sweet.

I really have missed my chance. I should have bit off his arm when he asked me out, but it was such a shock to me that I went and messed it up. Now he'll end up married to Blondey McBigTits, and I will have to bring them coffee every morning and watch them dance together at office parties.

I am *not* sitting around this hotel waiting for him to return, wondering what he is doing or who he is doing. No, I will go out and explore this beautiful city.

After our belongings are safely away in our respective rooms, I refresh my makeup, pull on my wool coat and scarf and make my way to the reception.

Owen and his friend are nowhere to be seen so I walk outside and hope that if I wander about, I will find something to do.

The company I work for has spared no expense for this trip. We are staying in The Nimb and it is the most gorgeous building. It is grand and glorious, and I am in awe of the majestic architecture. There are lights around outside, but they are understated and classy. It really is wonderful here.

As I soak up my surroundings, including the Christmas market at Tivoli Gardens, I am excited for tomorrow when I will be able to take in the full experience. I wistfully watch the happy couples all around me, holding hands and kissing as snowflakes melt into their hair and drip onto their faces that are filled with love and hope. In stark comparison, an empty hole opens inside me where my heart and soul used to be. I have never felt more alone than I do right now.

This is not the sort of place you go to alone; this is the sort of place you enjoy with your loved one. My mind immediately flashes to Owen, and I am floored by an overwhelming pang of longing. I need to leave this to rest. Owen is not going to revisit this 'getting to know one another' thing, and brooding over him is only going to result in me being lonely for longer.

I stop at the Anarkist bar, and after much debate I order the cocktail recommended by the bartender. Before I know it, some other tourists have joined me, and we have a laugh talking and drinking. After a couple of hours of drinking, I am definitely feeling the effects of the alcohol. Some kind of sense must kick in my brain, because suddenly I realise I haven't eaten yet. I best go back to my hotel and get something to eat. On my way to The Nimb bar and restaurant, I see Ms. Big-Boobs, who eyes me suspiciously but doesn't talk to me.

The menu is not in English… or maybe it is, and I am too drunk to read it, who knows, but I give up on ordering food. A few men look in my direction, expressing their interest in me. Men in suits, men in roll neck sweaters, men who still have their wedding bands on their fingers. But not one pulls my attention back; none of them are as enticing as Owen Matthews.

I have another drink, which I probably shouldn't have, before I call it a night and make my way back to my room.

In my drunken state, I decide now is the best time to get some things off my chest with Owen. I am going to knock on his door and tell him that I am happy for him.

I completely miss his door and fall against the wall next to it. I look up as his door opens, and I tell him to shush, because he'll wake people up. But when I focus, I realise Owen is standing in front of me with just shorts on.

"Oh my God. That's not fair… why do you have to be so hot, Mr. Owen?" His eyes widen when I say this. Maybe he doesn't know he is hot?

"Are you drunk?" he asks me, and I can hear him laughing at me as he tries and fails to sound stern.

"Just a bittle lit. YOU. Owen, YOU said it was best not to mix business and pleasure… So why do I feel so sad about it?"

I get up on my feet, but the floor moves causing me to sway, until Owen holds on to my arms and keeps me steady.

"Get in here. What am I going to do with you, eh, Jamie Knowles?

Turning up at my room all drunk and pink cheeked, looking like a sexy goddess." Before I can tell him why I am here, it registers that he has called me sexy. ME! He takes me into his room and sits me down before giving me a bottle of water.

"Are you on your Owen?" I start to laugh. I made a joke, and it is really funny. He laughs, too, and shakes his head while he removes my shoes. "Mr. Owen?" I ask.

When he replies, "What?" I blurt out something I shouldn't be asking.

"Did you fuck her? You know the blonde with the boobs." I even do the hand motion to demonstrate the big, massive knockers. He looks a bit startled by my question and slightly amused too.

Owen sighs as he sits beside me. "Yes. I did. I fucked her a few times a couple of years ago. Does that bother you, Jamie?" He's looking me dead in the eyes now, his voice is clear but soothing, he still has no top on, and his hair flops down over his forehead making him appear younger than normal.

"I suppose it does bother me. Yes, I think it does. I am jealous, which is ridiculous. You're a free man, and you can screw who you want. But I don't want you to." I start to giggle. I would never say any of this in the cold light of day. I am seriously going to regret this come morning.

However, there is a slim chance talking about all this will clear the air between us, and it will help us move on. "I want you to Owen me." Well, I am on fire tonight with my jokes. I start to giggle, and after a while, Owen joins in with me.

"It bothered me that you went on a date with someone else. But I tried to respect the fact that you didn't want to risk mixing business with pleasure when it came to dating me."

My heart is beating fast against my rib cage; I am a heady mix of turned on, drunk and terrified.

"I have wanted you for the longest time, Jamie. Now, be honest with me. Do you want me? Do you want to give this a shot? Because I think you do, if your drunk talk is anything to go by."

I reach out and touch his face. This gorgeous man with his dark hair, sexy stubble and his smouldering eyes. I want him; I want to give us a shot. But I am terrified I'll walk in on him in bed with another woman, too. However, I have been miserable at the thought of never having this chance; Billie says it's the things I don't do that I will end up regretting.

"I want you, too, Owen. I want to give us a shot. But first, I have to puke up." Way to go me on ruining our first romantic interlude.

Owen laughs at me as I hurl every drop of liquor that I have ever drank. But he is so sweet, too. He holds my hair away from my face, rubs my back, and gives me damp face cloths and sips of cool water in between retches so I feel more comfortable.

When I stop heaving, he picks me up and carries me to his bed. Even though I have spewed up all the alcohol, I am still drunk. "Will you stay with me? Please?" I ask him, and Owen laughs at me again.

"It's my bloody room, woman!" Oh yeah! I forgot about that. "But I will stay in case you're sick again." I bite my lip in anticipation, I wish I had a toothbrush. I don't want our first kiss to taste sick. But that's a minute detail. I am in Owen's bed, still horny as hell, and he has no top on.

I pull him into the bed with me, but he laughs and shakes his head. "Oh, no, you don't. This is how this is going to go, Jamie. Once you have sobered up, we'll have this conversation again. I want us to be straight about what we want. I want us to be completely open and honest with each other. In the morning, tell me you still want this, and I am all yours. Tell me when you're sober, when you can't hide behind your drunkenness, and I'll believe this is what you truly want."

The pig, he just wants to see me blush. Looks like I'm going to spend another day yearning for Owen to be in my heart and between my legs.

~ Owen ~

My meeting with Mr. Hansen lasts for about two hours. It is boring and tedious, made even more so by the fact that I can't stop thinking about Jamie the whole time. Once the meeting is over, Mr. Hansen calls Saffi back in. She brings dinner for us all on a silver trolley. Twice she bends down suggestively. She is not subtle, and when Mr. Hansen leaves to use the restroom, she tries to climb onto my lap.

"I have been dreaming of your tongue action, Owen. It's still one of the best orgasms I've ever had. Come to my room later. You can show me what your tongue can do again, and I'll show you what mine is capable of, too." I have to admit, I had been on fire that night. But I don't want this. Not with Saffi.

"Get off me. This isn't going to happen, Saffi. You're great and all that, but I'm in love with someone."

I gently push her away from me, but she acts like I have burnt her. "You are in love with the skinny woman, your PA? But I am much sexier, no?" She runs her hands down her figure, and yes, I'll be honest she is a knockout, but she doesn't even compare to Jamie; she doesn't even make the race against Jamie.

"We had a great time, Saffi, but that was then, and this is now. I don't want this now. I just want her." Rage bubbles inside her; I can tell from her expression and by the way she turns a dark purple from the chest up.

"You have a pin dick anyway!" she shouts out at me as she runs from the room. Charming.

Leaving the conference room, I head over to the hotel bar to see if I can find Jamie so I can explain what is going on, or more to the point; what isn't going on between Saffi and I. She isn't in the restaurant either. I look out at the hotel's gardens but I still can't find Jamie, I am stumped. I even knock on her door, but I can't find her anywhere. The look on her face when Saffi was being suggestive both intrigues me and makes me feel ashamed. She looked hurt and annoyed, and I have already begun to read far too much into her reactions. Especially seeing as at the first opportunity she had, Jamie is out having fun with God knows who.

Giving up, I go back to my own room and shower, ready for my morning meeting. I help myself to a miniature from the minibar and try to read the documents I will need for my meeting. As I analyse the information, a post-it note from Jamie falls out, and I sit and stare at her neat curly writing. *Smash it!*

And as if on cue, a loud crash sounds outside my room, as if someone is trying to break down the wall. I open the door to find Jamie splayed on the floor in the corridor, arguing with the wall.

"Who the fuck put that wall there? Stupid place to put a wall; it could kill someone." She looks at me, squints and then groans about it not being fair that I look fit.

Oh, how I love drunk Jamie! Drunk Jamie is the funniest thing I have ever seen. We have had a lot of office parties and Christmas do's and have attended many colleagues' birthdays, weddings, divorces and engagement parties over the few years we have worked together. We would all drink, but I have only ever seen Jamie drunk on two occasions, apart from tonight.

The first time, she decided she wanted to play Scrabble when we were at a house party. There were other games going on; someone was playing blackjack; there was a game of strip poker taking place. To be honest, it was meant to be a tame night that started to go a bit haywire. She ended up with about twenty letter tiles and kept misspelling words or spelling out rude words. She howled, laughing at herself. It's one of the cutest things I've ever seen. I promised myself if I ever did get a chance with her, I was going to get her drunk and make her play monopoly with me just so I could see what she would do.

The other time was at a retirement party. To be fair, everyone was drunk, but Jamie just stood out to me because... well, because it's Jamie. She and a couple of other girls had been singing and dancing when Jamie climbed up onto the tabletop. I felt like time stood still as she danced like no one else was in the room. In moments like that, as she laughed and giggled with her friends, I was completely spellbound by her, by her freedom and self-assurance, by her easy-going and happy nature and her lack of care for what others thought or said about her. But then as soon as Carl would show up, she would turn into a timid wallflower.

True to form, drunk Jamie didn't disappoint. Right before tossing her cookies — and by the sheer volume you would think she hurled somebody else's cookies as well —she finally told me what I've been waiting years to hear: she wants me.

I don't care about anything else now, from the things she's said and asked tonight it's clear that she feels something, too. Tomorrow morning I have a meeting, and then I am free for almost two days. I have two days with Jamie in Copenhagen. Two days to shower her in all the love and affection I have been holding inside. Two days to really break down her walls, and show her what is lurking behind mine. Two days to win her heart and make her mine.

I go to her room while she sleeps in my bed and move all her stuff to my room. I know she is going to feel like shit in the morning and having all her stuff close by, so she can shower, change and brush her teeth, will make her feel better.

As I make myself comfortable on the sofa that's ten feet from the king size bed Jamie is sleeping in, I laugh at myself. So many times I have dreamed of having this beautiful woman in my bed; I never once contemplated it being like this. I hope this is the last time she sleeps in my bed without me. I am just drifting off to sleep when I hear her voice. At first, I think she is calling out to me, but after sitting up and rubbing my eyes I notice she is still asleep.

The blanket has fallen off her, exposing her bare creamy skin. And that's when I see it:Jamie has her hand between her legs, rubbing herself while whispering my name in her sleep. My breath catches in my throat, and my dick is instantly stiff in response. God she is exquisite. I am terrified to move, or even breathe, in case I wake her. As she reaches her climax, she cries out my name. I can do nothing but watch and listen, completely enraptured with my sleeping beauty.

All this time I have been dreaming of her and dreaming of us... has she been doing the same? Something tells me this is a new development. A happy one.

I can't wait to be the one who fulfils her wildest dreams. Aching with longing, I lie awake for at least another hour thinking of the beautiful woman in my bed, the scent of her orgasm, another presence in the room. I can't get the sound of her sweet moans as she came out of my head.

That is the single hottest experience of my life and it's simply because it's her.

When my alarm sounds in the morning, she jumps up, her hair sticks up at odd angles and she looks about my room confused and disorientated.

"Good morning, babe. How's the head?" Her eyes go wide in realisation when she spots me. Once again, she doesn't challenge my endearment, something about it just feels so right. The first time I called her babe was a slip of the tongue. Now, it feels so natural, like that is what I should've always been calling her.

"Oh my God. Owen. I'm so sorry. I got pissed. I had a couple of cocktails when I went for a look around. And I ended up sloshed. Did I make a holy show of myself?" she asks as she covers her face with her hands.

Teasing her, I start to laugh. "Oh yeah, you did. But you were hilarious. Do you remember anything about last night?" I challenge. I am taking what is mine. I have fucked about enough. I want her and I'm certain she wants me.

"No, I don't remember a thing," she tells me, and my heart sinks until I see her radiant smile. "Of course I remember, Owen. I told you that I like you. I confessed to being jealous about that woman yesterday. I admitted I was sad that we aren't going to date." She meets my eyes for the first time; her face is pink, and her eyes are filled with honesty and vulnerability.

While my heart beats profusely, I make my confession back to her. "I have wanted this, you, us; I have wanted it all for the longest time. I just need a chance to show you that I can make you happy." Butterflies fill my stomach when she smiles back at me, making me braver and lightheaded at the same time. "Will you come out with me this afternoon, eh? We could go to the Christmas Market and look around, get some food and really get to know each other?"

I wait with bated breath for her answer.

"I'd love that, Owen." We sit apart grinning at each other. My heart feels lighter, warmer, and fuller. I'm finally getting my chance with Jamie, and this time I will not fuck it up.

"Good. Because I no longer want to be al-Owen." I tease, and she groans again before throwing a pillow at me.

"Shut up! Oh no. I just remembered. I puked up, too, didn't I?" She covers her face with her hands as my laugh echoes around the room.

My meeting lasts for three hours, and I am preoccupied thinking of Jamie and last night for the majority of it. I told her to stay in the room and get ready. She was supposed to come with me to the meeting, but I wanted to give her some time to really think things over without me looming over her.

She is keeping my room, so I moved my stuff to her old one. I am unsure of how fast things may progress between us, and I don't want her to feel pressured. I want this to play out organically. I want this to be exactly what it's meant to be, and if my gut is right: this is it, she is the one.

After the meeting, I go to my room and change into my warm and casual clothes and comb my hair before going to collect my date.

I knock lightly on the door and wait for her to answer. She shouts, "Just a minute," so I turn around, my back to the door, and look about the corridor to find something interesting. The door clicks open, and I turn around to face her. She looks amazing, with a deep red coat and a cream knitted hat and scarf. She could be straight from a Christmas film.

"You look amazing, Jamie. Are you ready for this?" I extend my hand to her, and she places hers inside it.

"More than ready. Tivoli Gardens Christmas Market, here we come."

~ Jamie ~

I am nervous and excited all rolled into one. I am going on a date with Owen; we are actually going on a date! As soon as the night before came back to me, I cringed at my behaviour. I thought I had definitely blown it once and for all. But Owen teased me, made me feel better and reassured me about what I had said and done. He ever so casually called me babe again. He's done that a couple of times now and although I was taken aback the first time he said it, I have to admit that I like it. It doesn't seem forced on Owen's behalf, it simply feels right.

There is something very liberating about being open and honest with each other. I don't feel the need to hold back with Owen, and I hope he feels the same way, too. When I recall asking him if he'd fucked that other woman, my cheeks flush red. I can't believe I did that, but I am so glad I did and that Owen answered me honestly. Yes, it hurt a bit, but the truth is so much more palatable than a sugar-coated lie.

When I was with Carl, we never talked about anything. I felt stifled at times and belittled. I never felt able to communicate with him. I bit my tongue over a lot of things that I shouldn't have acquiesced over. I put up with a lot of stuff I probably shouldn't have. I think I was too young when we got together. I didn't know who I was back then. I didn't know what I liked. And as I grew into the person I was supposed to be, Carl didn't like the changes. He liked the young unsure girl, unquestioning and yielding.

I would never have spoken to Carl about sex. We had sex, but we didn't talk about it. I wouldn't dare tell him what I liked or suggest anything new. Carl liked to think he was a man who knew what to do, and although he knew what buttons to press there was always something lacklustre about our physical relationship. I wanted more, but I felt too embarrassed to express that.

I think with Owen, I could tell him these things and we could discuss them together. We have built up a friendship, we know each other quite well already, and I don't fear him ridiculing me or becoming angry if I were to say something he disagrees with.

I think Owen could help me fulfil the sexual yearnings and curiosity I have. I'm not kinky, or at least I don't think I am. However, I do want to try new things. I want to try a sixty-niner. I want to ride him. I want to take some risks and have some fun. These are things I have wanted to experience; the stuff I've never done.

Owen knocks on the door, and when I answer, he turns around, his sexy brown eyes taking in the sight of me, and I blush in response. In that one look, he makes me feel sexy and desirable. Every time I think of Owen now, I am filled with a burning want right down between my legs. I like to think I'm in control of my urges, but the dreams are coming quick and fast now and feel more real with every passing moment. I am not going to deny it, because it would be stupid to do so: I want Owen. I want him more than I have ever wanted anything.

"I thought we could take a walk, get some mulled wine, check out the lights and decorations and do some shopping," he tells me, and I beam back at him. The Christmas Market is something I have really been looking forward to.

We make our way down to the park and Owen hands our tickets in, allowing us access into the most magical place on this Earth.

It is a winter wonderland. There is snow blowing everywhere and tasteful decorations assembled about. The festive music, instruments and singing are subtle and heart-warming.

There are unusual light displays that are simply magnificent, the bright colours and twinkling patterns adding to the overall effect. The signs say there are fifteen magnificently decorated trees, and I want to see each and every one.

As we walk down through the market stalls, I slip my hand into Owen's, and he grins down at me when I do. We stop at a traditional ornament stall and I spot a tin nutcracker that would look great in Tables & Fables.

"I want to get this for my sister," I tell him, and he smiles and pays for it before I have the chance to. "Thank you, Owen. You didn't need to do that."

Owen wraps an arm around my shoulders and directs me to another stall that has mulled wine simmering away in a large vat. There are oranges, apples and cranberries along with star anise, cinnamon bark and chunks of ginger root bobbing up and down in the crimson liquid. If I could bottle the smell of Christmas, this is what it would smell like, the fruity base and spicy undertones evoking feelings of festive love and togetherness.

My recovery from my hangover is still on thin ice. "I'm going to pass on the wine, for now, I don't think my stomach can take it yet," I tell him apologetically.

Owen gives a little chuckle as he kisses me against my temple. "Don't worry, babe. How about hot chocolate instead, eh?"

"That sounds amazing, actually." As I look into his eyes, our faces are mere millimetres apart. I want to kiss him so badly.

No, I should rephrase that. I want Owen to kiss me. I want him to take my face into his hands and kiss me deeply and passionately without holding back. However, I don't know if I would be able to hold back, and we are in the middle of a Christmas market with families and young children going about their business as if the world isn't changing at a rapid pace right in front of their faces.

I break eye contact but he doesn't give up, and that turns me on even more.

"What's up, babe?" he murmurs against my head. His voice sends shivers of need throughout my body.

"I want to kiss you, but there's too much of an audience." He places another kiss against my temple and leads me along the path to one of the large Christmas trees that is beautifully decorated in lilacs, whites and silvers and thousands of twinkling lights.

"I've wanted to kiss you all night, Jamie." I melt into his embrace, my body lights up from my centre as Owen pushes my hair back off my face and presses his lips against mine.

He lazily opens his soft lips against mine, and I wrap my arms around his neck allowing his tongue access. It's a sweet kiss, full of passion and promise.

As he deepens our ardent exchange, my body floods with pent up tension. I want him. I want his body to press against mine and into mine.

I want to see every part of him.

I want to give every part of me to him.

He pulls away from our kiss all too soon, and when I look into his eyes, I can see love and tenderness. I can see the future.

"Come on, babe, we have so much to see, and if I get my way, you'll not be getting much more sightseeing done. Are you hungry? We have a table booked at restaurant Promenaden in an hour." Oh wow! I've heard about the wonderful restaurant that has a balcony that overlooks the Gardens, allowing you to see the light shows while you eat.

"It sounds amazing. Thank you, Owen. Thank you for doing all this for me." He kisses me again before I can finish my sentence. This time Owen leaves no doubt in my mind of what he wants. My feminine core is practically burning in wanton desire because I want the same too.

"Shall we have a go on The Flying Trunk before dinner?" The Flying Trunk is a ride dedicated to the fairy tales of Hans Christian Andersen. Similar to the 'It's a Small World' ride at Disneyland, or a less sinister ghost train. You travel through the different depictions and displays of thirty-two fairy tales, and the one who can guess the most, wins.

The queue isn't too long, and after a few minutes, Owen is helping me into the treasure chest cart that will carry us through on our journey. He sits down close to me and casually places his arm around my shoulders again. It's comforting and a little intoxicating being this close to him. I rest my head back on his shoulder, and my body seems to simulate a jigsaw; my body fits completely with Owen's. He completes me.

The pressure that has been bubbling up inside me all day threatens to spill over. I have Owen's arms around me, the memory of his kiss on my lips and the rumbling of the cart acts as a stimulant to my aroused, wanting pussy. I hope Owen wants to take things further tonight. I think I'm just going to explode if I don't get to touch him soon.

To give him a clue what I'm thinking, I tilt my head up and graze my nose against his stubble. Just as I hoped, Owen immediately responds with enthusiasm. He no longer kisses me sweetly. This time, it's hard and carnal, and I moan in satisfaction. I cannot get enough. We kiss each other into a frenzy. A fire burns between us, and I don't want to stop it; bring on the inferno and burn me.

As he runs his hand down my body, I am delighted to hear a groan of approval. We are wearing too many clothes, and that annoys me. I need him. I need to see what is hidden beneath his clothes. I want to see the real Owen. The one no one else gets to see, at least not anymore. I want him to be mine.

I slip my hands down his chest, across his hard abdomen and lower, and I manage a teasing touch of his ample cock before pulling my hand away. This is too public.

I thread my fingers through Owen's hair and pull him to me to kiss him one more time. He is cradling my ass in both hands and pulls me to his chest. I land, without any grace, on his lap, and before I decide to respond even more boldly, several flashes go off all around us, startling us both. It's only when I see the end of the ride that I realise it was the souvenir camera. We have been caught on camera.

Having been caught kissing, I'm glad I didn't act on my instinct to get his cock out. The shame! And yet the thought of it, me sucking Owen's cock as the cameras flashed all around, seems to fuel my desire even more. I am seriously close, dangerously close, to surrendering and losing all control. As we head to the souvenir booth, Owen laughs while the man tells him he was unable to display our photos since young children may see.

"We were just kissing. I'll have every photo please." He turns to me, his eyes still clouded with passion, and whispers to me, "It's a good job I didn't do all the things I wanted to; we'd be buying our porno right now. How hungry are you, babe? Do you want to keep our reservation, or shall we make our way back to the hotel?

CHAPTER SEVEN

~ Owen ~

Being with Jamie is even better than I ever envisioned or imagined. When she said she wanted to kiss me, I just wanted to kiss the face off her in front of everyone. I don't care who sees, I want them to see.

She made it clear that I could have kissed her before now. Last night I knew she wanted to, but I waited because I wanted her to have her full faculties, and after all this time, I wanted to make it special. I have dreamt of this moment for the longest time, I just need to get it right. I want to leave absolutely no doubt in her mind that this is what I want, and for her to be fully aware of what I am offering in return.

As we check out the photos from The Flying Trunk ride, my heart misses a beat when I see for myself how great we look together. Jamie laughs as she fans through them.

"We have a lasting memento of one of our first kisses now," she tells me as she slips them safely back into their protective cover and into her handbag. I'm overjoyed that she wants a souvenir of it.

I try to persuade her to come back to the hotel; I am straining in my trousers now. I have been fully erect and ready to blow since I picked her up from her hotel room. I had to tuck my cock into my waistband so it's not too obvious. I want to take Jamie to bed; I want to do all the things that keep running through my mind, like touching every part of her and making her cum until she screams my name.

Jamie, unfortunately, has other ideas. "Easy, tiger, there's plenty of time for all that. I'm sorry to be a party pooper, but I really, really want to go to the restaurant so I can see the gardens from up there and the light show, too." I know right now that in the future I will give her whatever she wants. Whatever she asks for will be my command. I will do anything for her.

"Okay, okay. We will go to dinner, but can we skip starters at least?" I sound like a petulant child, but I sincerely don't know how I'm going to make it through the rest of the night without touching her.

When she whispers in my ear, the sensation makes me groan. "We can skip starters, and if you're a good boy, I'll be your dessert back at the hotel." Her words almost tip me over the edge. I'm seriously considering a tactical hand job in the toilets before I blow my load involuntarily. She knows what she has done to me, too, if her little grin is anything to go by.

We huddle together as we walk to the restaurant. The winter sun has long made way for the moon, making the temperature drop, but it serves to discourage the crowds, too. Families with little ones make their way back into the warmth, and the older couples also seem to be calling it a night.

I am surprised to find Restaurant Promenaden is a buffet-style eatery. I apologise to Jamie for bringing her to what would constitute a canteen back home, but she laughs and tells me she already knew it was from her research.

It isn't the romantic meal I envisioned, but it works out better this way. We are served instantly and are able to look at the local cuisine and ask questions about it before making our choices. When we have filled our plates, we head straight to the balcony.

The balcony is almost empty, with the rest of the diners opting to eat inside in the warmth. I lead her to the corner table which is obscured with ferns and other plants as well as Christmas decorations. It's private, secluded and very pretty.

We sit next to one another, looking out at Tivoli Gardens, and I don't know what looks better: the breathtaking view or my gorgeous date. We try the frikadeller, which are traditional Danish meatballs with a unique taste, and the 'must try' local pickled herring, and chat away.

"I want to ask you about the date you went on... what happened?" In all honesty, I want to know what made that one different from ours. Why did that one not work out, and can I learn anything from it?

"His name was Conor. He was a nice enough man, but there was no spark there. I am going to be honest with you, Owen. I don't want there to be any lies between us, especially if we are to become something long term." She pauses and gulps before continuing. "I had a one-night-stand with him. I don't regret it, but I didn't enjoy it either. Afterwards, I felt I had done it so Carl was no longer the last and only person I had ever been with. It felt good that I was able to put some distance between Carl and I, but now I also know that one-night-stands are not for me."

I knew something had happened; I could tell when I called her on Sunday. I am glad she is being honest with me and that we can talk openly about matters such as this. I am also glad she got her rebound out of the way and it wasn't with me. I don't want to be a one-night-stand or a rebound. I want so much more than that.

"A rebound is usually a good and healthy way to draw a line under a previous relationship, Jamie. There is nothing to feel bad about. I'm glad I wasn't your rebound. I'm also feeling really happy that you're not just after a one-night-stand either." Her whole body seems to relax, and I find it endearing that she worries about my opinion.

"I don't want this to be a one-night thing, Owen. I don't want to be a one-night-stand to you," she tells me plainly and honestly. I must be the luckiest man alive because all my dreams are coming to fruition.

"You could never be a one-night thing for me, Jamie. I have wanted you for the longest time. I meant every word I said last night. I want to be with you. I'm tired of messing about. I really like you, and if this doesn't work, then it doesn't work. But we'll never know if we don't try, eh?"

She answers by kissing me.

I have fantasised incessantly about how it would feel to kiss Jamie, and yet, this is beyond all fantasy. Her beautiful, plump, pink lips caress mine, almost feather light like a butterfly's wings across my own lips. I am overwhelmingly aroused. I thread my hand through her hair and hold her harder against me. The illicit moan from the back of her throat has me completely undone. I have never been this turned on; she is the most sensual woman I have ever spent time with.

As I run my hands down her body, I look into her fire-filled eyes. God, she is exquisite; she is perfectly in proportion; she is in the most perfect shape. She is everything. Once, I was shocked that I fell in love with her without meaning to. Now, I know I never stood a chance; she is the complete package. I lightly graze my hand between her legs and take great pleasure when she yelps, bringing the memory of her getting off in her sleep last night back to the front of my mind. I need her to chant my name again, but this time I want it to be because I made her cum; I want it to be my doing.

I am thankful for the tiny bit of privacy we have because I am never going to make it back to the hotel without touching her. While we continue to kiss, I slip my hand under her coat and stroke lightly down her sides. She doesn't protest; in fact, she moves closer and sighs when I repeat the action. This time, I hold her waist and pull her closer to me, and she moans quietly at the back of her throat as we continue to kiss. She doesn't stop me when I pull on her waistband. We look deeply into each other's eyes as she helps me to open the fastening on her pants. I whisper to her, "Spread your legs for me, babe, just a tiny bit, please." I've died and gone to heaven when she does as I ask, giving me better access to her pussy.

Jamie wants this as much as I do; her tight pussy is moist with her own arousal. I barely stroke her velvety lips and she shudders into me. Using my fingers, I spread her weeping slit open. Geez, I want to bury my head right in here and eat away until she cums all over my face.

When I finally connect with her clit, I can tell she's ready to go off. "Do you want me to finish you here, or do you want to wait until we go home?"

She pulls away from my lips, I love the pink glow of her cheeks, her lips are swollen from my kisses and her hair is tousled. I want her like this but completely naked and open to me, lying in the centre of my bed. I want it all.

"I want both," she says before laughing a bit and resting her head on my shoulder.

I gently rub the pad of my forefinger over her clit, causing her to moan again. I keep going in circular motions, adding a bit of pressure until she clings to me. I replace my finger with my thumb and slide my finger inside her. She is warm, wet and tight, and my finger feels like it's come home, it belongs here. "Oh, baby, you feel even better than I could have ever imagined. It's going to be amazing between us. Tonight I am going to make you cum over and over and over again." I slide in a second finger whilst continuing the assault on her clit. This time, it stretches her wide, and as I curl my finger slightly, I feel the beginning of her tremor in my hand.

"Oh my God, Owen!" she whispers as her body begins to shake and tremble. She's holding back, but I've got her. I want to see the full extent of her orgasm.

"Cum for me, Jamie. I want to feel your pussy clench my fingers as you cum. Then when we get back to the hotel, I'm having my dessert. I am going to lick up every drop of nectar you squirt out for me." She falls to pieces in my hands as she surrenders to her climax; she looks amazing, so strong, so sexual and so goddamn gorgeous. When she has finished, I remove my hand and lick my fingers; she is the sweetest honey. "Open your mouth for me, gorgeous. Taste how delicious you are." Her eyes are stunned and dazed, but she does as I ask.

As her little pink tongue skims my finger, I can only dream of how it will feel for her to use her tongue on me. Hopefully, I won't have to wait too long to find out.

She delights me by sitting on my lap. "I can feel how hard you are. I know you want me as much as I want you, Owen."

"I want you in every way, babe, but let's take this back to the hotel. I can't wait any longer to be naked with you."

~ **Lauren** ~

I have spent so much time with Tim this week: almost every day we have either met for lunch or watched a Christmas film together at home, both his and mine, in the evening. He seems to like a lot of similar things to me, and I've never laughed so much or had so much fun. I keep pinching myself; surely this cannot be right. A handsome, funny, and caring man spending time with me?

When I am with Tim, I can be myself, and that comes as a massive shock to me. I am a masker; I mask so that people don't see the real me. It doesn't hurt so much when I am judged for something that is not true, but it cripples me when people have me nailed and criticise me for the true me.

With Tim, I catch myself being myself. I am so comfortable around him, and he makes me feel so good about who I am, that I am less afraid for him to see what is behind the façade. He is such an amazing man that I cannot comprehend how and why he is interested in me. He could do so much better.

Tim has been very respectful towards me. I know that people tend to jump into physical relationships, but that is not my style. My mother is deeply religious, and being from Northern Ireland, it would be a sin for her daughter to go about cavorting. However, I have also never found anyone until now who I wanted to be intimate with. I have had the opportunity on a couple of occasions, but I held back; it wasn't a part of me I was comfortable sharing.

Until I met Tim.

Now, I am having all sorts of feelings deep inside that have continued to grow over the past few days. I think I might be ready to take things further than kissing but I know Tim is waiting for the cue from me.

I have no idea what I am doing. I haven't told him I'm still a virgin. I am worried that this might scare him off. Maybe I don't have to tell him? If it gets to the point where we do sleep together, maybe I could just tell him afterwards. It doesn't have to be a big deal, right?

One thing that has happened is that my writing has improved. I have ideas simply pouring out of me and not enough time to write. Even my circle of online writing friends are noticing the difference in me. They keep asking who has put a smile on my face and inspired me. It's almost like meeting Tim and allowing him to see the real me has broken down all the barriers not only in my personal and private life but in my professional and creative life too.

Tonight is the first night I haven't seen him, but Billie from Tables & Fables is holding an impromptu Open Mic Night since she has cancelled the one for Saturday as her husband is whisking her away for a romantic weekend. I sit with my writer friends; I am here to support them tonight. I am not ready to share my writing in this way yet.

Tables & Fables at Christmas has just got to be the most magical place ever. With the log burner roaring away, the festive lights and decorations everywhere creating an ambience of festive cheer, the Christmas music in the background and the delicious smells coming from the kitchen, it is one of my favourite places to be. I would love to bring Tim here, but for now I haven't told him about my alter ego, Lol Outloud, and everyone here knows me as that. I would show him this side in a heartbeat; Tim isn't the issue. The issue is everyone here seeing Tim with me and wondering what the hell he is doing slumming it with me.

Open Mic Night is not a usual way for authors to drum up interest. Outside of Tables & Fables, I don't know another place that does it. This is a novel way of generating interest in our work; you get up and recite a passage or a chapter that is meant to draw people in. They make a connection not only with the story and the characters you write about, but they get to know you, too. If you can win over the crowd, they request that you recite every time you're here. If you can get the crowd to relate to you, you generally have a fan for life. They will invest in you as well as your product.

Tim asked me about my writing, and I was shy at first about explaining to him that I am a steamy paranormal romance writer. I write full-time and have made a bit of success with it. I have never gone the traditional publishing method, preferring to write online on episodic platforms and sometimes I self-publish. I have a small cache of books now, but they have failed to reach the heights of my peers. I often wonder why. I beat myself up for chasing a dream that I may not be talented enough for. I doubt myself and criticise not only myself but my characters, the worlds I build and the storylines I develop. Surely, if they were worth something, people would see that?

One of my writer friends told me that my negativity about myself comes across in my writing and that prevents me from being successful and relatable. But how do I change the way I feel about myself and therefore about what I create?

My friend, Rochelle, knocks me, bringing me out of my daydream. "Lol, it's my turn. Mind my bag for me, will you?" she says as dashes up to the stage. The place is jam-packed, and I sit and watch Rochelle both with pride and with a little envy too. The crowd loves her; she is a crowd puller and rightly so. She is confident and talented and has no qualms about sharing her work with whoever will listen.

Tonight, Rochelle shares a recent chapter she wrote for her latest work of art which is centred around vampires. She makes vampires sexy like no other person I've ever met, but then, Rochelle has that effect. She once wrote a romance novel about aliens, and afterwards, I wanted an alien to come and whisk me away too. Rochelle is very sexualised in the way she presents, which again is a crowd pleaser. The men fantasise about being with her, and the women, like me, want to be her. She is up in front of a crowd of over 200 people simulating her female lead reaching orgasm; she writhes on the stool and moans and groans loudly.

My face turns a deep crimson as I simultaneously cringe at her words and blatant display and feel shame that I am also aroused by what she is both saying and doing. Rochelle looks like a goddess up there. As she builds up her orgasm, she throws her head back, exposing the dark, flawless skin on her neck. Her small, rounded breasts jut out perfectly as she does it. Her nipples, visible under the light, stand hard against the fabric restraining them. Everyone is in raptures. Rochelle makes it easy to feel like you are in her story; you are the lead and that is your orgasm.

Billie sits in Rochelle's vacated seat. "I'm going to have to start paying her; I swear half the people here only come for her porn," she tells me merrily. We have all joked in the past about Rochelle's ability to turn everyone into a lust-filled sex maniac. "Why aren't you getting up, Lol? I read your latest chapters online... you are on fire, girl. You are writing some amazing stuff at the moment. I read some out to Jonty last night, and he couldn't keep his hands off me; he was so turned on. I'm loving the relationship between Cathy and Nick. I think the crowd would go wild for it."

I love Billie. She has been a staunch follower of mine, and she has a great influence in the online network. If she recommends a book or an author, readers listen. They know she is straight-talking and honest in her critique. She has pulled me up many times about holding back in my writing. She is actually the first, and only, person to guess that I am still a virgin from my writing. She asked for a private word one day regarding a sex scene I had written, and she asked a couple of questions about it and then whispered, "Lol… are you a virgin?" When I told her I was she gave me a few pointers on why she had noticed. Now, if anything is off or doesn't come across right, she'll give me the heads up. She has never told anyone my secret, and I appreciate that so much.

"Not yet, Billie; I'm too shy," I tell her for the hundredth time.

She holds her hands up in surrender. "Okay, okay, just hear me out. How about I read for you next week? You could get some little business cards made directing people to your work, and I will just say I've been asked to perform it because you love my voice. Think it over, and let me know by Monday so I can exercise the old vocal cords." I nod and tell her I'll think about it. "Lol, I honestly think it's your time to shine, sweetheart. Take a chance."

It all sounds so simple, but lately all I seem to be taking is chances, and I worry: what will happen when my luck runs out?

The journey home is cold and dark. It's the only part I hate about Open Mic Night in the winter. It wouldn't be so bad if I wasn't alone. I instantly think of Tim and him joining that part of my life, too, where Lol and Lauren merge. I think I'll have to wait and see if things turn serious. I am seeing him again tomorrow night, and I am really looking forward to it. I think I am going to start to take things further; Rochelle has left me in a wanton state that I have to suffer through on this rumbling bus home.

Maybe Tim won't be scared off by the fat virgin?

~ Tim ~

This week is flying by. Since Saturday, I have spent time with Lauren every day, and yet it feels like it isn't enough. I miss her and just want to spend more time with her.

I have been left in charge at the office while Mr. Matthews and Jamie are away on business in Copenhagen, which gives me slightly more flexibility. I am getting in to work earlier and either taking a longer lunch or leaving earlier at the end of the day so I can spend time with Lauren.

My world begins and ends with her now. I am completely besotted with the shy beauty with the dimpled smile, sexy green eyes and curves to die for. I have tried to take cues from Lauren and her body language, and until last night she appeared closed off to anything other than kissing and holding hands.

I wonder if someone has hurt her and made her scared of opening up to me. I just want to cherish her and adore her. I want her to know how amazing she is. Maybe if I tell and show her enough, she will begin to realise it for herself.

Until last night, we had cuddled, but she had hardly touched me. And then from nowhere, we were kissing when she timidly moved her small hands from the sides of my face down and over my chest before cuddling into me. Her breasts pushed against my chest where her hands had just been while she rested her head between my neck and shoulder. This may seem so tiny to others, but to Lauren and I, this was a massive step. This was intimate and deeply arousing. I failed to keep my hard on away from her, but I felt that she also needed to feel the effect she had on me. I swear I saw a small smile on her gorgeous face when she did.

I am due to visit my sister and her family tonight, as I do every Wednesday. I invited Lauren, too, but she had prior plans. I think she might be willing to come with me next week though. I sincerely hope so. My sister will love her, and her approval means the world to me.

My sister, Felicity, lives in Essex, so it's close enough for me to visit, but I don't pass by daily or anything. She lives there with her wife, Marie, and their two children, Lyndon and Celeste. Our family moved down south when we were teenagers. We are originally from Liverpool, and although my accent has smoothed over time, my friends still call me scouse, a slang used to describe the famous Liverpool accent, because it's still very obvious to them that I am from there.

My sister, Fliss as I call her, has everything that I have ever dreamed of: the house, the wife, the kids. And yet, there was a time when she worried that she would never be able to have these things because of her sexuality. Fliss gives me hope that what I desire will come to me, too, and that no situation is hopeless.

I have been deliberately vague in my replies to her quizzing text messages, and the more obscure I am, the more it piques her intrigue, until this morning she sends me a message telling me she knows something is going on and she intends on interrogating me until I tell her every last detail. I can't wait to tell her everything and to ask her advice on how to proceed with Lauren.

When I arrive at their house, my niece runs to me with her arms outstretched so I can lift her. "Uncle Tim, Uncle Tim. Look at my tooth. It felled out, and the tooth fairy came and left a penny for me." Celeste opens her mouth up and shows me the gap where her tooth once was.

"Oh my word! You're growing up too fast, Celeste. Did it hurt?" She giggles as I swing her up and tickle her when she tells me it didn't hurt. "Where is Lyndon?"

"He's playing football in the back garden. He said he's waiting for you." I have been teaching my nephew a few moves since he signed up to the local football team. Now, he has me sitting duck in the goal while he tries to score anything and everything past me. "Did you bring some sweeties, Uncle Tim?"

My running joke with the children is that I bring them sweets every Wednesday and they hide them from their mums. Their mums know. I wouldn't keep stuff like that from them, but the kids think it's our little secret, our high jinks, just for us.

"Of course I have, my little butterfly. Here you are." I hand over the loot, and she jumps up and down on the spot in her excitement. "The bubble gum is in there; what you asked for."

"Thank you, Uncle Tim. I love you." My heart swells at her words; she's such a sweet little girl.

"I love you too. Now quick, take them to the stash before the mums see." Her little legs move at the speed of light as she hides the sweets away for her and her brother.

"There you are. Come on, get inside and tell me all your news." My sister pops her head out the door and invites me in. "Is she running to stash your sweets?" she asks with the hint of a smile on her face. I laugh in reply as I try to hug her, but her swollen tummy prevents a proper embrace.

"Wow! Fliss, you look ready to burst. Are you sure it isn't twins this time?" I ask her while I touch her tummy. Baby number three is due around Christmas and will be called Noel or Joy in tribute, or so my sister told me. I am on babysitting duty when the time comes, and I am looking forward to being an uncle again.

"Never mind all that. What is going on?" She is not giving up, but Lyndon saves me by knocking on the French doors and pointing to his ball.

"I'll have to tell you in a little while, duty calls," I say as I make my way out to see my nephew.

"So you admit there is something to tell at least." I smile back as I walk away, and she groans out loud in frustration.

Night falls quickly at this time of year, so, despite taking my flexi-day so I had extra time with my family, our practising is called off after only twenty minutes because we can no longer see each other.

When I go back inside, my sister-in-law has also returned from work and comes to greet me with a glass of wine for both of us which we clink together.

I love this time with my family. Since our mum passed away, it's just me and Fliss, and I cherish the time we get. I know how precious our time together is.

Once we've eaten, my sister lets the children play so she can interrogate me. I gush about Lauren and how lovely she is, and I can practically see the joy dancing about in Fliss' eyes. She is so happy for me. Before I leave to go back home, Fliss pulls me in for a hug. "Invite her for dinner. invite her for Christmas. I can see the change in you. Is she the one?"

I smile before I reply, "I think she is."

~ Jamie ~

The date with Owen is going even better than I could ever have dreamed of. From the way he acts and talks to me, I do wonder how long he's wanted to have a more private relationship with me. We know each other, we are colleagues and friends, but now I'm getting to know him on a whole different level, and I really like it.

I worried about things being awkward between us. Owen seemed like he was holding back until I stormed into his room drunk as a skunk without any sort of filter on what I was telling him. Now he is confident again, he seems more like the Owen I have always known and admired. I want him. I'm shocked when I realise that I never craved Carl in this way.

I love how bold he is with me. I love the public displays of affection; I'm not referring to him making me cum in the restaurant because hopefully no one saw that! But he held hands with me, and he wrapped his arm around my shoulders. He even kissed me in front of one of the fifteen Christmas trees, and it was so romantic. I am doing little internal squeals at the thought of it. It's almost as if Owen is proud of being with me.

When he says he wants to go back to the hotel, I take mercy on him. We are going to sleep together tonight; to be honest, I think we deserve medals to have lasted a whole night. I just want to get him out of his clothes and feel the delicious contact of his skin against mine. The way he brought me to climax on the balcony was so intensely hot. I am eager to find out what else he can do. I also have a few things I want to try out on him. Things I have never really tried, not enthusiastically anyway.

As we approach our hotel, I drop my hand out of his. We are here on business after all, and I don't want Owen to feel like he has to do this and compromise his own position.

"Get back here now. Do not think for one minute that I am letting you go tonight after we've come so far, babe. I know what you're doing, but do you know something, Jamie? I'm a grown man, and if I don't want something, I will tell you. Stop giving me an out. If I want out, I will tell you. All I want is *in* when it comes to you."

Holy fuck, my panties flood with desire at his words. He looks at me with passion burning in his eyes as I step towards him. I slowly wind my arms around his neck, pushing my own boundaries. I kiss him hard and unapologetically, and nothing has ever felt more right.

His strong arms encircle my waist before his hands travel to my ass. "Come on, babe, you're fucking killing me here!"

I have never been so brazen in public. Carl was never a public display of affection type of boyfriend, so my only other experience was from walking down Oxford Road with Conor where we held hands and kissed once, which is nowhere near the intimacy between Owen and me. It's not even comparable.

With Owen, it's not like he doesn't care who sees us together but more that he is happy for people to see us together. He's proud to be seen with me.

As we approach the door to my hotel room, we are frenzied with the need to remove each other's clothing as fast as possible. He made me cum less than thirty minutes ago, but I am so worked up because I am desperate to feel *him* inside me.

I drop to my knees as soon as we have the door closed behind us, my hands trembling with anticipation as I unbuckle his trousers and allow them to fall. I touch his cock that strains against his black trunks before helping him to remove them. His long thick shaft springs forward as it is released from its prison.

"Oh my goodness, Owen, where have you been hiding that? That's really quite impressive." He laughs a little, but it catches in his throat as I trail my tongue over and around his tip. I lick all the way down to the base of his shaft, and then I cup his balls as I lick all the way back up. He is a remarkable specimen. As Billie would say, 'He could have you walking like John Wayne!' I never knew what she truly meant until now.

I take more of his cock into my mouth and suck him. Owen lets out a gasp as he closes his eyes and throws his head back, holding onto the door frame for balance. I use my hand on the part of him I cannot fit into my mouth. I slurp him and suck him, finding a rhythm we both seem to like. When he gently threads his hands through my hair, guiding my head the way he wants, I know I am really satisfying him. His cock hits the back of my throat, and I can feel the tension building in him as the prominent veins on the underside of his impressive manhood harden and become taut.

"Oh, Jamie, baby. You're so good. My cock has never felt as good." He grips my head with a bit more force and makes a final thrust, spilling his load into my throat and mouth. He tastes warm, salty and manly. It's such a big turn on to know that I can please him this way. We are compatible. Owen told me we would be amazing together, but it's only now that I can see for myself that I can match him. I can satisfy him as much as he satisfies me.

I stand up when I have finished licking up all his spilled essence and look proudly at what I have achieved. I made him cum just with my mouth... What else can *I* do?

"You are so fucking sexy, Jamie," Owen tells me as he strips my final pieces of outer clothing, leaving me standing in my matching silk cream underwear set that I wore especially for tonight. "You are incredible, just absolutely flawless. I dreamed of us being together, but I started to believe it may never happen."

He scoops me up and places me in the centre of the bed.

"And now it's my turn to finally get a taste of you. I have wanted to bury my face in your pussy for as long as I can remember. I want to make you scream my name as I make you cum over and over and over."

My breath is coming out in pants. If this is the effect he has on me with mere words, I think I'm going to be a complete wreck if he does go down on me.

He removes my panties and pushes apart my thighs, displaying my very core to him. "Babe, it's even better than I imagined; you are perfect. Now last night when you were sleeping, you woke me up whispering my name. Tell me, eh, what was happening."

My face fills with heat; I can't believe he heard me. Last night's dream was the most vivid one, probably due to being drunk and horny.

When I don't immediately answer, Owen pleads with me. "Please, baby, tell me so I can make your dreams come true. It turned me on so much to watch you get off as you shouted my name, but now I want to be the one who causes it. So tell me, and your wish is my command."

I give in, speaking words I couldn't imagine saying out loud to any other man. "I have been having dreams for a couple of months of someone, a faceless man, going down on me. That was until you asked me out, and now, all I see and feel is you licking me until I cum."

He gives me a wicked grin that sets my heart alight, and my pussy throbs for his touch in response to his wondrous gaze.

"Then let's make both of our dreams come true. I bet you taste like honey."

CHAPTER EIGHT

~ Owen ~

She is a goddess; her golden hair looks like a crown as she lays back against the pillows. "Like honey?" she asks me, repeating my words, and I nod in reply.

"Yes, baby, like the sweetest honey. Sit up for a second." I realise all too late that in my haste to get between her legs, I forgot to take off her bra.

She draws her knees together, hiding my prize away from my view, and waits for further instructions. She is pliable; I like that. I want her to tell me her every desire, but I also like to be dominant at times. I like to take the lead.

I lean forward and kiss her. I can taste myself still on her lips; it's so fucking sexy. Then I trail my hands down her back until I reach the clasp on her bra, which I make short work of undoing. I sit back on my heels. "Show me, Jamie. Take it off and show me everything."

I deliberately ask her to do this part. I know she is self-conscious about her boobs. She often refers to them as 'aspirins on an ironing board'. I also heard Carl mocking her once about them and could see how upset it made her. I think she has lovely tits. They are small, but they are perfect, just right on her frame and anything more would look ridiculous. I am eager to see them in the flesh, to taste and devour them and show her how beautiful I think they are.

She lowers her head, and her shoulders slump slightly. I hate to see her looking and obviously feeling so vulnerable. She takes her time removing her arms from each side while holding the front of the bra to her chest. She looks up momentarily to see if I am still watching, then lowers her gaze once more before slowly pulling her bra from her body. However, she continues to obscure the view by drawing her knees up to her chest.

"You're perfect, Jamie. You're perfect to me. Every single part of you." Her head snaps up at my words. I wet my lips before biting my bottom one. God, I cannot believe this is finally happening. She is watching me intently now. "Lie back again, please, babe. Let me see you in all your glory."

She slowly lies back, but she keeps her hands over her boobs. "Are you shy?" I ask her in a whisper, and she shakes her head at me. "Then why are you hiding from me?"

"They're small. Tiny. I've never taken my bra off in front of someone before, Owen." Aww my sweet, gorgeous girl, she doesn't realise how perfect she is to me.

"I want to see them; I want to taste them, and suck them and nibble on your nipples until they stand on end... I wonder if I could make you cum just by playing with your perfect little mouthfuls." Her eyes darken and passion floods her. She is a bright little spark alright, just as I knew she would be.

"You... Do you actually like them?" I shake my head at her and her arms, that she had started to lower, spring straight back to cover them up.

"No, Jamie. I don't just like them. I fucking love them. Let me see them, baby. Let me see your gorgeous body, so I can see how perfect you are."

Her hands tremble as she slowly lowers them. I am so proud of her for being brave and putting her trust in me. She closes her eyes, but I will her to open them again. I shift slightly on the bed causing her to rock. She opens her eyes to see what I am doing just as I start kissing her ankle. I kiss all the way up her leg to the junction at the top. I thrust my tongue lightly just so I can sate myself with a tiny taste of her. I kiss up to her pubic bone and then her hip bone. I watch in pure delight as her skin puckers from my gentle kisses.

I head to her belly button, which is pierced, and kiss all around it before licking up to her rib cage. My eyes are now level with her nipples. "These are my little mouthfuls now; all mine and I love them and think they are amazing. Can I?" I indicate to her boobs, and she nods to me. I let out an involuntary growl of satisfaction as I finally get to suckle one of her nipples. It's amazing, and I know she feels it, too. She whimpers as I take a mouthful of her right breast and suck. I tease her with my teeth and flick her fully erect nipple with my tongue, causing her to jump from the sensation. Then I repeat the process on her other breast, not wanting one to feel left out.

"Owen..." she calls out my name as I slip my hand between her legs again; she is so hot and wet now.

"That's it, baby. Call my name. Call my name when I make you cum, eh?" She nods quickly, her eyes clouded with passion and built-up arousal. I kiss my way back down to her pink slit... now it's time to make her dream and my own come true. I use my thumbs to spread her wider and relish the first full stroke of my tongue against her wet, swollen and sensitive clit.

134

She nearly jumps off the bed, so I back up a bit, a little less pressure and smaller strokes with my tongue, and this time she practically gushes in her excitement.

"Yes, Owen. Like that, just like that." She leans forward slightly and rests onto her elbows so she can watch me eat her. I slip one of my thumbs inside and back out of her. Her moans tell me how much she is enjoying this. Her legs begin to tremble, and I lap at her faster and more deliberately, alternating between licking her clit and thrusting my tongue deep into her. As she edges closer, the urge to sink my throbbing cock into her over and over until we both cum almost overwhelms me. Until she starts to call my name, and I remember my objective, my primary motive for now and for always... making Jamie's dreams come true.

Last night, as she got herself off in her sleep, she whispered my name. Tonight, when I finally place my mouth against her gorgeous pussy until she cums, she shouts my name repeatedly loud and clear as she succumbs to wave after wave of pleasure.

I shift my weight, unable to wait to be fully inside her now. My voice is hoarse as I cover her body with mine and whisper sweet nothings into her ear, "That was the most exquisite experience of my life, Jamie, but I want more. I want to slide into you and screw you slowly until you cum again."

"I want to ride you hard until we both cum again. Do you have a condom?" Shit! I am so caught up in the moment, a condom hasn't even crossed my mind.

"Yes, there are a couple in my jacket. Wait for me a minute." I assess the room, trying to locate my jacket. Our clothes are all thrown about everywhere, which makes me smile. We were both so enthusiastic and caught up in the moment.

I find the jacket, bring the condoms back to the bed and sit on the edge as I slide it down onto my dick. This is it; I am finally going to be with Jamie. She surprises me by climbing onto my lap, straddling my hips. "Is this okay, Owen? I want to try this way first, please."

My kisses stop her talking. I have surely died and gone to heaven as Jamie lifts herself onto my hard dick and slides down slightly. She repeats the movement, this time she takes a bit more of me, and again and again, until I am fully embedded inside her.

We move together in unison. I am completely lost in this moment, the moment Jamie is finally mine. Her sweet moans and whimpers mingle with my grunts and groans. As we both approach our impending climax, I am overcome with the need to take control. I stand while I am still balls deep in Jamie and ask her to wrap her legs around me. Her whole body shakes, and I just want to help her find release now.

I carry her over to the nearest wall and pummel into her deep and hard. At first she gives me a startled look and I worry that maybe I am being too rough? But as she starts to chant my name, and her juices continue to flow, I realise she likes this as much as me. She sucks down on my shoulder as her orgasm takes over her body, and I allow myself to cum now that she has. Boiling hot cum pours from me like never before.

It takes me a while to realise it's me shouting her name, too. As I start to come back down to earth, I notice the tears on my shoulder and that Jamie is limp in my arms.

"Are you okay, babe? Did I hurt you?" I try to keep the panic from my voice, but I hate the thought of causing her pain.

"It was the most incredibly beautiful moment of my life, Owen. Thank you." She has floored me with her words. That's exactly how I feel, too.

I carry her back to the bed, and she yawns as I lay her down. "Don't leave me, Owen. Stay here with me and hold me."

The thing is, I don't know if she means just for tonight or for always. I want to stay with her forever and never leave. There is no going back for me. I knew I loved her, but until this moment I didn't realise just how much she meant to me.

This girl is the love of my life. After discarding the condom, I lie next to her and spoon her. She cuddles into me, and before long she is fast asleep, sighing contentedly.

Sleep eludes me once again as I try to formulate a plan. A plan to not just stay in Jamie's bed but in her heart forever.

~ Lauren ~

Today is a work at home day. I have a newsletter, a Facebook group, promotions, editing and writing to do. I also want to clean my flat and have a relaxing bath before Tim comes over tonight.

I am thankful I didn't have to wake up early this morning after Open Mic Night. I had been texting Tim into the small hours of the morning, and so I'm glad for the opportunity to catch up on my sleep. Tim told me all about his visit with his family and that his sister has invited me for dinner next week and for Christmas, too. I cannot believe he told his family about me! I never thought I would ever be a 'take home to meet the family' sort of girl, but Tim seems to think I am. As he spoke with love about his sister and her family, I couldn't help but be in awe. He can expect no such fanfare from my family, not when my mother will just use the opportunity to bring me down.

Tonight, we plan on watching White Christmas. I had

mentioned to Tim that every year my granny used to insist on us all watching it together when I was growing up, and it choked me up a bit.

I am going to make chicken curry in my slow cooker. I bought cranberry and white chocolate shortbread from Tables & Fables for dessert, and I will light Christmas scented candles all around my place. It's going to be warm and cosy.

As we settle down with our meal and movie, Tim shocks me by saying, "I think this is a good way to pay tribute to your granny. Who knows, maybe we can make it a tradition and watch it every year." He is being open and hopefully honest with me, and I feel he deserves the same back from me.

"Do you see us together next year, Tim?" He smiles in reply and kisses my head before taking a deep breath.

"I sincerely hope so, Lauren. I want to be, and if you want the same, then I can see a long and happy future ahead of us. What do you see?"

I hang my head. Do I answer a half truth or be completely honest with him? I think for us to work and for me to hopefully get what I want, I have to be honest. Are all my secrets safe with Tim? There is only one way to find out. "I sometimes see us together. But sometimes I see you running off with someone thin and better looking. Sometimes I can't see a future with someone like you wanting to be with someone like me. I think at some point you might wake up and realise that you want and deserve better."

There is hurt in his eyes when he looks back up at me. "Do you really think I'm that stupid and shallow? I just want to make something clear here, I fancy you. I think you are sexy, and the only person who doesn't like what and who you are... is you, Lauren. I think you are beautiful, all of you. In every single way. I wish you could believe that."

"I want to believe that. I'm starting to believe it, but it's scary. I've never done this before, Tim." He wraps a comforting arm around me. "I am so scared of being hurt, but I can't seem to stay away from you. I'm like a moth to the flame. It's so scary." He gives me another smile.

"We can just carry on at your pace, but, Flower, I need you to know this. I want you. I want you to meet my family. I want to spend the holidays with you. I want to get matching onesies and a little dog and decorate the Christmas tree together. I want to eventually get married, and have children and maybe move out into the countryside with you. So I will wait, and if you want these things too, I am here."

"I do want those things... and I want them with you. How do I know I will be enough in the future?" I feel like my heart melts under his gaze.

"Because you are already enough. You don't have to perform or be anything other than who you are, Lauren. And as long as we stay true to ourselves, and we don't get personality transplants, I don't see any reason why that would ever change. I'm falling in love with you. And I want to be with you, only you, for you." He finishes by kissing my hands.

I can't believe he is falling in love with me. I'm falling in love with him, too. This could be something incredibly special if I let down my walls. But first I have to tell him. I have to tell him the extent of my experience.

"I'm falling for you, too, Tim. And the thing is, I think I might be ready to take things further. But I am... that is I have... I don't really have much erm... What I am trying to say is that I have no... no... erm. Oh God, I suck at this." His face goes from open and smiling to confused to a full-on grimace.

"Geez, Lauren, for a writer you are making a right mess of this. Tell me what it is you think I need to know." He makes me laugh with his assessment of my speech; he's completely right of course.

"I'm not very experienced is what I meant to say, Tim. And when I say 'not very' I mean not any, really." I look at him and await his reaction.

"Do you mean in relationships or are you talking about sex?" he asks, his voice level. He is showing no outward reaction. I tell him I mean both. "Are you telling me you are still a virgin, Lauren?" My crimson is on fire. I feel so embarrassed. But now that I've told him I may as well wait to see his reaction.

"Yes. I'm still a virgin. I am a twenty-five-year-old virgin." I wait for the laughter that doesn't come.

"And why is that? I'm guessing you've had the opportunity? So, I therefore presume this has been through choice." He isn't laughing or running away, and I'm caught off guard by this.

"I just have never met someone who I felt comfortable enough sharing that with or who I fancied and respected and admired. Until now." Oh God, I feel like a schoolgirl telling him I like him.

"So, it wasn't about religion or saving yourself for someone in particular?" I shake my head, and I feel lighter for sharing this with him. A warm glow starts in my tummy, happiness mixed with desire.

"Thank you for sharing all this with me, Lauren. I think it's amazing. I think you are amazing. Just so you know, there is absolutely no pressure from me. I will wait for as long as it takes. Well I'll rephrase that. I would like a couple of children, but you've got a good decade before I nag you for them."

I smile at him. He is just taking all this in stride. "Well, that's the thing, Tim. I think I am ready to take things slowly forward. You're the person I trust and fancy. You're the person that will understand and help me. You're the one I have been waiting for."

His face lights up; he looks like a little boy at Christmas. "I don't know what I ever did to land a beauty like you, Lauren. I swear to God, I will spend my lifetime wondering how I ever got so lucky."

"It doesn't bother you that I don't have experience?"

He shakes his head. "Lauren, I am delighted and honoured that you shared this with me. I am looking forward to sharing what is to come with you."

He places his food on the coffee table in front of us and then moves my plate too. Tim takes both my hands into his and looks at me with such adoration in his eyes my heart pumps erratically. "I am proud to be considered worthy enough to do something so special with you, when you're ready. I'd like to make it special for us both. I want this to be a happy memory for you, the best. Especially because if you like it, you'll want to do it again and again and again with me."

He laughs a bit at the end of his beautiful speech, and I smack him on the arm lightly, feigning outrage. "Tim!" But I end up laughing with him. He wraps one of his arms around me, and I feel so safe as I snuggle into him.

"Just do me a favour, just one thing, Flower?"

He kisses my head, so I reply, "Anything."

"When you are ready to go all the way, will you give me a bit of warning so I can make it nice and special for you?"

I lean up and kiss him on the lips, and my hand goes to his chest. "Of course I will. But first, I'd like to slowly build up to the main event starting with touching."

"Can I touch you, too?" My face heats up once again as I nod yes. "God, you are so sexy when you blush like that. You are driving me wild."

Can I really be having that effect on him? It doesn't seem likely, and yet I can see his erection. And I have felt it a couple of times when we have been kissing. Tim wouldn't lie to me.

"Can I touch you?" I ask him. I get a little thrill straight down into my tummy and further down between my legs when I see the want in his face and the surprise in his eyes.

"You don't have to do this, Flower." I said these very words to him that first night he kissed me. I can think of nothing better than turning the tables and giving his words back to him.

"Oh but, Tim, I really, really want to."

His eyes darken, and I know I've said the right thing.

~ Tim ~

She is a minx. One cheeky little minx. I am so relieved that no one has abused or hurt her. I am elated when she tells me she is still a virgin. Once she learns that I am trustworthy, I can help her and show her how powerful and beautiful her body is and how to use it, too.

Then my innocent Flower goes and floors me by asking if she can touch me. When she told me she was inexperienced I had thoughts of me touching her and gently easing her into sensual activity and then she goes and blows that out of the water.

"Oh, but, Tim, I really, really want to," she says to me with a small, secret smile. I did not expect that tonight. I almost have to lift my jaw off the floor.

"Where do you want to touch me?" She answers by grazing her hand slowly over my crotch, and my dick jumps in response.

"Here." Her voice is full of curiosity and intrigue. She is blushing, but she remains determined. I'm overcome with awe.

"Have you ever touched a cock before?" She shakes her head at me. Geez, she really is innocent. I just cannot comprehend how she has managed to stick to her morals. I was dipping my wick as soon as I found a willing girl at 17 years old. Am I right for her? Does she deserve someone better? Someone with similar morals as her. I don't want to lead her astray, but she's a grown woman with her own mind, and she has initiated this.

"Listen, Flower, I am willing to do whatever you want. As little or as much as you want. If you are sure you want this to be with me, I am honoured. But I need you to show me or tell me what it is you want and need, okay?" She gives a stiff nod to my request. I think that's as far as it will go tonight.

"Can I see it?"

My head snaps back up to meet her eyes; she is full of surprises tonight. I can tell she's still feeling shy and unsure, but she is being so brave. She wants this; she really wants this.

"Come on, Flower, you can do better than that. What do you want to see? If you can't put a name to it, you might not be ready yet." Maybe I am pushing too hard, but I don't want this to be a childish experience. I want a woman. I want to be the man I am with her.

"Your dick, Tim. Can I see your dick and then touch your dick?" Well, well, well. An angel with a gutter mouth.

I stand up and pull down my zipper, and she stands, too. "How much do you want to see? Do you want to show me?" She nods slowly before dropping to her knees. All sorts of wild thoughts come into my head of Lauren whipping out my cock after dropping to her knees and sucking me until I cum in her mouth. I can't wait to try all this stuff with her in the future.

However, instead she touches me over my underwear, I try to mask my heavy exhale of breath, but the feeling of her featherlight strokes over my hard shaft has me ready to explode.

"It's already so hard, Tim," she says as she looks up at me through her eyelashes. A quick flash of that dimpled smile and I am putty in her hands. She has bewitched me. There have been plenty of others before Lauren, but nothing compares to this. No one compares to her.

"I am always hard when I am around you, Lauren. You're so fucking sexy and cute. I don't think I have ever been soft when you are near." I cannot suppress the groan I make when she lowers my boxers. "Fuck! Lauren, you'll have to be careful; I could go off like a rocket. I'm so turned on."

"Really? I'm not hurting you, am I?" she asks me when I groan again after she strokes the underside of my cock. I shake my head in reply. This is like torture and the best pleasure I've ever had. When her hand fully encircles my cock, I smile at the little noises she makes. So intrigued and enlightened at the same time. "It's hard and yet the skin feels so soft and smooth. And it smells a lot nicer than I imagined."

I laugh at her assessment. At least I don't have a smelly cock! "Well, I do wash every now and again, Flower. You're doing so well. But if you carry on touching me like that, I'm going to cum."

"Can I make you cum, Tim? Would that be okay?" I discard my jeans but keep my boxers where they are. I sit back down on her sofa and tap for her to sit next to me. "Shall I bring tissues?" she asks.

"Yes, bring tissues. And then come and sit here next to me." She does as I say and watches me attentively as I stroke my cock. "I have never been more turned on than I am right now. Just the thought of you touching me and everything is ready to just burst out from the anticipation and excitement. I want you to sit next to me so I can kiss your beautiful face while you make me cum... because no one could make me cum like you will." She bites her bottom lip at my words, her cheeks glow pink, but there is passion in her eyes, an eagerness to please.

"May I?" she asks before taking over on my cock. I tense in order to make it last longer. I have fantasised non-stop about these moments, and now they are here I'm going to blow before we properly get started. "Do I really turn you on, Tim?" she asks me as she awkwardly and beautifully jerks me off.

"I fancy the fucking bones of you. I can't wait to give you what you're giving me. I can't wait for you to be mine. Slow down, Flower, I will blow otherwise; I am so worked up." She slows her movements, and I don't miss the smile my praise raises. Those fucking dimples will be the death of me, so cute and innocent, and yet I can already see a cheeky side to her. Once she lets go and is able to fully trust me, we are going to have so much fun. "Ever since that first night, all I have been able to think about is you. Do you know how many times I have had to pleasure myself just thinking of you?"

"You jerk off and think of me?" I don't know if she is flattered or offended but I've got this far on honesty, so I'm sticking with it. I nod my head back at her. "Well, it's only fair if I do this one then." As she holds my cock more firmly and boldly, and moves her hand more deliberately, I feel my copious load leaving my balls. As hot cum shoots out from me, pouring down the back of her hand, I hear her gasp and mutter, "Oh my word!" under her breath.

"Holy fuck, Lauren!" I try to steady my breathing while looking into her eyes. Hers are filled with wonder and triumph. My cock continues to twitch and pulsate for a while afterwards. "That was... out of this world amazing. Everything feels so much more intense with you. I was falling in love with you. Now you have me hook, line and sinker, Flower."

We kiss passionately and clean up my mess intermittently in between. I want to reciprocate, I want to give her all the pleasure she has given me, I want to give her a lifetime of pleasure, but I am scared of pushing too far. Tonight has been a lot, and I don't want to pressure her or overwhelm her.

So instead I lay it out for her what I am willing and want to offer. "I want to touch you, and see you and make you cum, too. I want to give back what you have given me, because that is the best feeling ever."

"You really genuinely enjoyed tonight?" I make a face at her. I have just cum all over her and she's asking if I truly enjoyed it. You can't fake that shit.

"I more than enjoyed it, Lauren. It was the best. I want to take this at your pace. But I also want you to know that I want to do all those things back to you, and then maybe we can do them both together, when you're ready of course."

She nods her head and smiles. "Okay. But not tonight; that's far enough for tonight. But I'm free tomorrow night if you are."

I kiss her in response. She'll never ever know how much this means to me. For her to trust me and offer herself to me despite her insecurities and lack of confidence is the most humbling and privileging feeling in the world.

My sister asked me last night if Lauren was 'the one'. There is absolutely no doubt whatsoever in my mind that she is.

The one, the only... my everything.

CHAPTER NINE

~ Jamie ~

The sun streaming through the open voiles disturbs the best sleep I've had in a long time, and I smile when I realise I didn't wake up with my hand down my pants. Until I remember I am not wearing any. My eyes flash open as I take in my surroundings: the hotel room, the massive bed. Oh, my sweet Lord, I slept with Owen. Several times, in fact. It was the most sensational night of my life.

That's when it hits me that I am in bed alone. Owen and his clothes are nowhere to be seen. As embarrassment flushes my face, anger rages in my heart.

How fucking dare he?! The absolute bastard. I thought last night had meant the same to him as it did to me, and then he cold shoulders me without so much as a kiss goodbye.

My shame stings my eyes. How will I ever face him now? I'm definitely looking for a new job; I would be too ashamed to go back to work now after he has humiliated me in this way. He should have been straight with me. He said it wasn't a one-night-stand, the lying douchebag.

I run to the shower and scrub myself clean as tears of anger and sadness overwhelm me. I am going to slap him right across the face when I see him again. How dare he use me like this? I thought he liked me. I thought I meant something to him. God, I did stuff last night that I have never done before. It literally rocked my world. He rocked my world, and now I am a no one once again.

Fury fills me as I wrap myself in a large white hotel bathrobe and twist a towel around my hair. I will show him! I will make him regret the day he did this to me.

I am picking my clothes out when I hear the door of my room open. It's probably housekeeping, I think, but I get the shock of my life when Owen walks into the room with a Santa hat on his head and takeaway breakfast and coffee in his hands.

"Babe, why are you crying?" he asks me, dropping the food and drinks on the little table we screwed on last night before striding over to me and taking my face in his hands.

I lash out at him. "You fucking bastard, Owen Matthews. You fucking left me and humiliated me. You said this wasn't a one-night thing. You said you wanted more." I shout, ranting and crying at him as I pound his chest with my fists.

"Shhhh, Jamie! Babe? I'm right here. I just went to get breakfast for us. I did tell you when you were sleeping, and I thought you knew because you spoke back to me. You talk a lot in your sleep though."

Reluctantly, I stop hitting him and try to stem my tears.

"This could never be a one-night thing for me, Jamie Knowles. I am in love with you, and last night was incredible. Hands down the best night of my life so far. I am never leaving you. If you'll have me that is. I'm so, so sorry for worrying you, will you

149

forgive me?"

The rapid change in interpretation of this morning's events leaves me bamboozled. "You didn't run out and leave me?" I ask him straight up, and he shakes his head at me before kissing me gently firstly on my lips and then down my neck to my shoulder. The molten lava that filled my tummy last night is back with a vengeance. Just like that, I want him again.

"I am never going to leave, Jamie. Every word I said to you, every confession I made, is the truth. I have wanted this for the longest time. I have *loved* you for the longest time, and I am on cloud nine right now." His beautiful face, honest and full of love and wonder, is close to my own. I want to kiss him, but I don't want him to stop talking either. "I want you to be mine. I am yours; you have no choice about that, really. I'm so in love with you that I would literally do anything to make this work."

I'm a little overwhelmed by his speech and humbled. And, I will concede, turned on. "I'm yours, too, Owen. I might not be exactly where you are yet, but I want to be with you. Oh God, I'm exhausted again now!" I yelp as he lifts me and carries me to bed. "I'm so sorry for jumping to the wrong conclusion, Owen. I will have more faith in you, and in us."

He gently removes my robe, and I feel a twinge of self-consciousness in the cold light of day. Up until last night, I have never taken my bra off during sex. It is something I have always been paranoid about. My flat chest makes me feel so unattractive and unfeminine. In bed, I usually wear a padded bra, with extra padding, so that it looks like I have a bit of breast.

"There they are, my beautiful little mouthfuls. God, I missed them," he says before lowering his head to each one in turn and sucking them. He makes noises you'd make when you get to eat chocolate cake after being on a diet. This is the most erotic sensation I have ever felt. It's the first time I have allowed anyone to touch and see them, but Owen seems to love them. I kind of love the way he loves them, too! I can see them in a new light now and definitely have a newfound appreciation for them.

I'm just about to submit to the pleasure once again when my stomach growls.

"We'll have to continue later, babe. I can't have my girl going hungry. It's my job to take care of you. I got us coffee and breakfast." I groan and beg for him to suck my nipples one more time. His satisfied smile warms my insides all the more. "After breakfast. We have the whole day free. I thought you might want to go sightseeing... or maybe we could stay in bed all day?"

"Bed all day sounds amazing. Thank you for breakfast. No one has ever taken care of me like this before... Well, Billie might have when I was younger, because she had to." When I think back to being a young teenager, Billie looked after me and then Jonty too. Billie tried her best, but she wasn't my mother, and everything was a bit slapdash. We basically winged it between us.

"How old were you when your mother died?" The familiar twinge in my heart stirs, but it doesn't take my breath away the way it used to. I want to share this with Owen. My mother is still a massive part of me even in death.

"It was just after my eleventh birthday. She had ovarian cancer. It took her very quickly. I found it impossible to comprehend that she had died when she had looked perfectly beautiful and healthy just weeks before she passed away." Owen strokes my back as I tell him about my mother, then he brings the breakfast stuff to the bed while I brush my hair.

"It must have been hard, especially at that age." Thinking back on that time, it was hard. The first year after she died is like a fuzzy haze, and then within that year my father had met and married my stepmother, and she was expecting their first child together by the time the first anniversary of my mother's death came around. That was when I moved in with Billie.

"It was hard, but I had Billie. And then when she met Jonty, he helped to raise me too. I owe everything to them. I probably would have ended up in care if my stepmother would have had her way. She hates me. She says I am the mirror image of my mother, and Billie thinks that's why she didn't want me around. It's upsetting that I'm so distant from my father, and I hate that I don't know my siblings very well, but I have Billie and Jonty and the children. And now, I have you."

He looks intensely back at me. "And now you have me. Tell me about the future... Do you want a family? Do you want to travel?"

I laugh at his serious expression. "Stop frowning! Maybe I want a family... it didn't seem inviting or important before. I always worried about getting ill like my own mother, and I didn't want to risk my own children being without a parent. Billie tells me that I have as much chance of being knocked down by a car. What about you, Owen? Tell me about your future."

He contemplates my question before he answers. "I'm no good with kids, Jamie. I never have been. I think one or two of my own wouldn't be too bad, just not yet. I would like to travel a lot more first. Will you come with me?" I crawl over to him. I am still naked and wiggle my bottom at him causing him to groan in gratification.

"I will *come* wherever you want, Owen," I tell him. I take great pleasure in kissing him lightly on the lips before biting his bottom lip.

Owen jumps up and starts to unbutton his shirt. "Stay right there, you naughty girl. You say you'll *come* wherever I want. I want you to cum right here, right now, while I fuck you from behind. Is that okay, baby?"

Oh, yes. That sounds like perfection. "I'm sure I can be persuaded. But, Owen, go easy. I've never done this before either." He lightly smacks me on my bare ass. and when I feel his tongue thrust into me first, I melt against his mouth and fall to my elbows. Owen seems to know exactly how to please me. I don't even know how to please myself. Carl certainly didn't know how to please me.

Carl didn't like to 'rut like dogs'. He said he only liked missionary. It haunts me that when I walked in on him with that woman, she was riding him like he was a bucking bronco. Afterwards, Carl told me he had been finding things lacking between us and didn't know how to approach me about it. I guess it was easier for him to turn elsewhere than to develop a deeper and more satisfying connection with me.

Until I really tried other stuff with Owen, I had thought that my relationship had broken down because of my lack of imagination and sexual prowess. Now I know, it just didn't work with Carl. Things fall apart everyday so better things can come together. And boy did Owen and I *cum* together.

When I broke things off with Carl, I was shocked to find I didn't actually miss him. Most of my heartache came from being humiliated, and at losing my home and dog, because Carl didn't want us to finish. Despite him being the one to hurt me and be unfaithful, I in effect had to leave him when he refused to leave me. Carl continued to rub salt in my wounds even after the incident that led to us ending. I know Owen would never be so cruel.

I am falling fast and deep for Owen. Is it possible to fall in love this fast? I'm not sure, but it feels good. It feels so right and easy and like we've been together for a long time already. I am comfortable, happy and satisfied with Owen. I am looking forward to the promise of the future with him. I feel like he knows me and my soul… and I believed him when he told me he has wanted and loved me for a long time. Could it be possible that I loved him too, without realising it?

~ Owen ~

I didn't realise how insecure Jamie is. I know she has little doubts and a lack of confidence. We've spent a lot of time together on these trips and in the office. The first time I realised she was scared of flying, she didn't actually tell me. We were on one of the shortest flights, and she freaked out and couldn't breathe.The issue is always with take-off and landing.

I knew about her insecurity about her body, because so many times when we have had to attend meetings, dinners, galas and events for work during business trips, I would overhear her ask Tim or one of the other PAs, 'How shit do my boobs look in this?' or, 'Do I look like a boy?', and the things she said about them to us all in the group often felt like she made fun of her boobs before anyone else could. Her reaction to Carl's put down about her 'non-existent, pathetic excuse for tits' killed me inside and had me ready to fucking strangle the jackass. How could he treat her so poorly?

The way she attacked me when I came back with our breakfast shocked me. Surely, she didn't think after all this time, and the most incredible night, that I would get up and leave her? However, when I look at her past, it doesn't take a genius to work out why. Everyone apart from her sister has left her or hurt her. She expects people to leave now, because that's all she knows.

As she crawls towards me on all fours, swaying her hips, I just have to have her. She is the sexiest woman I have ever known. To me, she is perfect: there is nothing I would change. Not even her insecurities, because they make my Jamie exactly who she is. I'll do my best to help build her confidence up, but at her pace.

My whole body reacts to her; my cock has been hard since I walked back into the hotel room. As soon as she wiggles her ass, my cock throbs and aches. I *must* have her. I need to have her.

I walk around the bed in a determined daze, tearing my clothes off. I was just going to slide right into her from behind, but when she asks me in her husky voice to go easy because she's never done it this way before, I change my mind. I'm going to make this the best experience of her life.

Her tight pussy is just visible to me through her shaven lips, and before I can help myself, I plunge my tongue right into the heat of her. Her nectar is an aphrodisiac, one drop on my tongue and I crave more. As I eat away at her precious flesh, I hear her surprised moan of pleasure, and so I continue to probe and lick her clit. She falls to her elbows and rests her cheek against the bed.

"I will never ever get enough of you, Jamie; I want you all day, everyday, for the rest of our days. In every way we want. I want it all with you, babe."

When her legs start to shake, I climb up on the bed next to her and slide a condom on. "Tell me if it feels too deep or it hurts. It will feel different from this angle, okay?"

"I will," she promises as I line myself up with her entrance. Just that tiny amount of contact and my dick is jumping with glee, wanting to play and ready to shoot already. It really seems to have a life of its own around Jamie.

I press into her slowly, groaning as I do. Her pussy is exquisite. She is wet, warm, tight and perfect. I keep checking that it feels good for her; I don't want to hurt her.

"Erm… Owen. I need you now, faster." She is getting bolder. I like that, and since this position is a favourite of mine, I want her to really enjoy it. Seems like I'm not doing my job if she's having to ask for more.

"Sorry, babe, I was trying to go easy," I say as I start to slam into her, her groan of satisfaction pushing me almost to the edge. She pushes back against me, forcing harder and rougher movements from me, and then shouts my name as her body surrenders to the overwhelming climax. Her legs give way, and I slam into her once more as I blow my load. We both pant as our sweaty bodies continue to convulse with pleasure. Every time feels even more spectacular than the last. I could die a happy man right now.

"That was amazing, Owen. My legs are still shaking." I reluctantly pull out of her, and she moans when I do. "I feel empty when you're not inside me now." It pleases me to no end when she says little things like this. I chuckle and lay down next to her, and she snuggles into me.

"Don't tempt me. I need to go out soon. That was my last condom." She tickles my chest hair absentmindedly.

"Can I come with you? Maybe we can take a look at some other stuff while we are there." My wayward cock starts to harden at the thought of taking Jamie to one of the adult stores I know are around here. "Oi, stop it, we have no more condoms, remember?"

The glint in her eyes tells me she likes that I find her irresistible.

"What do you want to do about this long term? Were you taking birth control before?" She nods yes before she replies.

"I'll make an appointment when we get back home, and then we won't have to worry about running out of condoms anymore." I kiss her hard. This feels like a proper confirmation that we are together and that we are a couple.

"Shall we go and explore for a while and get some supplies? I know a shop or two in Copenhagen that might tickle your fancy." Her eyes gleam with curiosity and intrigue.

"I think I'd like that, too. Don't laugh, but I've never been to one of those kinds of shops before, Owen." That settles it, I have to take her shopping.

"Come on then, babe, get dressed. The quicker we get going, the quicker we can come back for more fun."

She giggles as I chase her into the bathroom. I love her playful nature, because it shows me that we are going to have fun, much more fun than I had initially thought or dared to hope for.

We walk down the street hand-in-hand. Jamie looks amazing. Her cheeks glow, she's smiling and there is a buzz about her. I can't keep my eyes or my hands off her. She insisted on us both wearing Santa hats and I don't have it in me to refuse her.

After stopping by a chemist where I pick up the biggest box of condoms I can find, we carry on walking past The City Hall Square and over to Stroget, which is a long shopping street in Copenhagen that has all the leading brands. I lead her to the end of the block of shops, and on the corner is where I want to take her: DMasque, an adult pleasure store. Jamie smiles and bites her lip when we arrive, so I double check she's still feeling up to this. "Are you sure, babe?"

I needn't have worried; she practically drags me inside. "I'm so excited," she whispers to me with enthusiasm.

I have been in this shop before, it was a couple of years ago which is why I know it is here, but last time I wasn't really interested in what was on offer. Now I'm here with Jamie, and I couldn't be more eager. I want to experiment with her. I want to buy her toys and dress-up. I want it all with her.

An assistant greets us, shows us where everything is located and encourages us to peruse their repertoire of products.

Jamie's eyes are wide, trying to absorb everything around her. "Some of this stuff is downright scary, Owen!" she whispers.

"We can leave; we don't need any of this stuff," I offer, but she cuts me off by shaking her head at me.

"Some of it looks scary, but some of it is... interesting. Like this, what does this do?" She picks up the feather duster that the shop assistant has just used to clean the shelves.

I can't help but laugh at the wonder in her voice; she is so cute. "Babe, that is a duster the assistant just used to clean the shelves."

Her face is red as she drops the duster. "Maybe I'll just get a vibrator or a whip instead. Oh my God, how embarrassing!" She laughs, too, and it's too perfect an opportunity to not kiss her. Everything about her, everything she does, it's just perfect. She is perfect.

We go through to the next alcove and there are several dressing up outfits that draw her attention. A nurse, a French maid and a patent leather skin-tight crotchless body stocking. I indicate to the assistant that I want them all while Jamie continues to browse. When we arrive at the sex toys, she doesn't seem impressed by the large multicoloured phalluses and cringes at the thought of a glass dildo.

"No, no, no! What if it smashes inside me? That'll be an embarrassing visit to Accident & Emergency, Owen!" I pick up the small lady finger, a g-spot stimulator, some lube and nipple clamps.

As I make my way to the till to pay, Jamie strikes up a conversation with one of the assistants, who passes her a card and air kisses her. I'm glad she is distracted so I can pay without her noticing too much.

When she approaches the till, she has three items in her hands: strawberry body paint, a pair of handcuffs and a slim leather riding crop. "Owen, love, I don't think I'll take the feather duster," she jokes as we pay.

My heart sours at her casual endearment, I know what she is saying is in jest, but that word is one I have waited a long time for. She may not be exactly where I am *yet,* but all these little steps edge us closer and closer to where I want us to be: A proper couple. We are going to have so much fun along the way. She calls me 'love' so effortlessly, it feels as though I have always been her love.

With our bag of goodies, we giddily make our way back out into the street where snow is falling; it won't stick but it feels romantic. I got my Christmas present early. Jamie is finally mine, and we have so much to look forward to.

~ Tim ~

Time seems to drag until I see Lauren again on Friday night. I am both nervous and excited. How can a beauty like her still be so innocent? I am both flattered and honoured she trusts me to be the man to guide her. I have been on pins all day waiting for my turn to show her a good time.

My biggest issue is… I want to show her the best time, so I know I need to make her cum. I feel like I have one shot to get this right. So do I use fingers or go straight for the big guns and lick her out? I don't want to scare her off. I just want to make her feel like a million dollars.

If I was being selfish, I would just play with her jugs all night. I cannot wait to get my mouth on them. She has a big, healthy set of knockers. They are absolutely mesmerising. The way they strain against her tops, the subtle hint of cleavage and her nipples hardening through her clothing just drive me wild. She has caught me on a couple of occasions looking at them. I'm no better than the teenage version of myself. All I can think of is the heavy, sensitive flesh in my hands, being free to lift them and push them together, and her wanting me to kiss every inch of them ending at her large nipples, dark and hard screaming to be sucked and tweaked.

But I am not selfish. Well, not that selfish. Tonight is not about me. Tonight is all about Lauren; I am going to make sure of it. I want this to be earth shattering for her.

I call her as I make my way back to her flat and tell her I am bringing Chinese food. She squeaks back at me which makes me laugh. "Are you ok, Flower?" She says she is and then rushes off, telling me to hurry up.

As I stand at the intercom waiting for her to let me in, butterflies dance around in my tummy. When I finally see her, less than twenty hours after I last did, I plonk the food on the hall table, take her face in my hands and kiss her passionately. She gives my tongue access after letting out a surprised yelp at my sudden display, before she melts into my embrace. "I missed you so much," I tell her in between my kisses, and she smiles shyly back at me in response.

"Do you want food first?" she asks.

I shake my head. I am being forward and dominant tonight, because somehow, I feel that is what she needs. "I want you; I want you first, please?" Her eyes widen but she nods her consent. "Can we use your bedroom this time?" She smiles and pulls me along to her bedroom.

"What do you want me to do, Tim?" She stands in the dim light looking vulnerable and shy, and I just want to reassure her that everything will be okay.

"I want you to trust me. I want you to trust me to touch you and give you what you gave me last night. Can you do that?" She moves her head very slowly up and down. "Good, I want you to take off your clothes from the waist down and lie on the bed for me, please."

I watch her intently as she follows my instructions. When she removes her panties and stockings, I look away to allow some privacy. Her bed squeaks when she climbs into it.

She keeps her skirt on, opting to roll it up around her waist instead, and when she sits on the edge of her bed, I tell her to stop. I take off my jacket and kneel down in front of her. "Just shift your ass back a tiny bit, Flower." She does as I ask, and I place my hands on her legs and feel her shaking. "Don't worry, Lauren. Everything is going to be okay; I promise you. Now, just lay back and close your eyes. And trust me."

She follows my instructions perfectly. I place little kisses all the way up from her ankle to her knee and then repeat on the other leg. Her legs are white, smooth and shapely. Lifting one up, I bend it gently so I can place her foot on the edge of the bed. After repeating the process with the other leg, I try to spread her knees apart, but she resists and holds her legs shut like a vice.

"Lauren, I promise I am not going to hurt you. When you're ready just let your knees fall to the bed." Like magic, she opens her legs to me, revealing soft thighs and her juicy pussy that is already glistening. I kiss my way up from her knees to the junction between her legs and suck, kiss and nip at her womanly thighs as I do. I have dreamt of these thighs wrapping around my head as I eat her out.

Her response is timid at first. Her hands are fisted in the bedspread, and her breathing seems heavier. But once I spread her lips open and gently trail my tongue over her moist, velvety folds, she gasps in response. I slowly swirl my tongue over her entire sex before concentrating on her little clit that is hidden from immediate view. Her legs tense against the overwhelming pleasure this action brings and I smile in reaction.

"That's okay, Flower, just relax. You're really going to enjoy this. You taste exquisite, and you feel even better. It's like my wildest dreams are coming to life right now." She relaxes to my words. This time, there is no let up as I eat away at her; I lick, nip, suck and rub until I feel her natural wetness in abundance. It's like the finest elixir, a sure indicator of my success in pleasing her.

With her legs shaking and her breathy moans, I know she's getting close. I slide a finger inside her tight hole as I clap down on her clit, and as she starts to cum, she moves against my mouth and threads her fingers through my hair, holding my head in place. I slide a second finger in, too, curling them up to find her g-spot and encourage a second orgasm just as the first starts to finish.

She shouts my name this time, and as I continue to slowly lap at her, she mutters incoherent words under her breath. "That was amazing, Flower. I could seriously stay here and go all night."

Her little voice is clearer now that she has regained some

control. "Oh my God, Tim! Don't tempt me."

I laugh at her remark. As I stand and try to help her up, too, she looks down at my tented trousers. "Does doing that turn you on, Tim?"

"Doing what?" Her face reddens, and she bites her lip and looks away. "Lauren, I have just had my face buried in your perfect pussy. Of course that turns me on. My woman, crying out my name as I make her cum. Too right, I am turned on. I've never been more turned on than I am right now. I still have your juices on my face and can still hear you chanting my name. I have never wanted someone as much as I want you. I have never wanted to please someone as much as I want to please you."

She kisses me, gentle little strokes on my neck and up to my ear, tugging on the lobe with her teeth before kissing me full on my lips. "I want to please you, too, Tim. I want to please you like you pleased me. I have never desired anyone. I have never wanted anyone. Not until you. I want you more than I could ever tell or show you, Tim."

She drops to her knees and starts to undo my pants. My dick springs free, and she enthusiastically slides her lips and mouth down it. I know she's never done this before, and just the thought of her awkwardly trying to suck me off makes me want to blow my load right now. I hold my cock still for her, pulling back the tight skin so she can explore me more freely. I hold on to the doorframe above my head with my other hand as she fucks me with her mouth. I close my eyes and imagine I am slamming into her tight wet hole, but it's too much.

"Lauren, I'm going to cum. Fuck, you're good at that! Are you sure that's your first time, Flower?" Her eyes sparkle in triumph, and she sits back on her feet as I slowly rub myself and cum into my hand.

"Tim? I think I want to do it. I want to go all the way."

Thank you. Thank you, God!

~ Jamie ~

This trip has been amazing. This morning we attend a business meeting, and I am required to take notes for Owen and schedule other meetings for him in a few months' time. I expect Owen to maintain a professional front, but he holds my hand as we walk in and introduces me as his PA and, more importantly, his girlfriend, to the chagrin of Saffi.

Owen laughed when I told him about my secret name for her, he told me there was no reason to be jealous but laughed at my creativity. Saffi is pleasant enough to Owen and Mr. Hansen but completely ignores me, looking through me and talking over me. However, I take it all in stride. I would be gutted, too, if Owen had knocked me back, so I do have a little sympathy for her, no matter how childish her behaviour is.

The flight home is a breeze with Owen. He holds my hands and keeps up a steady flow of chatter to distract me. And when it comes to landing, we are too busy kissing to even notice. It's the first time I have been able to fly without too much anxiety. I could actually get used to flying with Owen.

"Can I take you out to dinner tomorrow night, babe? We could go out and then end the night at my place?" I agree, it sounds like a great plan, until I remember I promised Billie I would watch the children for her again.

"I can't. I've just remembered that I promised Billie that I would babysit… but why don't you come with me? We are going ice skating at the National History Museum." The reluctance is evident in his face, but I flutter my eyelashes and pout, and he groans and agrees.

I call Billie to ensure this isn't an issue, and she shouts down the phone about wanting all the dirty details and that she knew we would make a great couple.

I arrive back at my apartment on Friday evening, and I am like a new woman.

Everything seems to be falling into place.

CHAPTER TEN

~ **Jonty** ~

It's been seven days since our dogging exercise, but it feels more like seven weeks. Both Billie and I have been buzzing all week. The sex is phenomenal once again, and I feel ten years younger. As I place my signet ring back onto my little finger on my right hand, I am ready to take my wife dogging again.

The ring was given to me many years ago at a club in Europe, an exclusive club for like minded people with similar interests to me and my wife. As a discrete way to identify one another, we simply need to show each other the emblem.

While we wait for Jamie to arrive to babysit, Billie does chores to keep herself busy. She had an early appointment at the local beauty salon. Last night, Billie was all of a frenzy when Jamie told her she is seeing someone and that is nothing to how crazy with joy she was when Jamie added that her new man is her boss, Owen Matthews. I smile to myself as I recall how excited Billie appeared by the news.

"I don't know what is more exciting, Jonty: Jamie's news or the night you have planned for us," she teasingly told me with a glint in her eye.

"I'll make you pay for that later when we are alone," I whispered against her ear as I lightly spanked her ass.

She looked back at me seriously. "I'm hoping you will."

Jamie and her man arrive earlier than planned, which is a blessing. Billie wants to get all the details from them, and I selfishly don't want to hit the gridlock out of London. With a couple of weeks left until Christmas, the roads are bound to be busy. After introductions are made and hands are shook, I press my wife out of the front door and to my waiting car.

We arrive at our destination bang on time. I booked the same hotel as last time. Billie likes it here, and I know the way to the dogging site from here and back again.

"Are you still okay with all the limits, Billie? Are you still sure about us performing a scene tonight?" She nods back enthusiastically.

"Jonty, feel... feel how wet I am. I cannot wait." She pushes my hand between her legs and sure enough, as promised, her waxed pink slit is slick with her juices.

"Just a little taste?" I beg, dropping to my knees and hungrily trying to nose my way through her clothing to her hidden delight.

"No! Wait for your supper. You'll enjoy it all the more that way." She tells me off sternly like a school headmistress. I like the thought of that, and so I file that idea away for future use. I still make a show of groaning in disappointment that I have to wait for my treat.

My beautiful wife is dressed like an irresistible slut ready for our scene tonight. We have agreed on oral and full sex in front of the crowd, but we both don't want any crowd participation. It is to be just me and her and everyone else watching us.

The crowd is promised to be large, and there are some semi-professional performers attending from around the country, too. It is the Dogging Scene Christmas Party.

As we pull up, there is an attendant working the car park. He tips his hat at me when he spots my ring and asks if we want a stage or viewing area. We pay the required fee for our stage area and towards the security measures, and the attendant gives us a pack for tonight. Inside is a traffic light sign: red is for no approach, amber for watch and talk but don't touch, green is for all in.

Billie moves our sign to amber. "Are we still agreed, Jonty? Any last minute changes?"

I kiss her hard. "No changes; I'm happy with our decision. What about you?" I ask, but she has already started to remove her outer garments and all that remains is the skimpy kitten outfit she has covering her vitals. She looks superb, busty, voluptuous and lascivious. While she is checking her make-up and hair in her compact mirror, I set the scene.

I get out of the car, set our traffic light up on the windscreen and then arrange our 'stage', which is a raised platform that links up to the bonnet of our car. I lay out the fur blanket and leave the small bag of supplies I may need within reach. Although it is December, the night air is cool, but not cold. Still, the addition of outdoor heaters is greatly appreciated.

A small crowd is starting to gather around: two couples and a couple of single men. One calls out to me, "What is your scene? Are you alone?"

"The star of my scene will be out in a moment. She is a horny little kitty, and I'm hoping she'll show me a good time.

Maybe you could stay, watch and give her some tips and encouragement?" Billie steps out of the car, and I couldn't have timed it any better. The crowd murmurs its appreciation. She has cat ears on her head, and as she climbs on to the platform her tail swishes suggestively.

Billie lays back on the rug. Her boobs spill out of her sheer negligee; big round globes and soft peaks which harden as she slips her hands over them and tugs at the little sensitive buds.

The crowd seems to swell with anticipation. One man shouts out, "Good pussy cat, what else have you got?" and a couple mutually masturbate one another as they watch my wife.

Billie moans louder than normal for the benefit of the crowd. She slowly sits forward, making eye contact with her audience and then runs her hands down her curvy body until she reaches the top of her thigh. She raises her knees slightly and the crowd goes wild.

"She isn't wearing panties." "She's completely naked underneath." "I can see her juicy pussy." Maintaining eye contact with her appreciative viewers, Billie spreads her legs wide and slides her hand between them. As she finally touches the very heart of her femininity, she groans, and the crowd groans along with her. Grown men strain their necks to get a better view. Their wives and partners nod their approval.

Billie rubs and strums herself in front of the adoring gathering, and I know, as her husband, she is getting off on the undivided attention they have all freely given her. Her pants become harder and faster. I know she's on the edge, and that's my cue. "Stop right there, you naughty little pussy".

Billie pretends to be shocked by my interruption. The crowd goes wild. "That's my pussy, all for me." I crawl towards her on all fours, licking my lips. "My pussy," I tell them all one last time.

"Your pussy needs you," Billie simpers to me. I bury my head between her legs and hum. The tiny vibrations against her warm lips and swollen clit bring her first climax; the crowd is in raptures when she does. A couple of others join her in her pleasure.

Some people move along, and others come and join the show. Billie instructs me to open up my pants for her. I do as I am told and then close my eyes allowing my other senses to fill in the gaps.

Billie plays up to the crowd. She implores them to tell her what they want her to do.

"Get his cock out." "Jerk him off." "Suck that dick and give us a cum shot." "Ride him or let him fuck you doggy-style."

Her soft, warm lips gently graze the underside of my shaft. She keeps going until she reaches my balls which she cups and gently caresses causing my dick to twitch all the more.

I open my eyes and look down at my beautiful wife with pride. "Suck me, sweetheart. Let my cock hit the back of your throat." I hold her head in place as I start to thrust into her warm, inviting mouth.

Billie makes a big show of sucking me off. She moans and groans in all the right places, and the crowd loves her.

"Finger yourself while you blow him, kitty. Let us see if you can cum for us again." The excitement builds rapidly within me as she fulfils every request put to her.

The time comes for the big finale. I am not as young as I once was, and it would take me too long to be ready to cum again, so Billie and I had previously agreed that she would suck me for a short time, but we would quickly move on to full sex to give the

170

crowd what they all desire.

The cum shot. The crowd shouts for it. They want to see me pummel her and ride her ragged in every way, but what they want is to watch me blow my load all over her.

I fuck my wife while people watch; I fuck her in every position until I feel her quivering in my arms. "Shall I let her cum again, guys?" I look around; people are fucking in the audience, imitating what we are doing.

"I'd let her cum. She is such a good girl. She has been the best little kitty for us all. She deserves the reward. Make her cum for all of us. We would all love to fuck her until she cums."

The man's words catapult Billie over the edge. She pants and groans as she cums, and she seems to cum for the longest time. I pull out of her just when I think she has finished, but then she squirts. The crowd erupts in overexcitement. The ones that miss it beg for a description from the lucky few who saw it. I continue to stroke myself until I also cum all over her back and ass giving the interactive audience the cum shot they've been heckling for.

The crowd explodes into raptures. Many shout their thanks or hoot; some are too busy pleasuring themselves.

"That was great, Bilbo. Was it as good for you as it was for me?" I think she enjoyed it, but I want to hear the words directly from her.

"Best night ever, Jonty. That last orgasm was sensational."

I cover her up in her robe and bring her sweet hot tea from the flask in my supply bag. There is a definite chill in the air now, and I don't want her getting cold once the adrenaline wears off.

We talk to the crowd for a while before I insist on Billie needing time to change and warm back up. I carry her to the back seat while I tidy up the stage. When I get back to her, she is dressed once again, with a glow in her cheeks and a spark in her eyes.

"Do you want to go viewing the others, Bilbo, or are you done?" She kisses me and rubs my face.

"I'm more than happy to go now, Jonty. Nothing is going to top that, and I want to leave on a high."

We wave goodbye to our fellow doggers. They made this the kinky and exhilarating experience that it was, and I will always respect and thank them for doing that.

~ Owen ~

I need today to go well; I need Jamie to see a potential future with me outside the bedroom. I am crapping myself because I have never really been around children, and I feel awkward and exposed. It's not that I don't like them, I'm just a bit lost with how to act with them.

Jamie is obviously an absolute natural when it comes to children. She told me she feels more like an older sister than an aunt to her sister's children because she lived with them when they were born and they are all really close as a family. It is evident from their interactions that they love one another deeply, and for the first time in my life, I get a glimpse of what the future could look like for me. Maybe children and the whole family thing wouldn't be too bad after all. With Jamie by my side, everything seems like a possibility.

It helps that the children, Oscar and Chloe, are decent kids. Oscar asks me about my football team, and we hit it off over a game of FIFA on his games console. Once he starts talking about football, he doesn't stop. He is obviously passionate about the sport and the game, too. It is a great sport for us to bond over even though hockey would be my first love. I have grown to love football since I moved to England twelve years ago. Jamie keeps looking over to us. She seems so happy as she plays with little Chloe.

"We have tickets for 4 p.m. at the ice rink, guys, so one more game, and then we best make a move so we don't miss it. Are you excited, Chloe?" Chloe nods to Jamie as she clutches on to her Barbie Doll.

"Daddy said I could get a penguin so I don't fall over, Jim-Jam," she tells her aunt earnestly. I laugh when I hear Jamie tell her she's getting a penguin, too.

"Oscar? What are they talking about?" I whisper to my new little sidekick, and he rolls his eyes as he explains that a penguin is a skating aid to stop people falling over on the ice.

"Can you skate, Oscar?" I ask him as we continue to battle against each other in the computer game.

"I'm okay. I don't need a penguin; that would be so embarrassing! Chloe still needs a penguin but she's younger than me. If Jim-Jam gets a penguin, I'm going to pretend I don't even know her." I laugh at his statement. "Can you skate, Owen?"

I used to play hockey when I was growing up in Canada. I haven't been on the ice in years, but I know it'll be like riding a bike. It's a skill you never lose. "I'm okay, too. Don't worry, mate, I don't need a penguin either."

We make our way in a black hackney cab to the Natural History Museum. It's not far from the house but Jamie wants to preserve all Chloe's energy for ice skating, telling me, "She only has little legs."

We continue to team up; I stay with Oscar, and Jamie helps

Chloe. Both girls look cute in their knitted hats and fingerless gloves. They really could be sisters; the resemblance is that strong.

Oscar has a fierce independent streak but he does let me help him put on his rented skates. I show him how to place his socks so they don't rub and give him blisters. "You've done this a lot really, haven't you, Owen?"

I chuckle at his astuteness. "Shhh, don't tell Jamie yet, but I used to play hockey. I'm going to try and impress her." He wrinkles up his nose.

"She's so bad; she'll be impressed if you don't fall down, Owen. Ice hockey is a really tough game. My mum says I can't play it because I'll break my beautiful face." He rolls his eyes and shakes his head. He's a real character, alright. After I help him tie his laces tight, we go to meet the girls who both have a penguin, much to Oscar's dismay.

It's busy because it's the weekend and it's the run up to Christmas, so we try to stay huddled together. Chloe frets and is still unsteady even with her penguin for support, whereas I suspect Jamie only has a penguin to make Chloe feel better.

"Oscar, I'm going to give your sister a skating lesson. Will you look after Jamie?" He rolls his eyes again but glides over the ice to his aunt.

"Okay, okay, but at least abandon the penguins for a minute." I relent; he seems steady enough to hold Jamie up, and I think Chloe's confidence would grow if she believed she could do this and wasn't so dependent on the skating aid. I move their penguins into the middle, and then I hold my hand out to little Chloe.

"Chloe, instead of using the penguin you need to learn to walk

like one of them on the ice. You've seen a penguin walk, eh?"
I start to do the penguin waddle march, and she giggles as she joins in too.

"Look! I'm not falling over!" she shouts to me as we waddle along the ice. Her giggles of glee at not falling over just melt my heart. Kids aren't so bad after all.

Jamie's eyes, filled with love, longing and passion, catch my attention. She almost falls over when she attempts to wave at me.

I bring Chloe back to her aunt, and she boasts about getting all the way around the rink without falling once. It is heart-warming to see when she pushes her penguin this time, she does it with a bit more confidence.

"Owen, shall we have a race?" Oscar shouts to me. I bend and kiss Jamie before I leave. Her nose and cheeks are now bright red, and she looks adorable with her little penguin and her look-alike niece.

I can't remember the last time I had such good, innocent fun. It's amazing how children change a dynamic; they have so much joy and energy. Oscar has a natural athleticism about him and he picks up the basic skills very quickly. He will make a great sportsman in whatever pursuit he chooses.

When our time on the ice is almost up, I ask Oscar to watch his sister for a couple of minutes. I just want a moment with Jamie.

"You're not going to be making out, are you? That would be so gross!" he mutters in disgust.

"Oi, it wouldn't be gross. Just look the other way for a minute, young man," Jamie adds through her laughter.

I take her hand, and just as I thought, she isn't too bad on her skates. I spin her around in the middle of the rink and then pull her to me. "I've had a lovely day, babe, much better than what I thought we would have. I was terrified of the children but they are cool."

"I have loved today. Thank you for sharing this with me. Those little people mean the world to me, and just watching you interact with them made my heart flutter. I'm really falling for you, Owen. This all feels so right and so natural."

I lift her chin with my cold fingers and kiss her tenderly. She is the sweetest, most intoxicating honey, and I am addicted to her. Today confirms I want the full package with Jamie. I want her to be part of every aspect of my life, and I want to be part of every aspect of hers too.

We go back to the children who are pretending to vomit, and once we have our normal shoes back on, we go to the café upstairs to have dinner and hot chocolate. It's been a long time since I have had any sort of semblance of family time, and it's a shock to find how organic and exciting this all feels. We are having an awesome time, and with the Christmas music playing, the lights and decorations all around us, it's hard to not get excited about the impending holiday.

We make our way around the small Christmas market. There are little wooden huts serving food and drink and selling little holiday items. It's no Tivoli Garden but being here with Jamie and the children makes it extra special.

Chloe wants a new hat that looks like a reindeer, and Oscar picks up a hand-crafted tin ornament. "I want to get this for my mum; she will love this for her café." Jamie helps him pay, kisses him on the head and tells him his mum will love that he has been so thoughtful.

I pick out an ornament for Jamie and me. It's two elves kissing with a toy workshop in the back and a banner over their heads that says "Our First Christmas". The lady serving quickly etches Owen and Jamie onto the bellies of the elves before wrapping it in tissue paper. I slide it into my pocket; I'm going to ask her to come to my home tomorrow to help me decorate my Christmas tree and I'll show her the decoration then.

We head back to Jamie's sister's house with the children, who look worn out and ready for a big sleep.

Jamie helps her niece and nephew get ready for bed. Chloe runs to me after she has brushed her teeth and cuddles me. "Thank you, Owen, I've had loads of fun today, and I didn't even fall over. I'm glad Jamie brought you. I knew you were special when she kept saying your name when she was sleeping." I ruffle her hair and wish her goodnight as she runs back on her little legs to get her bedtime story off her aunt.

Oscar comes to fist bump me and makes me promise we will play FIFA again in the morning before his parents return. "Definitely, buddy. I'm going to kick your butt."

"Challenge accepted, Owen. You are going down!" he replies with a grin.

I wait in the living room for Jamie. She comes in after about ten minutes with a bottle of wine and two glasses. "Do you want to watch a Christmas film, babe? We can snuggle up and drink wine and make out." The look on her face sets my soul on fire. Happiness oozes from her, and the feeling is mutual. I have never been as happy and content as I am right now.

Jamie kicks her shoes off and tells me to do the same. We lie together on the sofa watching the film *Love, Actually*. We kiss, cuddle and laugh as we watch the sweet movie. Jamie cries when they all declare love for each other, and part of me has to acknowledge that I would probably do the same if Jamie was to fall in love with me. She knows how I feel about her, and I know she is falling for me; she told me. The icing on the cake would be those precious words and feelings.

Life would be perfect.

~ Tim ~

Lauren wants to go all the way, and as delighted as I am that she is ready, I don't want her to regret a rash decision. I also want to make it special for her. It isn't only our first time together; it is her very first time ever. She is so precious to me. I want this to be the best experience ever for her.

At first, she backs off from me, thinking I am rejecting her. As if I would.

"Flower, please, listen to me. I just want to make it special for you. You deserve for this to be special. Please, let me do this for you and for us," I try to explain as I pull her to me. It is heartbreaking to see how fast she doubts both me and herself.

"You definitely still want to?" I quickly realise I am the problem. I am treating her like a delicate flower; no wonder she doubts me. I need to get back to being more like me. Then she will never, ever doubt how I feel about her.

"I want you more than I can tell you, Lauren. How about this? Tomorrow night, we can make it special, and if you still want to, we can go all the way and do every little thing you desire. But for tonight, I want you to lay back down on your bed and let me eat you out again and again. Let me show you exactly how much I want you. Let me show you how much I want to please you and make you happy." I push her towards her bed. Desire flows through me, and the same desire reflects in her eyes. With the blush that covers her cheeks and her slightly parted lips, my want for her rises once more, and I start to harden again.

I make her cum with my mouth and fingers a couple more times before we eat our Chinese food. And then, when watching another Christmas special, I lick her out just one more time. She has a healthy sex drive that pretty much matches my own. Now that I have had a taste of her, I can't stop; I just want more and more of her pulsating pussy as she cums all over my face. After the second time, she didn't even bother putting her panties back on, which is fine by me. I have free and easy access to her beautiful pussy, and all I want is to make her cum over and over again.

She lets me sleep over at her place. Every night until last night has ended with a kiss before heading home. Tonight, I get to kiss her clit and hole as well as her mouth before we fall asleep, and I am on cloud nine about it.

In addition to the physical progress we are making, I love that she trusts me to sleep in her bed with her. Getting to cuddle her and spoon her tonight and hopefully every night from now on is a dream come true. Her beautiful soft curves against my hard body is the most exquisite feeling in the world. We fit together perfectly.

I am staying over again this evening. However, this time I hope I get to see my beautiful girl fully naked, and when she cums I want to be inside her, making sweet love to her.

We speak during the wee hours of the morning when the room is pitch dark and the rest of the world is sleeping. She confesses she is worried about being fully naked with me, but she is excited that she finally found the one to share this moment with.

I ask her about how she had envisioned this moment, and it is the usual stuff like soft romantic music playing, candles flickering around and most importantly, a sweet and tender moment.

So after we have enjoyed our morning together, I tell her I have a few jobs to do but I will be back at 7 p.m.

I hate leaving her, but I know this is only temporary and it will give me the opportunity to put everything into place.

I stop by Camden Market armed with my list of supplies that I will need. It's absolutely crammed full with Christmas shoppers, and I can't help but wish I had thought to bring Lauren with me, too.

After locating rose petals, pillar candles and handcrafted chocolates, I head back home for a shower and freshen up. The hours seem to drag by until I can go back to Lauren's. On my way back to her flat, I pick up a bunch of flowers I had ordered earlier and then purchase a bottle of champagne from the shop next door before hailing a taxi.

Excitement and nerves bubble up inside me. I don't think I've ever slept with a virgin; well, not knowingly at least. I don't think I have ever slept with someone who I have felt this deeply for either. This night has so much riding on it because it means everything to me that I get it perfect for *my* perfect woman.

She opens her door in a red silk nighty with a dressing gown over it but open. Her hair is swept over one shoulder and is curled. She looks gorgeous. I know from the look on her face that she is fronting this out. She is blushing, and her big green eyes are downcast.

"Hi, Tim, come in." I hand her the flowers and the champagne which she thanks me for. "Are you hungry? Dinner shouldn't be too long."

I pull her to me, kiss her hard and then whisper into her ear, "I am starving, but only for you, Flower." I kiss her ear and lick down the outer ridge before biting the lobe playfully. She tries to pull me to her and into the bedroom. "No. Go and turn off the oven. Get two glasses for the champagne, give me ten minutes in your room alone and then you can come in."

She nods and goes to do my bidding. I go into her bedroom and arrange the rose petals and candles. I play the Spotify list I made last night for us and lower the volume so the romantic music plays softly in the background. I light the candles, strip down to my boxers and lie on the bed. I place a rose between my teeth and wait for her.

She knocks first before gingerly entering carrying the two long stemmed glasses I requested, plus a bucket of ice for the bottle of champagne. Her face lights up when she looks around her bedroom, flashing those cute-as-fuck dimples at me.

"Tim, it's all so beautiful. I can't believe you did all this for me. I'm so lucky. I'm so glad I waited for you." I kneel up, pull her to me and give her the rose from my mouth.

"A flower, for my Flower. I'm glad you waited for me, too. I want to do stuff like this and make you happy for always, Lauren. You've come to mean so much to me. This means more to me than I can tell you."

"I changed my mind though, Tim. Can we do it another night, please?" My heart falls to my stomach, but she smirks at me. "I'm joking, silly!"

"I'll spank you if you carry on, missus," I tease and she bites her bottom lip in response. "You are so naughty, Lauren... I think you might actually want me to spank you and so you are being a bad girl on purpose."

She giggles as I pull her onto the bed and kiss down her neck. However, within those few moments, the atmosphere changes, the very heat between us changes and we start kissing each other passionately while touching each other over our clothes.

"You're wearing too many clothes," I tell her, trying to remove her dressing gown, and that's when I notice a slight reluctance in her face, "You know I think you are beautiful, Lauren. To me you are all woman. You're absolutely perfect. I cannot wait to worship every inch of your whole body. I can't wait to make you completely mine and to be completely yours."

She is filled with a steely determination as she removes her dressing gown. I pull her back to the bed. "Let me?" I ask as I play with the spaghetti strap of her silk nightdress. When she gives me the nod, I pull the nightdress down to the swell of her breast giving her time to adjust and protest if she wants to. "Since that first night I have been dreaming about these bad boys. So big, round and juicy; they are fucking amazing, Lauren." I edge the material down a little bit more.

"You like my boobs?" she asks in surprise. She evidently hasn't paid attention to the amount of staring I have done at her tits the past couple weeks. I nod yes, and then she treats me. She tugs on the bottom of her night dress and her boobs bound out. Big, full, and complete, with large pink nipples and areola.

I groan as I latch on to one, and then the other. Palming them confirms she has more than a handful, and I am in heaven right now. "Even better than my imagination, Lauren. Fuck, these are amazing. You shouldn't hide these babies away. Well, not from me, anyway."

My obvious adulation and appreciation seems to feed her confidence. She becomes bolder and more daring until finally she is completely naked in the centre of the bed just like I have been dreaming of. Her pussy is slick with arousal, and it feels like she could be ready for me.

"I have been dreaming and fantasising about this moment since the night we met, Flower. I am completely and utterly besotted with you. I am falling so fast for you, and now we are going to share something that will bond us together for life. This will live in my heart forever. Do you want me to wear a condom?" She shakes her head no; we have already discussed the issue of protection, she explained that she's on the pill to regulate her hormones.

"Tim, I will remember this forever. You will be my first, and I want you to be my last too. I think I'm falling in love with you." Vulnerability mingles with her passion, and all I want is to give her all the words that want to spill from my heart.

"I love you, Lauren. I think I have loved you from the moment we met," I murmur to her as I line up my rigid cock with her soaked entrance. "Don't tense. It'll hurt if you tense. Just try to relax. I promise I will stop if I hurt you." She relaxes back into my embrace, and we kiss again. I try to press into her, but she is still so tight. So, I use my fingers again trying to limit the amount of pain.

I line up with her once more. "Lauren, this is going to hurt a little, but then I'll try and make you feel better again. I'm sorry, baby." I push with a little bit more force this time and hit her barrier of resistance. She cries out as I finally embed myself inside her.

CHAPTER ELEVEN

~ Lauren ~

As Tim presses into me, my insides feel like they split apart. I don't mean to cry out, but it really hurts. Tim immediately stills inside me, and apart from the throbbing where the pain once was, I feel okay.

"Lauren, look at me please." The concern in his voice brings tears to my eyes. "I'm going to stop, okay. I'm sorry. I didn't want to hurt you." I hold onto him. I'm scared if he moves it will hurt even more.

"Don't. Don't move, Tim. God, it hurts. Just stay where you are." I hate that I have tears running down my face; I'm such a weakling.

"Lauren, please look at me. I'm sorry. I never want to hurt you. Please don't cry." His concern makes me want to cry all the more.

"It'll be okay. Just don't move," I tell him. He chuckles a little and wipes away my tears with his thumb. I kiss his hand on the way past, and he looks at me with love and passion before kissing me softly, but it isn't long before all that pent up arousal and desire ignites in my tummy again. The undercurrent of pain subsides, and the overwhelming need to move takes over.

"Flower, you said not to move. You are moving." A primal moan leaves my lips as I move against Tim. There is pain but the pleasure is exquisite. This is it. I'm having sex with Tim; I am no longer a virgin. "Can I move, too?" Sweat beads Tim's forehead, he has been so restrained and patient.

"Yes. Please. Move." My legs start to shake as he moves slowly inside me. His groan worries me, am I hurting him, too? I touch his face so he looks at me. "Is it okay?"

His voice is harsh, but his words set my heart on fire. "It's better than okay. You feel fucking amazing, Lauren."

My core is filling with what feels like molten lava, and as I climb towards an eruption, I beg Tim to go faster, to go harder. We are frantic; this is not the sweet moment I thought it would be. This is carnal, primal and passionate. It is the most magnificent moment of my entire life. My control shatters as I cum. I cry out Tim's name, and I think I scream.

Tim groans as he cums, too. His seed is hot as it pumps inside me. "Fucking hell, Lauren. Holy shit. That was... that was stunning! Are you okay, Flower? Was it good for you, too?"

He quickly holds my face in his large hands, assessing my reaction. "It was. Oh my God. It was the best." Tears fill my eyes once again. "Thank you. You make me feel so special and sexy. You make me feel like I could fly if I wanted to." I have never felt so alive.

"You're incredible, Lauren; you are the most amazing woman I have ever met. That was out of this world. Thank you for letting me be the one. You are the one. I love you. Marry me?"

I stiffen below him. He is still inside me; I am still processing losing my virginity, and he is talking about getting married.

"Tim, don't. You don't have to do that. I'm really enjoying getting to know you. I am falling for you, and you know how special you are to me. I am looking forward to what develops between us. Let's just enjoy tonight; let's enjoy what comes from tonight. There is no rush."

He gives me a radiant smile. "Okay, Flower, but just so you know, I am going to marry you one day, just as soon as I've persuaded you of how right and perfect we are for each other. I am going to marry you in front of the whole world so they know you are mine and how much I adore you."

My heart beats fiercely in my chest. Things are moving too fast. It's one thing to sleep with Tim, but what if I actually allow myself to fall in love with him, too? Would he really declare me as his in front of the whole wide world, or would he eventually grow to be ashamed of me like my mother? What would I do if he left me for another woman, someone slim and self-assured, someone from the world he inhabits and one I will never belong in?

After we clean up, Tim falls asleep holding me. There isn't a part of my body he hasn't touched; there is no part of me that he hasn't cherished. He didn't flinch when he saw my fat butt or squirm at the sight of my roly, poly belly. Could he truly find me sexy and desirable? The burning question is how can he say he loves me when I can't even love me? What could he possibly see in someone *like me?*

I fret until the small hours and eventually get up and make myself a hot chocolate to drink while I stare out the window at the city I now call my home. I have waited so long to find someone like Tim. I waited so long that I gave up on such a man existing. Now I have the man of my dreams giving me everything my battered heart has ever desired, and I'm frightened. I am so scared because what will I do if one day he wakes up and realises he wants more or better?

My mother's words of criticism about my weight and appearance echo around in my mind. If my own mother can think and say those things about me, why would some random man see me any differently?

I weep silently into my hot chocolate as fear takes hold. I don't notice when Tim comes in, not until he kneels in front of me and holds my face in his hands. His touch is featherlight and yet calming and reassuring.

"Lauren, sweetheart, why are you crying? Are you sore? Tell me how I can make it better." All I can manage is a shake of my head. His eyes are wide with concern and panic. "Are you regretting what we did? Is that it?"

"No. I don't regret it. I don't know why I'm crying, but I feel so scared," I admit with a sob. He's going to think I am so pathetic now.

"Come back to bed, and we can talk." Although he is still sleepy, he is full of calm reassurance and compassion.

I pathetically stand and take hold of his hand. The rush of affection I have for him nearly knocks me to my knees.

"I'm falling for you, too, and I am frightened, insecure and feeling kind of vulnerable right now."

He kisses my head then pushes me to sit on the bed while he removes my slippers and climbs in beside me.

"All this is new to you. You gave away something very precious last night, and that's bound to make you feel vulnerable. I feel scared, too. Scared you'll end things, scared my heart will get broken and scared that I'll never feel as alive as I do when I am with you."

I stare at him in disbelief as he explains all this to me. "How can you feel all of these things, Tim? Why haven't you run away?"

His smile is just the sweetest I have ever seen. "Because, Flower, I am in love with you, and I will do anything to show you. I will remind you every day if I have to. This sort of thing doesn't just happen. We are so lucky to have found one another in the sea of people milling around us. I feel I am the luckiest man alive right now. I don't give a fuck about the rest of the world. All that matters is us. All that matters to me is you. You're all I want, Lauren; all I could ever want and need in life."

He holds me close and my heart starts to settle. It is scary to put your trust in another, but life is for living. I could protect my heart from feeling and walk away from Tim right now, or I could live life to the fullest and appreciate this for all it is. This could be the start of the rest of my life. I just need to be brave enough to go for what my heart desires.

Tim. It desires Tim. And I think it always will.

~ Jamie ~

Billie and Jonty return home at lunchtime on Sunday, and as much as I love my sister, Owen has invited me to his house and I want some alone time with him. There is something freaky about staying in my sister's house that has stopped us wanting to have sex. Is this what happens when you have children? Geez, no wonder my sister wanted nights away in a hotel; she must be permanently cock-blocked.

It has been adorable watching Owen interacting with my niece and nephew. He confessed to feeling out of his depth with children because of his lack of experience, but I honestly couldn't tell. We spoke briefly about the future and about what we both want and it's the first time having a family in the far future looks like a possibility. However, I think I have a good few years before either one of us will be ready for that.

Owen lives in Knightsbridge, which isn't too far from my sister's. As soon as we get through his front door, we are ripping clothes off each other in between frantic kisses and moans. He rolls the condom on expertly before saying, "Welcome to my humble abode. I hope you'll spend lots of time here, with me, doing this." I am spread across his dining table, and he slides into me, groaning in pleasure. "Fuck! Baby, I have wanted this all night."

His moves become deeper, harder, and tantalisingly fulfilling as he takes long, steady strokes deep inside me. It is measured and delightful. "I want you to play with yourself, babe. Flick your clit now while I fuck you hard. Let me see you make yourself cum."

My core gushes at his words, and I clench him deeper inside me. I stroke down the sides of my body, his greedy eyes taking everything in. God, he turns me on so much. "Okay, Mr. Matthews, I will get myself off thinking of your hard cock deep inside me, but next time I want it to be you that makes me cum." As I start to rub my swollen clit, he gazes down at me and watches me as I build up to my climax. His continued thrusts egg me along. My pussy is slick with wetness, and as Owen's cock tenses and becomes rigid inside me, I start to cum. I chant his name, and it pushes him to his climax too. His body drops to mine, his head on my shoulder as he continues to pump deep inside me.

It's not just the sex that is exhilarating, everything I do with Owen just feels exciting and right. Even the mundane things like us washing up simply feel so much more pleasurable because it's another moment shared with him.

We have to go back to the office tomorrow, and back to reality, but with a dinner date set up and the office Christmas party to navigate, we have much to look forward to.

I agree to help decorate Owen's Christmas tree, and he makes my heart flutter when he shows me a decoration he had made yesterday. It has our names etched on it and across the top it says... Our First Christmas.

"I hope this is the first of many, babe," Owen says sincerely through kisses.

Me too, I think as my heart swells with happiness. Me too.

~ Billie ~

I am still buzzing with excitement from Saturday as I open up Tables & Fables on Monday morning. Everything in my life seems to be falling into place because of the happiness and fulfilment I have in my heart and soul right now. Jonty says I'm glowing but Jonty is biased and always tells me I look beautiful even when it is evident I look completely gross.

However, there must be some truth in what he said. Jamie first told me I looked younger and happier. She then told us she would watch the children for us more often so we could enjoy extra time together as a couple, which is so sweet of her, especially now she has a new boyfriend.

I couldn't be happier about the situation with Jamie right now. I've seen the way her boss looks at her and Jamie, no matter how hard she protested she wasn't interested in him in that way, was definitely harbouring some feelings for him but denied them because she was with Carl. You could see a chemistry between them, a chemistry that's hard to diffuse and fake. In my humble opinion, they could be really happy together.

When the staff at the café comment on my carefree happiness, despite the busy season upon us and customers pouring out of our ears, I know Jonty's compliment isn't wholly biased. Dana even asks me for my secret. Am I taking drugs? Have I been inspired by an epiphany?

Imagining her reaction as I tell her I got fucked on the car bonnet by my husband while loads of people sat and watched and that since then I have felt on top of the world, I think she'd have a heart attack.

Last week, Dana recommended a book she has been reading that Lol, one of my favourite regular customers, highly suggested, and so last night, as Jonty and I settled back into our normal life, I pulled up the book on my Kindle and started reading. Before I knew it, a couple of hours had passed, and Jonty was snoring away at the side of me. I didn't want to put it down, even the threat of an early start for work didn't dissuade me. I can't wait to discuss it with Lol today.

Greenwich is in full swing for Christmas. The shoppers and socialisers are flocking; therefore, our footfall has doubled now we are on the final countdown for the big day. The seasonal lattes and hot chocolate are going down a storm, and festive themed treats constantly have to be refilled. Our bakers and confectioners are working around the clock at the moment just to meet demand. The children are lucky if I manage to save a treat or two for them.

The day goes by so quickly that it is after lunch before I manage to grab a few minutes to sit and talk with Lol. As I approach her, I notice she has a massive smile on her face. It is like looking in the mirror. "Good weekend, Lol?" I ask when I am near her.

She looks up at me, flustered. "Yeah. Sorry, I was just thinking." She smiles again, and I notice how beautiful she is when she smiles and I wonder what put that smile on her face.

"What's his name?" I ask jovially. In all the time I have known her, she has never expressed much interest in anyone apart from telling me her preference is for men. There have been a couple of men interested in her, but she had never taken a flying bit of notice. I just assumed she wasn't ready for anything heavy, or they weren't her type.

Lol laughs at my question. "Who said anything about a him?" Despite her deflection, there is a definite twinkle in her eye and a radiance that only comes from falling in love. However, it isn't my place to pry. Well, not too much anyway. "Dana said you started *Mismatched Mates*. What do you think?"

After explaining how I hadn't been able to sleep because I was so engrossed in the book, Lol laughed. "She has a load of books on Amazon. You should check them out. She is my idol, that is who I would love to emulate."

I arrange with Lol for me to read a passage from her book this Thursday at Open Mic Night. I am excited and hopeful that this sweet woman will start to get the recognition she deserves.

When walking back to the counter, I get an idea... I am going to email Melody Tyden and see if she would like to be our star contributor for our New Year's Eve Open Mic Night party. She is bound to pull a bit of a crowd and it will be a treat for the admirers of her work, too, including Lol.

However, I am distracted by the text message on my phone from Jonty:

The agency has located a pretty female matching the description you gave me. We can talk it over tonight. Love you, Bilbo x

Oh my, I have to clench my legs together. "I just need the bathroom," I shout to Dana as I take a couple of minutes to pull myself together. Our final 'gift' to one another is a threesome. At first, I thought I wanted a second man but the thought of another woman once again intruded into my thoughts. That first encounter with Jonty watching me as I was intimate with another woman and then the both of us pleasuring her together as one was so hot. That is what I am missing. I don't need another man. Not yet anyway. What I want is something different, and I have missed the female form, with its soft curves and womanly attributes.

The rest of the day will drag now that I cannot wait to be home with my husband.

~ Tim ~

My sweet and sexy flower has been so vulnerable this weekend, but that's okay. I am more than happy to reassure her and be here for her so she knows she can depend on me. She gave herself to me, and although I couldn't give her my virginity, she has completely stolen my heart. I love her. I am head over heels in love with her and everything she is. I want to marry her; I want her to be my wife and the mother of my children. She is my future, my destiny. My everything.

Once I managed to calm her, she slept in my arms, and it has become one of my favourite things. It takes a lot to trust someone enough to fall asleep next to them, and that tells me that Lauren doesn't trust herself as much as she trusts me. I am determined that eventually she will see herself through my eyes. I want her to know how absolutely incredible she is.

We have sex a few times over the weekend, and each time just gets better and better. I know she is self-conscious, and I don't know how to demonstrate to her that I love every part of her body, even the parts she doesn't like. I mean everything I say to her; I love her fuller figure, I love her round bum, and I love her massive boobs, too. I love every aspect of her fuller, curvy body, and I want her to love it, too.

I go back to work on Monday, but the boss is back, too, and so I can't be taking two hour lunches to meet up with my love. I am so distracted by my own love life, I don't notice anything different between Jamie and Mr. Matthews until Wednesday.

I look up from my desk and see Mr. Matthews wink at Jamie, and when my head snaps around to her, she is sharing a look with him, while a blush creeps up over her face, then she looks down and bites her lip. Something has definitely happened there. I took my eye off the ball for one minute and my best pal at work is hooking up with the boss.

Once Mr. Matthews returns to his office, I whisper to Jamie, "Did you two fuck?"

"TIM! Shhhhh... Geez, have you ever heard of being discreet?" She has got to be kidding me, they were practically eye fucking each other across the office. "We're seeing each other, yes, but we're trying to keep it quiet in the office. The last thing I want is people gossiping about us. I really, really like him, Tim."

Through my massive grin, I whisper, "My little sis is all grown up. You look so happy, Jay. You both do." It looks like the song is right. Love is all around. "I'm taking Lauren to meet my sister tonight; I'm nervous and excited. I just hope they all get along. I think she might be 'The One', Jay. I'm in love with her."

She hugs me and squeals. "Owen and I are going out to dinner tomorrow. We're going to the OXO. Promise to tell me all about it?" She holds out her little finger to me which I link and shake while I roll my eyes at her. "I can't wait to meet her, Tim."

We both look up as Mr. Matthews leaves the office. "Are you two going to get any work done today, eh?" he shouts back to us from over his shoulder. When the door closes behind him, we both burst out into laughter.

"The office party is on Friday, are you still going?" Jamie asks once we recover. I had thought about missing it but now I'm intrigued to see how these guys plan to keep this quiet once the liquor starts to flow. Office romances are usually made or finished at these parties. I'm hoping this is just the beginning for Jamie. I don't think I've ever seen her as happy as she is right now.

"Yeah, maybe I will bring Lauren with me so you can meet her."

Mr. Matthews doesn't return to the office. I notice that Jamie is fretting. "Didn't he have a meeting pencilled in?" I ask, trying to reassure her, but she shakes her head in reply.

Jamie's shoulders visibly relax when we get to the main lobby and he is waiting for her there. "Good night, Tim, Jamie. I will see you both bright and early tomorrow."

"Tim knows," Jamie admits. "I told him."

Mr. Matthews looks shocked at first and then grins. "Good. No more pretending in our little office then. Good night, Tim. And you - get in that car you're coming with me!" It's a side to Owen Matthews I have never seen. Who knew Mr. Serious could be... playful and fun?

As they drive away, I walk to meet Lauren at the tube. I can't wait for my family to officially meet her and for at least someone to see how happy and right we are together too.

~ Jonty ~

I arrive home from work as usual on Wednesday evening. We are taking the children Christmas shopping at Harrods tonight, and then to see Santa. My little Chloe is on the ceiling with excitement, and her enthusiasm warms the cockles of my heart. She reminds me so much of Billie. I sincerely didn't get a look in where our little girl is concerned, and I am thankful for that.

"Daddy, are we getting a Harrods Teddy Bear for mummy again?" The Harrods Teddy Bear is a well-known Christmas institution: for decades now, they have designed a new bear every Christmas with the year stitched into its foot.

When I met Billie, she had tons of them. At first I ignorantly thought it was childish; who had teddy bears at 22 years old, for Christ's sake? However, I then found out that they were bought for her by her mother, from the year Billie was born until the year before we met, just after her mother had died. She cherishes those bears because it was something she shared with her mother. The one from the year her mother died was missing and it broke her heart that she didn't have one. So, I went searching and finally tracked one down. That was the day she agreed to marry me. I turned up at her flat soaking wet with the bloody bear she was missing in the iconic green and gold Harrods bag, and through her tears of grief and gratitude, she thanked me and finally agreed to marry me.

Now, every year we have to get her the new bear. Her mother's story becomes entwined in ours and every year that I buy her a new bear, it reminds me of the lengths I would go to for my Billie.

Oscar doesn't take notice of these things, but Chloe does. She helped me buy last year's teddy bear, and now she has her own collection too.

"Yes, I'll need you to help me again." Her massive smile tells me how much she loves to be included in this tradition.

"What are you two whispering about? Come on, Glo-worm, you need to get your hat and gloves on." Billie catches us hatching our plan, but she knows all about our father-daughter task.

"Sorry, Bilbo, my fault, I was just asking our girl all about school." Chloe giggles as she runs to find her hat and gloves, giving the game away.

"Remember, Jonty, Oscar wants to see the virtual reality stuff, too. If you could take him when I take Chloe to pick out her dress, they shouldn't become too restless." Kissing her, I reassure her that I cannot wait to spend a bit of bonding time with my son. "Did you hear back from the agency?" she whispers to me after checking that no little ears are listening.

I nod to her. "Yeah, we are all set for Saturday. I have booked the hotel and arranged for the children to go and stay with my mother and father for the night." Her excitement is palpable, and the way she jumps and hugs me tight is all I need to confirm this is something we both really want and are both eagerly anticipating.

Everything has a rosy hue over it, like we are living life inside a kaleidoscope, and all because we no longer have to hold back that part of us. This release has been exactly what we needed as a couple, and I cannot wait to give my wife her final gift from this experiment.

~ Lauren ~

Tim introduces me to his sister and her family, and beforehand, I thought I would feel shy and out of place, but I instantly feel part of the family. The house is beautiful; clad in all its Christmas gear, it looks like something you would find in a film. The children are adorable, and as I watch Tim play football with his nephew, Lyndon, my heart flutters at the prospect of him doing that in the future with our own children.

Children have always been high on my agenda. I would love a small brood of my own; however, I was diagnosed with Polycystic Ovarian Syndrome a couple of years ago and although I was not declared infertile, the consultant basically explained that I would have a very hard time conceiving.

Tim's sister, Felicity, hugs me when he introduces me. She gently places her hands either side of my face. "Yes! You are exactly as I pictured you. Tim didn't exaggerate how beautiful you are. And yes, Tim, I see how cute the dimples are." My face flames with embarrassment, but her partner, Marie, laughs as she pulls her wife away from me.

"Fliss, give the girl some space. You're going to chase her off." She looks at me apologetically.

"Oh, Lauren, I'm so sorry! I am over excited to meet you because it's the first time I've seen my little brother in love." Marie rolls her eyes at her again and we all end up laughing.

Last night, I dyed my hair again; it's now a deep purple and little Celeste looks at it in awe. "Mummy, I want purple hair, too."

I quickly apologise to her mums, but they wave it off.

"Don't worry, as soon as Celeste is old enough, she can have whatever hair she wants. It's good for her to have positive role models and feel able to express herself."

I don't think I've ever been called a role model before, but a warm feeling, a sense of pride I suppose, fills me up inside at the thought of being a positive role model for this little girl.

I tell Celeste to go and get her hairbrush and bobbles and allow her to brush my hair and play with it. When she is finished I wouldn't look out of place in an 80's rock concert, but boy, does she look happy about her masterpiece.

Tim laughs when he comes back in with Lyndon. "Who did your hair, Flower?" he asks with a sparkle in his eye.

"I did, Uncle Tim; do you like it?" He lifts Celeste up to him as she chatters away, and he tells her how beautiful I look with my newly styled hair while winking at me.

Before we leave, Fliss calls Tim upstairs, and he looks upset when he returns. "Come on, Flower, let's get the tube back before it gets too late."

We are staying at Tim's flat tonight because it's closer to the tube station, and I will be going home and out to Open Mic Night tomorrow night.

"Are you okay, Tim? You seem distracted, and a bit upset. I thought everything went well." I hope I didn't do something to change their minds.They all seemed nice and welcoming, but I can't help noticing the sudden change in Tim's demeanour.

"It went better than well; it went perfectly. They all love you, and you just slot right in like you've always been a part of our family." I let it lie because I truly want to believe that I could slot right into his family. How perfect would that be?

As we get to the steps of Tim's building, there is a drunken man waiting at the entrance.

"Tim? Where the fuck have you been hiding, buddy? Any chance I could crash with you tonight?"

I recognise him. He's the one Eryn went home with the night I met Tim. I think his name is Jason.

"Sorry, not tonight, Jason. I'm busy." Tim tells him bluntly.

Jason looks between the two of us, squinting as he tries to focus. "What the fuck are you doing with the beach whale, Timmy?"

~ Owen ~

My world has just flipped on its axis. I need to talk to Jamie, but I don't want to upset her, and I certainly don't want to put a jinx on us. The timing is far from ideal, but that's something I have no control over.

I wait in the lobby for her, and she smiles luminously when she sees me. My heart pounds against my chest reminding me that *this* is what it means to feel alive.

We get into my car, a pretentious sports car I have as part of my employee benefits that Jamie is not even slightly impressed by. "I need to talk to you, babe." She nods at me; she already knows something is happening because I didn't return to the office.

"Okay, tell me. I can take it." She assures me as she flinches away; it is as though she expects this to physically hurt her, which it may well do.

"I have been offered a promotion," I tell her bluntly, and I can tell from her look of pride and happiness that she doesn't understand just yet. But she will.

"That's brilliant news, Owen! Whose job have you got? Can I move with you, or will I be getting a new boss?"

I stop at the traffic lights and look at her. "The new position isn't in our office."

It's finally starting to dawn on her what I am saying. "What office is it?"

"I haven't accepted it. I don't know if I am going to. What do you think?"

She won't look at me. "Where is it, Owen?" My heart beats faster; I know she'll insist that I take the job, but I don't want to take it if it means I can't be with her.

"New York. They offered me the big fish. A promotion, pay rise, benefits and relocation settlement."

The realisation washes over her and through her pain-filled expression, she smiles at me. "You would be a fool not to take it, Owen. You have worked so hard, and you deserve this. I am so proud of you. Will you take me home, please? I'm not feeling too good."

"Jamie... I haven't accepted it, not yet. I don't want to leave this. I don't want to lose us over a job." Any other day, the roads would be gridlocked but not today; I'm at her flat in Greenwich within ten minutes.

"We've only just started dating, Owen, and it isn't just a job. This is your career. I just need some time to think things over. I don't want to lose you over a job either. When will you give them your decision?"

"I have asked them to consider some additional benefits before I will agree. I made a few counteroffers. I know we've only just started dating, Jamie, but we are more than that. I'm in love with you, and I want to be with you. No job could ever be more important than that." I kiss her to bring home the truth of my words.

She looks up at me, her eyes brimming with unshed tears. "I want to be with you, too, but if this doesn't work, you would have thrown away your big opportunity for nothing. I am not going to be the reason you're unhappy, Owen. I just need time to think. I will see you tomorrow at work." She kisses me on the cheek before running to her door.

She takes my heart with her as she closes the front door on me. I have waited for her all this time, and now, the job of my dreams threatens to put a stop to it.

Jamie is so upset that I am starting to believe she is falling in love with me, too. I know she feels something, but how do I get her to admit that? Not just to me but to herself?

My counteroffer to the company is that I get to bring my PA with me, that she be offered the same relocation package. I don't want to tell her about that yet, not until they agree to that stipulation. The truth is, I am not sure she feels strongly enough for me to move to New York with me. We are still so new and fresh that this may be too early for her to consider.

There is always a long distance relationship to consider, I suppose, but I know that is practically dead in the water. I would only be able to come and see her once every couple of months and Jamie is terrified of flying on her own. What a fucking mess.

As I drive myself to my own home, I am overwhelmed with longing for her. This will be the first night we have spent apart since we got together in Copenhagen. If this is how I feel at the prospect of one night apart, then how the hell am I going to relocate to New York without her?

CHAPTER TWELVE

~ Tim ~

My fist connects with Jason's jaw before I even decide I am going to kill him. How fucking dare he? He is obviously shocked by my reaction because he doesn't defend himself and he now looks around in confusion as to how and why he is sprawled out on the pavement outside my apartment.

"What the fuck happened then?" he shouts indignantly.

"I fucking punched you, and I will punch you again, you slimy, no-good piece of shit if you ever, EVER speak about my girl like that again."

I can barely contain my rage right now; I am so fucking angry. But once I have told Jason exactly what I think of him, my thoughts immediately go to Lauren. She stands open-mouthed, looking like a shocked goldfish.

"Apologise to her right now, Jason, or I swear to God I will total you." Tears fall silently from her beautiful, emerald-green eyes, and I want to hurt Jason even more now.

"I don't want his apology. I want to go home, Tim. I want to go home. Alone. This isn't going to work. I don't belong in your world; you don't belong in mine. This was amazing, better than amazing, but can't you see the gulf between us is just too big? Thank you for the time of my life, Tim. I know you'll find the right woman who'll fit in with your world." She turns on her heel and walks away from me.

"Lauren, please, wait. I love you, and I want to be with you. You say I don't belong in your world and you don't belong in mine so let's build our own world. A world for you and me where we can be happy together. I don't give a fuck what the Jasons of the world think. You are the woman I love, the woman I want to spend the rest of my life with."

I get down on one knee and slip the ring box that my sister gave me earlier out of my pocket.

"I have never met anyone as incredible as you. I want to spend the rest of my life loving you and being loved by you. I want us to be a family and grow old together. There is no one else in this world I would want to face my triumphs and failures with. I will cherish you from today until my last day. Please, Lauren, my love. Will you marry me?"

This wasn't the proposal I had in mind. In fact, until my sister called me upstairs and gave me this ring, I was still trying to calculate how long it would take me to save for the ring Lauren deserves. Fliss told me my mother had made her promise on her deathbed that she would look after me and ensure I didn't settle for anyone but the woman who owned my heart. She left her ring for me to propose with. Both me and Fliss sobbed, remembering our mother and her dry humour and wise words. Fliss gave me the nod of approval. Lauren owns my heart; she is the one.

The tears continue to flow down Lauren's face. "If there was anyone I would have said yes to, it would have been you, Tim. But eventually, we have to come out of our own little world. This is the hardest thing I've ever had to do because I love you too. But I'm not the one. Everyone will tell you that we aren't meant to be, and I don't think I could ever survive you realising it, too." She wipes her tears as she backs away from me.

"Lauren, don't go. We can work this out," I shout after her.

"I don't want to, Tim. I'll see you around." She runs to a waiting taxi that sits waiting for a fare in a nearby rank, and I stand watching her leave with a hole where my heart once was.

"Fucking hell! That was intense. So, can I crash at yours now you don't have plans?"

I'd almost forgotten Jason was there, and I look at him in disgust.

"Go and fuck yourself, Jason." I open my door and slam it behind me, howling like a wounded animal. She's gone; my wonderful Flower is gone, and I am dead inside without her.

~ Jamie ~

As soon as I get into my apartment, I puke up. I honestly feel as sick as a dog when I relive what Owen just told me. New York. It's not just down the road; it's a whole continent away. Just the idea of the flight makes me break out in a cold sweat. I don't think I can do that flight on my own. I wish I could. I want to tell him, 'don't worry, I'll come and see you every weekend,' but the mere thought of the flight has me quivering.

On the other hand, the thought of Owen being so far away, of not seeing him every day and of not being in his arms and feeling his passionate stare drinking in my body completely crushes me.

I want to get drunk and fall asleep for a week, but that is a potential week I could spend with Owen before he leaves. My next instinct is to go to Billie for advice, but she isn't at home.

What am I going to do? I am really falling for him and now he is going to move to the other side of the world. He has been right there, right under my nose this whole time, and when I finally realise how right we are together, he's snatched away.

"Why is everything so complicated, Smokey? Why can't I be a dirty bitch like you and stick my ass up in the air for every Tom cat that comes along, no feeling and no strings. Life would be so much simpler." Smokey, my cat, meows and purrs at me, obviously in agreement.

I draw myself a bath and as I soak, I think of how happy I have been since Owen and I started seeing each other. He has been so loving and caring and attentive. He is an animal between the sheets... and outside of them, too. I smile to myself; I am having the best time and I am so sad that it might have to end.

I sit up abruptly, forcing water to slosh over the side of the bath as the realisation hits me: we still have time. Owen won't be leaving for at least another couple of weeks, so what the fuck am I doing in my flat wallowing and pining for him when I could be in his bed, in his arms and wrapped around him?

I quickly get out of the tub, get dried and dress before calling a cab. It's going to cost me a fortune but I don't care. I miss Owen, and I am going to miss him when he has to leave. But right now I want him, and if he wants me too, I am willing to enjoy what time we have left.

I feel less confident and sure of my decision the closer I get to his apartment, but I've come this far. Owen has put himself out there for me many times. Now, it is my turn to put myself out there for him.

I ring his buzzer and wait but there is no answer. I ring again, begging him to be home when the door swings open. Owen stands in front of me with a towel wrapped low on his hips, his hair slicked back and water droplets glistening his skin.

"Jamie?" he says in shock when he realises it's me.

"I'm so sorry I acted like such a dick. I was shell shocked. I don't want to miss a second I could have with you." Now that I'm here, I'm not as confident as I felt. I still mean what I am saying but the gumption I had before seems to desert me, leaving me vulnerable and exposed.

"How did you get here?" he asks me as he pulls me inside by the hand.

"In a taxi. I realised how stupid I was being. I missed you and you might be leaving in a couple of weeks. I want to make the most of the time we have left, and spending the night apart just seems ridiculous when I quite obviously want to be here".

Holding me close, he murmurs into me, "I missed you, too, but don't do that; it's dangerous getting taxis this late on your own. You could have been hurt or kidnapped. Call me and I will come and get you. Promise me now." I draw an X over my heart before he continues. "I don't want the fucking job. All I want is you."

"Yes, you do want the job, and that's okay. But for now, let's just forget about the job and moving away and all that shit. Let's just enjoy what we have right here, right now."

My heart soars as he kisses me; a deep, beautiful kiss that tells me a story. "Okay, we won't worry about the job and the move. Tonight, I want to make love to you, baby. We've fucked and screwed and its been amazing; however, now I want to connect with you emotionally."

Usually, when we are alone, we are frenzied, unable to wait or keep our hands off each other. Going slow seems to go against my natural inclination when I am with Owen, but my core throbs and floods at his words. I want him to make love to me, too. I want to make love with him.

As our bodies intertwine, my heart is soothed by the outward show of affection that Owen gives me. In a matter of days, he will be out of here for a new life in The Big Apple; however, for right now, especially tonight, he belongs to me, and I can allow myself to feel loved and cherished by the man of my dreams as we make love.

Will the memories be enough? I don't know if they will; I don't know if anything but the real thing will ever be enough, but it's better than no memories. At least I will have a small part of our time together kept safe in my heart, for me to bring out when the bleakness of life without Owen threatens to take over.

We make love into the early hours of the morning, and I fall asleep naked in his arms with a smile on my face and my body humming in satisfaction.

The alarm buzzing wakes me up, and when Owen starts to kiss down my neck, shivers of delight flow throughout my whole body.

"Last night was amazing, baby, same again tonight?" he whispers softly in between kisses. I shake my head at him.

"We have dinner reservations, remember? But once you've fed me and romanced me, I'm up for more of the same."

I can't wait to tell Tim all my gossip, but when we get into work, the receptionist passes a note to me that tells me Tim won't be in today because he's sick.

I make a note to call him at lunch so I can ensure he is okay. Tim has never taken a sick day. I wonder if Lauren has worn him out? I chuckle to myself at the thought of Tim finally meeting his match.

~ Billie ~

I am absolutely shattered today; it ended up being such a late night last night. When we got back home, Jonty showed me the photographs of the girls who were available for us on Saturday, which really turned me on. Jonty found it hilarious that he had to make me cum three times before I was finally satisfied. The girls available to us are so goddamn sexy that it's a hard job choosing just one. Finally, I decided I would be happy with any of the beautiful women on offer, so Jonty will have to choose for us.

It's like a yawn a second between me and Dana, and I am thinking of texting Jamie to tell her I'm sneaking up to her flat for a nap because tonight is Open Mic Night, and so this is set to be one hell of a day at the office.

The morning rush is just starting to die down when Lol walks in looking like a bagwash woman, or a walking clothes horse. She takes one look at me and bursts into fresh tears. Lol is usually so positive, so jolly and happy that I am having a hard time believing this is really her.

"Oh, Billie. I've fucked everything right up," she tells me through her sobs, so I take her through to the back room. I settle her in a comfy armchair, and Dana brings through hot drinks for us all.

"Come on, Lol, tell us what happened. I'm sure whatever it is, we can find a way to sort it out."

She starts to tell us the story right from the night she met a man at a club... and ending where his friend called her a beach whale, and after punching his friend, her fella got down on one knee and proposed.

I grab her hand to see the ring, but her hands are devoid of jewellery. "Don't tell me you turned him down?"

She nods as the tears stream freely down her face.

~ Jamie ~

Owen is called out of the office again, and after giving him a tight smile that I hope at least looks supportive, I throw caution to the wind and call Tim. I'm curious to see if he really is sick or just enjoying extra time in bed with Lauren. I'm also going to tell him about Owen's job offer and ask his advice on what to do.

After three rings, I am about to give up when Tim finally answers. "What?" he spits out through his teeth.

"Tim? Are you okay?"

"No. No, I'm not, Jamie. I could really do with a friend right now. Any chance you could take your flexiday this afternoon so you can give me some advice, please?"

I explain to him that he will have to come to my flat because Owen is taking me to dinner this evening which he says is fine. Owen still hasn't come back when lunch time approaches, so I leave a formal note explaining I am taking my flexiday and then I send a cheeky text to fill in the blanks.

Tim is waiting on my front doorstep when I get there; he hasn't shaved or brushed his hair. I am being conservative here, but he sincerely looks like a bag of boiled shite.

"What the fuck happened, Tim?" I ask him but I quickly regret my harsh tone. I have never seen Tim this way, especially not over a girl. "Come on, mate, let's get you a warm drink and a shoulder to cry on."

I take him up to my flat where Smokey is sprawled on the windowsill taking time to soak up the last of the December sunshine. After making a pot of tea and plating up some biscuits, we settle in my lounge and I sit attentively.

"I took Lauren to meet my sister last night; everything went brilliantly. My sister even gave me this." He throws a little black box in my direction, and when I open it, my mouth falls open. Inside is a beautifully detailed diamond ring. An *engagement* ring. "Yes, it's an engagement ring; one that my mother left to me before she died with the instruction that I be told about it when I have found the one."

I'm not sure of the direction of this story but up to now this all seems very romantic and sweet. Why does he appear to believe that the world is ending?

"It was all going so great. I know she was a bit on edge because when Fliss told me the story behind the ring I got upset and she didn't know why. So she asked me a couple of times if I was okay. But in all honesty, that's Lauren's ring, and I was worried she wouldn't accept it."

Dread fills me; my heart is breaking for my friend. She actually turned him down? Poor Tim, putting himself out there like that, with his mother's ring, too, and she shot him down. I would have been devastated last night if Owen had turned me away. Taking Tim's hand in mine, I try to offer him some comfort, and when he places his head on my shoulder, I know he is feeling soothed by me just listening and being here.

"I wanted her to at least know how I feel about her and what I see in the future for us. I had it all planned out in my mind; I was going to put candles out and play the soft music she likes, and I was going to tell her how much I adore her, how I had started truly living the moment I met her; that I wanted her in my life for always."

His voice has taken an edge and his tears fall on my shoulder, the wetness seeping through to my skin.

"And then the shit hit the fan big style. That knobhead Jason was sitting outside my flat, absolutely plastered, wanting somewhere to crash for the night, and when he saw me with Lauren he called her a beached whale, and everything we had built together, the trust she had put in me, just shattered into a million pieces, Jamie. I have never seen someone look so hurt. Those words from him destroyed her and nothing I said or did could change it." I hug him tight as I cry with him, too. This hasn't only destroyed Lauren, this has destroyed Tim, too; her pain was now his because he loved her. A love that is precious, pure and true.

"Oh, Tim. I'm so, so sorry. Do you think she'll change her mind about being with you once she calms down and realises that's not how you see her?" I ask hopefully, but Tim shakes his head at me.

"She is strong, Jay, really strong, determined and stubborn. The thoughts she has about herself are pretty hardcore and toxic. I don't think anyone has ever had a kind word to say to her. She's a bigger woman, but to me she is perfect; she is everything. She is mine, and I want her and will always want her, but she just can't see that. She says she'll never be enough but the fact that I can't make her believe how much I want her and love her shows I'm the one who isn't enough."

Tim is a stand-up guy; he is a brilliant friend and a true gentleman. He is funny and kind and has been a rock to me these past few months when my own confidence was rocked. He calls me his little sister, and I am blessed to regard him as my big brother.

Now, my big brother needs help, and I know just the woman to help us. I call my sister; she should be at work downstairs but Christmas is a busy time for her so I just want to check if it's okay to bring Tim down for a chat and advice session first.

"Of course, bring him down. I am actually sitting with Lol at the moment; she has had her heart broken too and I could do with some reinforcements right now. We are in the back room, come straight in."

We take the back steps into the café. Billie is always telling me off for not using the front door, but it's cold out; I don't see the point in walking all the way around when I can just slip through.

I can hear Lol crying as we approach. I have met her a load of times from helping Billie at weekends and of course Open Mic Night and she has always seemed quiet and assured; it's strange to hear her crying.

As we walk through the door, Tim stops, causing me to knock into him. "Lauren? What are you doing here?"

Lol's cries stop as she looks back in shock. "Tim? How did you know where to find me?"

"Do you two know each other?" my sister asks as she rises from her seat. And then it clicks... Tim calls her Lauren but to us she is Lol Outloud; she did tell us it was her pen name, but I'd never actually asked her what her real name was. She was Lol and she suited it.

"Lol... you're Lauren? Tim's Lauren?" I ask her, and she nods her head to me while closing her eyes to allow her tears to freely fall.

"He's the man you're in love with? The one you stupidly turned down last night?" my sister questions Lol, and she cries harder as she nods again. "Well, I think this is fate giving you a sign, Lol. Take the opportunity or live with the regret, sweetie. He's absolutely crazy about you. Allow yourself to be loved and to be happy. You are the sweetest girl I know. This is your time now."

Lol wipes her face and turns to stand facing Tim. "I'm scared of not being enough and I dread that one day you'll regret choosing me."

Tim steps towards her. "I told you once and I'll tell you again; I'll tell you every fucking day if I have to, Lauren. You are more than enough; you are everything I have ever wanted. You're all I have ever dreamed of. I love you. I love every single part of you. And if you walk away now, I will have to accept it, but I will always love you and fancy you, whether you agree to be mine or not."

Oh my God, Tim is so sweet! I can feel the unconditional and irrevocable love he has for Lol; I hope she can feel it, too. It would be a crying shame if these two amazing people couldn't find a way to be together.

"I am yours, Tim. I love you, too. I am sorry for running away, but this is scary. I don't know if my doubts about myself will ever go away, and I don't want to hurt you with my pain and insecurities."

"Lauren, can you trust me? Can you trust me as a grown man in love with you to do the right thing? To support you and love you and to know my own mind?" Lauren nods back to Tim. "Then marry me. I love you, insecurities and all. I will remind you when those feelings and thoughts get too much, that no matter what, you are beautiful, kind and most importantly you are enough."

I pass Tim the ring box back, and he gets back down on one knee.

"This isn't how I imagined asking you to marry me. I want to give you the world. Lauren, I love you with all my heart, please say yes."

There is a short silence before Lauren quickly nods, crying again but this time there is joy mingled with her pain. "Yes, I will marry you."

There is a collective cheer not just inside the back room but within the whole of Tables & Fables; naturally, everyone had been listening in.

I offer them both my warmest congratulations before excusing myself. Owen will be picking me up soon and I want to look exquisite for him, which is no small task. Something Billie said has my mind ticking overtime about my own future. About my own happiness.

Can I be brave enough to ask for what I want and need in the future?

~ Owen ~

I finally get out of the meeting with the CEO and Human Resources, and I am completely pissed. No matter how much I negotiate, the one thing I want more than anything is denied.

I want the firm to relocate Jamie with me, but they are not biting. I get it; I sincerely get that there is no financial sense in relocating my PA; they would simply fix me up with a new one once I settle into the New York office. But I don't want another one. I want Jamie; I will always yearn for her. So if they want me, she has to be part of the deal.

I reject their job offer, and the stupid bastards offer me another twenty percent pay rise on top of the increased salary the new role commands. What good is all this money if I don't get to be with the woman of my dreams? It simply isn't worth the sacrifice I will have to make. No amount of money is worth leaving Jamie behind.

The irony of the whole situation isn't lost on me. I prayed that Jamie would be mine and now she is. I also worked hard to secure promotions in my career that would see me able to settle with a family by my mid-thirties. And yet, one is going to come with the sacrifice of the other.

They can take my career. I am not giving up Jamie. I have waited and waited for her to be ready and there isn't a chance in hell I will put an expiry date on the beautiful union that is growing between us.

"I am sorry, Mr. Cosgrove. No deal. I am not going without her. If you want me that desperately in New York, you will do whatever you can to give me what I want. I don't want more money; well, not for me. Arrange it so Jamie has a position as my PA and I will relocate in the new year. If not, you will have to find someone else."

When I get back to the office I hope for an hour alone with Jamie. I have been fantasising about fucking her over my desk, and with Tim absent, this is the best opportunity we will get.

Disappointment washes over me when I read her letter telling me she is taking her flexiday, but I am quickly laughing when I read her text messages which detail exactly how she is going to be spending her time. She even sent an explicit one that graphically described how she is going to shave her pussy for me.

I am standing to attention, making a massive tent in my work pants, and my date with Jamie is still a good few hours away. I envisioned surprising her with news of her new job offer and I had imagined us celebrating back at my apartment with champagne and nakedness, but I guess that was too ambitious of me.

After a quick shower, I begin to get ready. Tonight, we will both be dressed up because that is the dress code. Jamie and I are going to the OXO Tower restaurant. The OXO Tower is a prominent building near the Thames, and the views from the restaurant are said to be second to none. With all the lights on for Christmas it should be pretty spectacular, and I know Jamie will love it. London will look amazing tonight when the sun sets and the city comes to life.

It is the ideal place to have a date because of its position in the South Bank cultural sector of London. If we want, we could walk around Trafalgar Square or go on the London Eye. However, there is no reason to go anywhere but the Tower itself. It is also home to arts and crafts and the first couple of floors are bursting with prestigious vendors selling their unique creations; from paintings to sculptures to vintage clothing and jewellery, there is an array of beautiful makes to be seen and bought. There is also an award-winning gallery we could wander around if we have the inclination.

The restaurant is a Michelin star eatery, and it's somewhere I have wanted to go for a long time, but this is special. I didn't want to go there with just anyone. I am excited to be sharing this with Jamie. I just wish I wasn't in such a crappy mood about work. I can't seem to shake it and it's annoying me that I have looked forward to this night with Jamie, and now my shitty mood could ruin it.

I decide to drive tonight; the wine selection is said to be amazing but I know if I have a drink, my mood is likely to sour even more, so I'm sticking to soft drinks.

I pull up outside Jamie's apartment and I'm surprised to see her sister's café is bursting with customers. It's never open this late usually. I don't see Jamie approach me, but when she calls out to me, my mood instantly lightens. "Oh, baby! You look amazing! Let's skip dinner and go upstairs, eh?" Her face lights up when she laughs at my compliment.

"Sod off, Owen. I'm starving, and you promised to feed me first." I can't help but be happy when I am with Jamie, so I try to push all work related matters from my mind and enjoy my date with my girl. "Besides, I didn't go to all this trouble for you to just take it all off me."

She twirls in front of me, giving me a full view of her dress, which scoops low on her back; any lower and I would see the crease of her ass. Her hair is starting to grow out now, too, and she has styled it so it falls in waves around her shoulders. I loved her long blonde hair but when she broke up with her ex she cut it all off into a short smart bob, which looked nice too. I am hoping I will get to see those long blonde tresses again. I kiss her possessively. "I am so proud to have you on my arm tonight, Jamie. You are stunning, my love."

I drive us to Coin Street, where the OXO building is located, and Jamie tells me about the drama that happened with Tim this afternoon. "So, he's getting married? Wow, that's kind of fast, isn't it." I'm quick enough to notice the crestfallen look on Jamie's face. I could kick myself for being so callous, but marriage is a big deal to me. I only want to do it once, so I want to get it right. The thought of rushing into something makes me break out into a cold sweat.

She replies with a tight smile, the one she uses when she doesn't want to upset people, and I do my best to make it better.

"I'm happy for him. We'll invite them to dinner next week to celebrate, eh, if you like?" That raises a proper smile from her.

"Like a double date? That would be great, Owen."

When we arrive at the building, I open the car door for Jamie and take her hand. I want to be close to her; I want everyone to know we are together and she is mine. She is luminous; she shines like a beacon of hope and happiness, and I am completely besotted with her. Every time I see her, my feelings grow deeper and deeper. If Tim feels a fraction of how I feel, it's no wonder he put a ring on his girl.

We take the elevator to the eighth floor and are shown to our table; it's a window view and Jamie gasps when she looks out at the London skyline that lights up with festive cheer. We order our starters and talk away about places we've been and places we want to see when the maître d' brings over another couple to sit at the table beside us.

Jamie groans with dread and displeasure, so I peer around to find the source of her dismay. A loud, whiney voice grates down on my nerves. "But I wanted the window seat, Carl! Why didn't you book a window seat?"

I can't fucking believe it. Jamie's ex is here and they are going to be eating at the table next to ours.

EMMA LEE-JOHNSON

CHAPTER THIRTEEN

~ Jamie ~

Owen is acting weird. I can tell something is wrong and he is putting a happy face on for me. I really want to enjoy tonight but something feels off.

He has been the perfect gentleman, even down to opening doors and pulling out my chair. He is everything I could ever want and need, but my stomach continues to swirl in apparent nerves.

I should learn to trust my gut instinct. I finally start to relax into our date when a voice I have heard before, in a circumstance I have tried my hardest to forget, assaults my ear drums.

"Jamie. What are you doing here? Are you two on a date?"

My ex-boyfriend, Carl. Geez, how did I ever find him attractive? He looms over his table at me, looking like a prize prat with a bloody cravat tucked under his shirt collar. His eyes are filled with a simmering anger and his cheeks turn red.

"Yes, we're here on a date." Owen stands and shakes his hand and introduces himself to Francesca, Carl's soon-to-be wife. I stand

and greet them, wanting the ground to open and swallow me whole. Why, universe? Why me?

Francesca greets me like a long-lost friend, hugging me and kissing both my cheeks. "Darling, you look lovely, so much better now that you're over the shock." She starts to laugh at her poke at jest. I don't find it funny.

"How lovely to see you, Francesca. I almost didn't recognise you with your clothes on." It's a cheap shot, but let's not forget, she was the one who was screwing my boyfriend, in my bed, behind my back.

"JAMIE!" Carl gives me a warning stare as he states my name, and when the back of Owen's neck turns red, I know this is riling him.

"It was… nice… seeing you, but we'll let you get back to your date now." I thank the lord that Owen is such a diplomat; however, Carl and Francesca are not taking hints. They ask the waiter to pull the tables closer, and I nod in agreement when Owen mutters under his breath… "For fuck's sake."

"I always knew there was something going on between you two." It's not so much a statement but more an accusation from Carl. There is a petty part of me that would love to get one over on him and say, 'Yes, we were also screwing behind your back,' but it simply isn't true.

"Actually, Jamie and I only recently started dating," Owen replies, and I place my hand on his and give it a gentle squeeze of support.

"She never wanted to come to places like this when we dated. She never wanted to do anything when we dated," Carl sulks, and I want to punch him right in the face. How dare he blame this all on me? It wasn't as if he had put any effort into dates and stuff.

"I suppose coming here on a date with you and your friends just wasn't appealing. But hey, you're here now with your fiancée so it doesn't matter any more, does it?"

Francesca clicks her fingers at the waiter and orders an expensive bottle of wine. She's going to need a couple of them if this night continues this way.

Whenever we try to break off into our own chat, Carl ruins it by trying to draw us back into a conversation. I had been looking forward to coming to the OXO with Owen but now I can't wait to leave. This whole situation leaves me feeling awkward and out of place, and the feeling just continues to grow.

"Are you seriously telling me nothing happened between you two until a few weeks ago?" Carl continues to press the issue, and I know Owen is starting to lose his composure. I don't blame him, but I don't like the turn this is taking. This isn't a pissing contest. I am no one's prize.

Francesca orders another bottle of wine. And as she gets drunker and drunker, the accusations start to fly my way. "I mean, the backlash Carl and I faced because of you, Jamie, was just ridiculous; we can't help it that we fell in love. We had to invite you to the wedding because Ted and Gerry are business partners, but I found it crass that you accepted with a plus one. Carl is in love with me now, so your little parade won't make him jealous."

"I am here on a date with my boyfriend. I couldn't give two hoots about you or Carl or what your opinion of my relationship status is. I left him, remember?"

The maître d' comes over to warn us that we will be asked to leave if we continue to raise our voices. Carl makes another snide remark, and Owen comes over all caveman about how I am his girl now.

I excuse myself to use the bathroom, but it's just a cover. I walk right out the door instead. I flag down a taxi and return to my flat. This has been one of the worst dates I have ever been on. I pull on my new pyjamas, the ones I got to match the slip I left at Owen's. When my phone rings, I answer, and it's Owen.

"You walked out and left me here? What the fuck, Jamie? Your ex and his new tart are arguing away, and I got left sitting like an idiot on my own."

"Don't you dare shout at me. You made me feel like a fucking possession, the booby prize for winning the pissing contest with Carl... What the fuck was that all about?"

"I know. I'm sorry, he really got on my nerves, and I was already in a mood. You didn't have to bail on me though, Jamie. Just talk to me."

I'm too angry to talk to him right now. I knew there was something wrong, but I am not having him thinking he can act all macho man because my ex-boyfriend makes him feel insecure.

"I need some space. Just leave me alone, Owen." I cut him off and then burst into tears. What a mess. I had been looking forward to spending time with Owen and this is what happened. We are wasting so much of the little time we have left together that it breaks my heart.

I realise I am being harsh on Owen. He isn't responsible for how Carl treated me, or how inadequate I feel around Francesca. After I finish crying and have calmed down, I call Owen back, and then my doorbell rings. I place my phone on the kitchen island while I answer the door, hoping it's Owen so we can make up properly. But when I open the door, I get the shock of my life.

"Carl? What are you doing here?"

His knuckles are bleeding, so I quickly bring him in and wash his hands and try to patch him up. "This is a nice place you have here. How long have you been dating him really, Jamie? I knew there was something between you; I could sense it. The way you would talk about him all the time and the way he would constantly look at you while throwing daggers at me."

"It's none of your business, Carl, but we really only started dating recently. Did you honestly believe something was happening between us back then?"

"I did and I didn't. I used to say to myself you talk about Tim a lot, too. But when you would whisper his name in your sleep, I knew you had some feelings for him. You never talked about Tim in your sleep, only 'Mr. Matthews'. You talk a lot in your sleep, Jay. I asked you once if you loved me when you were asleep, and you said no. I started seeing other women after that."

I knew about Francesca because I had walked in on them. I didn't know about the other women. I thought it would hurt to hear his confession, but it doesn't. If anything, I feel relieved.

"Where is Francesca now?"

"We had a fight; she says I still love you. But how can I love you when all I really want is to hurt you, Jamie, because you didn't love me back? I punched the door, and she ran off and told me to sort myself out, so I am here to sort this out once and for all. Do you love me?"

"No, Carl. I don't. I'm sorry. I don't love you. I don't even miss you. You love Francesca; you're just having wedding nerves, that's all. I hate that you both humiliated me, but I am happy for you. I'm glad you get to be with someone who can love you back just like you wanted. But I don't think I have been in love with you for a long time, Carl."

"You love him, don't you? Owen, or Mr. Matthews, whatever you want to call him. You're in love with him; I can tell."

Am I? It comes as a shock. I know I have feelings for him, but I hadn't put a name to them yet. And with him moving to New York soon, I didn't really want to put a label to it. Owen has told me and shown me he loves me countless times, but I hadn't been quite there.

Until now.

"Yes. I love him. God, I love him!" I am overwhelmed with the surprise of realising I love Owen. I don't care if he must leave; it doesn't change how I feel about him. I'm in love with him.

"Well, don't you think you should put the poor fella out of his misery and tell him? He looked distraught at the OXO. I think he loves you too, Jamie; I think he's loved you for a long time. I'm happy for you, too. I'm sorry about tonight, and I am sorry for how I acted and for everything. I'm going to go and make up with Francesca. I'll see you and Owen at my wedding, I hope?"

I make a non-committal noise as I open my front door. Carl and I embrace and part, maybe not as friends but no longer enemies. My heart drops when I look out and see Owen leaning against his car.

"This isn't what it looks like, Owen. I promise you this isn't..." I don't get to finish my sentence because he pushes me inside my flat.

"I know. I heard everything." He points to his phone, and I realise my call must have connected; he has heard the whole conversation. "You love me?" he asks me sternly.

My tummy turns and my heart beats faster and faster; I have never been so scared or vulnerable. I have said these words before and not meant them or understood properly what they meant. It is only now, loving Owen and knowing how it feels, that I realise nothing else compares. Yes, I love him; I am insanely in love with him. I nod my head and look up at him to gauge his response.

"Say it, I need the words, Jamie."

My mouth is as dry as the Sahara Desert and my tongue is stuck to the roof of my mouth. I take a deep breath and say the words my heart and head know. "I love you, Owen Matthews. I am so in love with you." My eyes well up and my voice breaks, and he stands looking back at me for a small eternity.

"I love you, too. I have wanted to hear those words for the longest time. I didn't think we'd get there, especially after tonight." He kisses me gently, and I melt into him, wrapping my arms around his neck. "I want to ask you something. I feel I can ask you now that I know you feel the same way about me as I do about you. I want you to move to New York with me. Will you come with me?"

~ Billie ~

Open Mic Night is always raucous, but as we approach Christmas, I am starting to consider setting up a booking system because it's becoming jam-packed. Dana asks me to consider opening both Friday and Saturday for Open Mic, but I tell her I will need to look at employing a manager to oversee it; I am already beginning to feel overstretched.

"What about me? I would love the opportunity to start taking Tables & Fables to the next level. I am talking about writing sessions and workshops, graphics and marketing classes, art workshops, music sessions." Dana is really excited, and I am too.

"You've got some great ideas, Dana. How about in the new year we sit down and discuss this more? In the meantime, write me a business proposal." She smiles back at me and salutes.

I go to greet Lol and Tim, who have been home to 'freshen up'. Yes, apparently that's what we are calling it now! Lol gives me the passage she wants me to read, and Tim asks why she won't do it herself. "No, Tim, I'm too shy. I'm nervous enough for everyone hearing my words; I can't say them, too." As I watch him kiss her on the head, I am thankful to him for making my friend happy; there truly is a perfect someone for everyone.

"Next time, you should read it yourself. I will get up there with you if you want. I could bring my guitar and perform, too," Tim tells his new fiancée.

It is lovely to see Lol so happy. I hang the mistletoe over their heads, snap a couple of photos of them kissing and post it to the Tables & Fables social media account.

When I get up and read Lol's passage, the crowd is deafeningly quiet and at the end, the applause brings the house down. Tim whispers in her ear and gives me the wink. So I introduce her to the crowd and tell them to come back at New Year for an exclusive with Lol Outloud. When Lol stands, the crowd applauds again, and afterwards, she completely runs out of paperback copies of her new book, all of which have happy owners who requested they be signed by her, too. It is just the confidence boost she needs.

I take a long weekend off, leaving Dana in charge, and on Friday I finally finish my Christmas wrapping and book in at the salon for some special grooming and treatments. I am on pins with excitement.

When the children come home, I order takeaway for us all,

and we get into our matching Christmas pyjamas and watch *Christmas Chronicle* and *The Polar Express.* Then the children write their letters to Santa. As I help my little Chloe, I realise how lucky I am. I have a beautiful family, a wonderful, open-minded, handsome husband, brilliant children, a gorgeous and kind sister, a thriving business with friends and colleagues I can count on, and a chance to embrace my kink and be myself with the love of my life. Life can't get any better.

Jonty takes the children to his parent's house in Kensington on Saturday morning. Oscar scowls at us but once he gets there he'll be fine. Jonty promises that he'll take him to watch the football over the Christmas break if he behaves himself. My little Glow-worm waits excitedly by the front door with her Hello Kitty pull along suitcase. She is taking her play make-up with her to make grandma look pretty; that should be a laugh.

While they are gone, I pack for Jonty and me. The place we are staying is an exclusive hotel and spa in the grounds of a protected area of natural outstanding beauty. Jonty has rented a villa, which is detached from the main hotel and has its own private grounds. There, we also have our own exclusive hot tub and a tiki bar.

When Jonty returns, he asks if I am ready. I excitedly take his hand as we get into the rental car. It should take us a couple of hours' drive, and I have packed us some lunch for on the way. As the radio blasts out Christmas tunes, I feed Jonty, and I cannot help a little bit of fun on the way. I sing along with Chris Rhea, Mariah and Slade and suggestively slide my hand up Jonty's thigh. When he doesn't take the bait, I stroke myself instead. He can never resist that.

"Stop distracting me, you horny little bitch. We'll never get there, and I'll be fit for nothing." He chastises me as we laugh together.

The villa is as beautiful as described, and I quickly unpack our stuff and set our scenes for later. Jonty told me he has a present for me but I have to be patient.

After showering and changing into a red baby doll with a white fur trim, fishnet stockings and stilettos, I join Jonty in the lounge where he has champagne on ice as well as a selection of soft drinks and beer, toys, snacks and other paraphernalia we might need. Jonty stays in his casual trousers and shirt that he has undone at the collar. He's showered and looks like a dashing silver fox; I seem to fancy him more and more lately.

"Bilbo, you look so sexy, come here. I've got something to show you." He pulls out a small box that I recognise as Viagra. "Did you know you can get these over the counter now? As you can tell I have no problem getting it up, especially when my gorgeous wife is dressed up like a hot slut, but this should give me some staying power." I kiss him in thanks but step back quickly.

"Down boy, you don't want to be going off before our guest arrives." The agency we are using is the same one we used years ago. The people are vetted and tested and compensated generously for their time. This was the only way I could have sex with a stranger; I wouldn't risk it any other way. I could have asked someone to join us last week when we went dogging but they could be anyone, with anything. That is a hard limit for me.

I check my watch; it's almost 7 p.m. And that's when the doorbell rings.

It's time!

~ Jonty ~

It's time to surprise Billie, so I ask her to stand while I fasten a blindfold around her head to prevent her from seeing what I am up to. Her excitement in anticipation for her gift from me is clear, as her arousal builds up, she has to tense her thighs together. Someone will have to relieve her soon. She's already worked up. I slip my hand between her legs and skim her sweetness, licking her nectar from my fingers. "Hmm, you taste so good. I can't wait for my main course now, Bilbo. You're such a naughty girl, but I like naughty girls. And naughty girls get prizes... Are you ready for your prize, Billie? Are you ready to see what I have arranged for you?"

"Yes, sir. I want to see what you've got me." She remembers to call me sir; my cock twitches when she does, clearly liking being dominant and in charge.

"Good girl. Sit here and wait, and if you do as I ask, there is going to be a prize for you. All for you, my sweet girl."

Her nipples stand erect as I move away from her. I desperately want to suck them, but I will have to wait. I have to organise the scene I have planned just for her.

I open the front door and, as arranged, the three girls Billie and I couldn't decide between all stand there. My present to Billie is that she can try all three. They are booked for the entire night, and I hope Billie likes what I have in mind. I asked them to dress as Charlie's Angels and they did not disappoint. I will be taking on the role of the elusive Charles Townsend, and they make up my harem, whose main mission is to please my favourite. Whatever my favourite wants, my Angels want to provide; we are at her will and mercy. We will do anything to make her happy and most of all satisfied.

I sit next to Billie and whisper in her ear, "My name is Charles Townsend; you can call me Charlie. My main mission tonight is to fulfil your every fantasy. Would you like to meet my Angels? They want to give you a night to remember." The girls stand in the usual formation, shaping their hands into guns and kissing or licking them.

"Yes, I want to meet your Angels... How many are there?" she asks. She is already panting and clenching.

I untie the blindfold. "Why don't you open your eyes and see for yourself? Merry Christmas, baby. I hope you enjoy your gift." She opens her eyes and groans as I make the introductions. "Billie, this is Jill, Kelly and Sabrina; they are my Angels. They are yours to command."

Jill is tall with long legs and red hair. Her enhanced boobs are straining against the pvc dress she is wearing. She has a gift bow attached to the strap of her dress.

Kelly is medium height, dark straight hair and super curvy. She isn't quite plus sized; it was so hard to find a plus sized woman, but she has healthy, ample curves and plenty to grab on to. She has her gift bow tied around her waist.

Sabrina is also tall with dark, glowing skin, a short dark afro and beautiful dark brown eyes. She has small boobs but her ass is big, high and round. Both Billie and I had been in awe of her beautiful derriere. Her gift bow sits like a bunny tail just above her ass.

Billie bites her bottom lip and leans forward. "You did this for me?" she asks me. Her voice doesn't give any indication of what she is thinking, but I know my wife: if she was angry, she would have stormed out of here already.

"All for you, my Queen. As you are my favourite, it is the Angels' job to cater to your every whim. What would you like them to do?"

As excitement flares in her eyes, my cock throbs. "Thank you, Charlie. Could you tell your Angels I would like them to perform a floor show while you go down on me? I need to cum; I can't think straight. Limits are... don't kiss my husband on the mouth, please. And it's such a pleasure to meet you all. I think we are going to have a lot of fun tonight."

The girls hearing Billie's request quickly go to work kissing and undressing each other; they are clearly comfortable with girl on girl action and it's a big turn on watching Billie get turned on watching them perform. "Please, Charlie, just make me cum quickly, and then I'll be able to relax and enjoy this. I am over excited at the thought of three girls all for me."

I rip her panties from her and lick her pussy while she sits on the edge of her seat. She grabs a fistful of the hair at the top of my head and pushes my head between her legs, forcing more pressure on her clit and controlling the speed of my movements. I glance up at her and smile in satisfaction. Her eyes are fixed on the other girls and their show. She whimpers and moans, which I know means she is close to fulfilment. I cannot wait to watch my girl get her freak on with my Angels, so I motorboat her pussy. She screams out in ecstasy as she cums in my mouth. As she throws her head back, I continue to lap at her bundle of nerves.

"I want to have a go now, Jonty. Who should I lick out?"

"Angels, line up for my favourite," I instruct the girls, and, as agreed, they all chorus: 'Yes, Charlie'.

"I would like the one with the big tits, Charlie. Tell her to put the heels back on." The girl does as she is instructed, and Billie takes her time exploring her curvy body. "Hello, beautiful, you have an incredible body. Would you like to have some fun?"

Kelly kisses down my wife's body. "I can't wait to have some fun with you... What would you like me to do?"

Billie whispers in her ear, and Kelly smiles and nods as she lies down on the rug.

As my wife kisses the other woman's body, tugging on her nipple and fingering her, I instruct the other two girls to imitate her, copy what she does. I sit and watch all four women pleasuring each other while I rub myself; my cock is rock-hard solid, and I haven't even taken a Viagra yet.

This night is going to be wild.

~ Billie ~

Kelly is roughly the same height as me, but she is super curvy and sexy as fuck. I pull her towards me using her gold gift bow and tell her I would like to lick her pussy until she cums.

"Oh yes, absolutely, Ms. Favourite. I would love that." I love my husband and his body, but I absolutely adore the female form. I love inflicting pleasure on beautiful women, with their soft voluptuous curves, round boobs and tight asses. Then the jewel in the crown... the delight between their legs. I love pussy. I love the difference between each one and yet they all function pretty much the same.

As I kiss down Kelly's body, I stop at her peaked nipples, nibbling them and twisting them with my fingertips. Kelly moans as I do. I slide my hand over her wide hips and down between her legs. She is well groomed with a neat and tidy wax job not dissimilar to my own.

Sabrina is wild. She whispers to me, "Do you like a bit of bum fun, Ms. Favourite? It's my speciality." I tell her to go for it. Jonty instructs Jill to pleasure Sabrina from behind and then Kelly to finish off our daisy chain with Jill sitting on her face. With Jonty sitting up and us being on the floor, he can see everything.

I take all of Jonty's shaft into my mouth, and his cock bounces off the back of my throat. I will never tire of sucking off my husband. This was my signature move to get what I wanted. I know Jonty really enjoys the feel of my mouth and tongue as it wraps around him, and even to this day, cumming in my mouth remains his favoured place.

Simultaneously, Sabrina laps at me. My nerve endings buzz with arousal, and when she rubs my clit with her finger instead of her tongue, I shudder with pleasure as she licks all the way up to my back passage. "Hmm, Ms. Favourite does like a bit of bum fun," she announces as she rims me. I moan into Jonty's cock as my orgasm brews and blows from nowhere.

"That's my girl. Go on, Bill, cum for me while Sabrina licks your ass." Maybe it's the taboo of it, or it's the millions of nerve endings in that area. Or maybe this has been my fantasy for so long that the best orgasm of my life was inevitable.

Jonty calls for a break while I clean up and recover. He doesn't want to cum yet. He insists that the night is young and we have lots more fun to come. I load up with snacks and tell our guests to help themselves. Jonty brings me a large glass of diet coke with ice.

We sit around together in the kitchen on stools and chairs. Our characters are forgotten for this short time, and it feels wonderful and relaxing talking to these three beautiful and intelligent women. My husband kisses me and holds me to him, and I don't know where I would ever be without my Jonty. This is a shared experience with him, but I could never do this without him. I wouldn't want to.

We return to the lounge area, and I wonder what else Jonty has planned for us. When he slips back into his character, so do the Angels, and I am therefore Ms. Favourite once again. I think of inviting Jonty to have some fun with me and Jill when the doorbell rings again.

No one knows we are here, so who could it be? My heart starts pounding and I look to Jonty for what to do. However, he stands up confidently, still in character. "I hope this isn't our nemesis and all-round bad guy, Thin Man," Jonty shouts theatrically. He smiles at me and winks as he goes to the door. My man always has the ability to thrill and surprise me.

A deep voice travels through to the lounge. "We meet again, Charlie. I am here to destroy you and your Angels." A tall handsome man in his late twenties walks into the lounge wearing the iconic pin stripe suit and slicked back hair. He takes in the scene. "But wait, who is this? Another Angel? She looks like one, so beautiful and yet dressed like a whore. What's your name, sweetheart?"

"Stay away from her; she's Charlie's Favourite; she's our favourite." Thin man laughs manically while rubbing his chin as the Angels try to protect me from the evil villain.

"At last, I have found your Achilles heel, Charlie! I have a proposition. I want one night with your favourite and I will let you and your Angels live."

"Never!" Jonty shouts back. Now comes my turn, my chance to indirectly give my consent to the scene put before me.

"Wait, Charlie. I will do it. I will spend the night with you, Thin Man... but only if Charlie and his Angels can stay and join in the fun, too."

"It sounds like we have a deal."

CHAPTER FOURTEEN

~ Jonty ~

Hearing Billie's agreement is like receiving an electric charge to my whole body. I want to share the most amazing night with her, and it is going great.

I know how much she used to like double penetration, but no matter how much we try to replicate that with toys, it just isn't the same. It's not just the penetration she craves, it's the feeling of being wanted by two men at the same time. It's the way three bodies join together, sandwiching her between us with our hard, masculine bodies. It is the intimacy, contact and the feeling of fulfilment.

I love doing double penetration because she always insists that I stay to the front. She wants to kiss and see my face, and she wouldn't enjoy it as much if the other man was in my place. It didn't matter who was behind, not really, all that mattered was that we were all having a good time and all getting what we wanted and desired.

I love fucking my wife, but DP is on a whole other level. Her pussy squeezes me even tighter when her ass is also filled, and the thin wall of muscle between the two dicks offered very little barrier. I can feel the other man's rubbing against mine. It sends a thrill right through me, just thinking about it. It's been a long time since I have been with a man, or even wanted to be with a man, but that little act always got me going. It is so forbidden, so taboo and yet utterly beautiful.

Having the other girls with us is also incredible. As I lie on my back, Billie slides down my cock and she instructs Jill to sit on my face while things are getting going. Billie tells Jill she will warn her when she wants her to move and then she should join Sabrina and Kelly. She would like them to perform a scene for her; we would be two trios for a short amount of time.

While I kiss Jill's pussy, Billie kisses her passionately on the mouth. Billie always found it strange how I didn't want another man to kiss her but I didn't mind another girl. I know it sounds strange, but I find kissing very special. I can kiss her and give her what any other man can, so I don't want to see her kissing another man. Kissing another woman was okay since they are different, soft and sexy, and it is hot to watch.

Once Thin Man has prepared Billie with lube and put on his condom, he gets to work stretching her out so she is ready to take him. I can already feel his fingers as he slowly presses inside her. My girl thanks Jill and tells her to join the others as she starts to moan at the sensation of having both holes filled. Thin Man kisses down her back and winks at me as he does.

"Charlie, do you want to control her clit, or can I have the honours?" I tell him he can have it first before sucking mouthfuls of my wife's rounded globes. I have enough fun to contend with at the moment. Thin Man straddles me before pressing into Billie. Her eyes widen and she moans and shudders as her body is completely stretched and filled.

Wrapping an arm around her, Thin Man slips his hand further

down to her clit, and as we all find a natural rhythm, my gorgeous wife exhales against me in pleasure. Billie is in raptures. As her orgasm grows and peaks, I revel in her expression of sheer delight, the passion in her eyes and the warm wetness that seeps from within her and coats me.

"Kiss me. Oh, Jonty, I'm going to cum. Kiss me." I thrust up into her again and again as my lips crash over hers and my tongue rubs against hers until she calls out in surrender. Her body trembles and contorts as we both continue to move within her.

"I'm ready to blow, too, Charlie, are you?" Thin Man asks me as he quickens his pace. I can finally allow myself to let go now.

"I'm ready, Thin Man, hold on." We both pull out of Billie, and she kneels for us as we both shoot our hot cum over her tits. My cum feels like it pumps directly from my balls. "Fuck! That feels good," I shout and I start to laugh in between satisfied grunts and groans. It's exhilarating, and I have missed all this stuff so much.

The Angels rejoin us, but right now all I want to do is chill out, relax and enjoy each other's company. We all relocate to the hot tub. We will have more fun later, but for now I just want to chill with my wife and our temporary friends.

Tonight has been the perfect gift for us both. For over seven years, we have buried this side of us, but now it's clear to see that to deny that part is to deny who we are. We've had a massive blow out and although I know it cannot continue at this pace… it has to continue at some pace; I don't want to lose this side to us again. I just hope that after this amazing night Billie feels the same.

~ **Owen** ~

The office Christmas party is always a good night. The company pays for everything including accommodation, and after everything that happened on our date last night, Jamie and I decide now is as good a time as any to walk out together. I can't wait for everyone at work to finally discover that we are now a couple.

However, the only ones surprised are Jamie and me... Everyone assumed that we had been seeing each other for months. If only!

Whispers of my impending promotion have travelled like wildfire throughout the whole company, and many people are speculating on how Jamie and I will maintain our new romance long distance.

What they don't know yet is that earlier this afternoon Jamie signed on the dotted line, accepting a temporary position as my PA in the New York office. It feels like that is the most they are going to offer, and to be fair, Jamie keeps wavering and the temporary position makes her feel more in control. If she doesn't like it or we don't work out, she only has the position for six months. All that matters to me is that we have struck a deal.

That gives me six months to win Jamie over. Or hide her passport. But in any case, Jamie has agreed to move to New York with me. Not only will we be working together and moving to a new city in a new country together, but we are also moving in together. I am over the moon. On top of her telling me she is in love with me, everything is falling perfectly into place.

Jamie looks beautiful tonight; no matter where I am in the room my eyes automatically seek her out. I am head over heels crazy about her, and I am proud to have her by my side. I'm not going to deny that I'll be even happier in a couple of hours when I get to take her to bed and strip her out of her very sophisticated dress.

A couple of the fellas from marketing and finance corner me and ask me how I managed to bag Jamie. Apparently, she turned them all down over the past few months when they asked her out. I smile with pride as I shrug to them and say, "I simply must have chosen the right time."

When Jamie has finished mingling with her friends, we slowly gravitate towards each other and the rest of the room disappears. We dance together like no one else exists. I pull her under the mistletoe as Bing Crosby croons 'White Christmas' in the background, and we kiss without a care for who sees, because I love her and she loves me right back, and we don't care who knows or sees it.

"Get a room," someone shouts, and my dick stiffens and lengthens at the mere thought.

"I'm ready to call it a night when you are, handsome," my gorgeous girl tells me, so I pull her into my arms as we say our goodbyes.

The walk to our room takes a lifetime, but as soon as I open the door, it's like the room is on fire. The passion between us could cause an inferno.

We don't make it past the hallway because when I lift her she wraps her legs around me and I find she has no panties on. "Are you trying to fucking kill me, Jamie? No panties all night?" I groan before I slide inside her. "Fuck. Babe, it feels amazing not having to wear a rubber. I can actually feel you, all of you. It's like our first time all over again."

"Owen, I can't wait any longer, shut up and fuck me. I can feel you against me, too, and I'm going to die if you don't move soon." She is already so wet, warm and frenzied. It's going to be another amazing night finding pleasure together. And now we have plenty more nights ahead, too.

Jamie practically splinters apart in my arms as I press into her faster and harder. The direct feeling of her wetness against my impaled hard shaft is my own undoing. My knees buckle as I push her back against the wall and unload deep inside her for the first time.

The first of many, many times.

~ Lauren ~

I'm still on a high from getting engaged to Tim and my roaring success at Open Mic Night, but I suppose it has to end sometime. Tim wants to tell everyone immediately that we are getting married, and that means going to see my parents. I am still overwhelmed with the love and unabashed affection Tim showers me with, and I must pinch myself at least ten times an hour just to check I am not dreaming, that this is all very real and happening.

Tim loves me and wants to spend forever with me, and luckily, I feel exactly the same way about him. I am actually marrying the most amazing man I have ever met.

If only telling my parents could have been a simple phone call. That is how Tim told his sister. I love that they're so close. He simply dialled her number and told her, 'She said yes'. To which Fliss screamed and hollered down the phone until Tim told her to calm down or she'll go into labour.

As we travel by train to my parent's home in Cornwall, my nerves and trepidation grow. I want my parents to be happy for me, but my mother is difficult and rude and my daddy is meek and does as he is told. I just hope my mother isn't rude to Tim; I can take her being horrible to me but I'm going to kick up a stink if she is rude or impolite to Tim.

"Don't worry so much. I will ask your dad's permission and I'm sure once he realises how much I love you, he'll be happy for you." I give him a tight smile; Tim has no idea what we are up against. Not when it comes to my mother.

When I called my parent's house to say I would be visiting, my mother said, "You may as well bring your Christmas presents to save you bringing them in a couple of days." I guess that means I'm not invited to Christmas this year! Not that I'm bothered. I am going with Tim to his sister's house, and I couldn't be happier about it. I'm really looking forward to a family Christmas.

We are staying at Fliss and Marie's over the festive period as Fliss is due to have her baby any day now and Tim and I will be watching Lyndon and Celeste when her time comes. I can't wait!

My parent's home is next to the beach, looking like a postcard in its idyllic wonder. If only people knew about the darkness that lived inside.

I knock on the door and my dad answers almost straight away. He's probably been waiting by the door. "Dorothy, she's here! Our lollipop is here and she's brought a… friend with her."

"Dad, this is Tim. Tim, this is my dad, Lyle." They shake hands and my dad invites us into the lounge.

This room hasn't changed since I was a child: the same wallpaper, the same carpet, and the same furniture. My mum didn't believe in being frivolous; well she was very generous with her snide comments and backhanded insults, but that hardly counts. The whole house is old and dated but nonetheless clean and tidy. I find it suffocating, like the past is trying to claw me back so I don't move forward.

Tim and I sit on the settee together, while my dad nervously hops from one foot to the other as he waits for my mother. My father is a slight man; he is nervous and quiet. I often wonder if he has always been this anxious or if years of tolerating my mother made him this way.

My mother walks in like she is the Queen of Sheba. "Lauren, it is rude to invite guests without telling the host. And what have you done to your hair? Purple hair? I hope the neighbours didn't see you. Sit up straight; your tummy won't look as huge that way."

Tim tenses next to me, and I hold his hand to reassure him. I'm used to this talk; it's like water off a duck's back now. "Hi, Mum, I want you to meet Tim. He's my fiancé. He asked me to marry him, and I said yes."

My mother doesn't immediately respond, and then she smiles and my heart soars. She is happy for me. She is finally proud of me.

My delusion doesn't last long once she starts to speak. "Is this some sort of joke? I never get your sense of humour, Lauren. I thought fat people were supposed to be funny."

My stomach turns as I am filled with an anxious sickness. I don't want Tim to see or hear this. I have such shame about the way my mother sees me; I don't want Tim to see my shame.

"This is no joke. I have asked Lauren to marry me. I think your daughter is incredible and I cannot wait to marry her. With your permission, of course." My dad smiles as he extends his hand to Tim, ready to shake it and welcome him to the family.

However, my mother is quicker than the two of them. She slaps my father's hand away and turns on Tim. "Has she paid you to tell us all this? Are you an actor or a gigolo?"

"Mum, please stop. Tim and I are in love. This is genuine." But my mother doesn't believe me; I can tell by the way she laughs mockingly at me.

"A man like him would not be seen dead with a fat waster like you, Lauren…"

I don't get to hear the rest of her spiel. Tim stands up, takes my hand and tells me we are leaving.

"How the hell did someone as sweet and as beautiful as you come out of a horrible old dog like her? It's no wonder you feel so bad about yourself when your own mother is a bullying hypocrite. I'm sorry, Flower, but no one is ever going to speak to you like that again."

As we get to the front door, my dad tries to stop us from leaving. "I know she can be difficult but she means well. Please, don't go like this."

"Why haven't you ever stood up for your daughter? How could you let her be destroyed by her own mother? You should hang your head in shame. You are just as bad as her; you may not have said the words but you stood by and let her continually hurt your little girl."

Tim is furious on my behalf. No one has ever stuck up for me like he has. I have never had someone I could depend on to have my back, until now. The tears roll down my face as he continues to tell my dad exactly what he thinks of him and my mother.

"You allowed the mistreatment of your child, sir. And now she is mine, not you or anyone else will treat her that way ever again."

My mother remains in the lounge and doesn't say anything more. I am just about ready to let Tim take me home when anger rises within me.

How dare she! How dare she try to ruin the one true happiness

I've ever had?

I march back into the lounge, ready to get to the bottom of this once and for all. "Why do you hate me so much?" I shout at her. There is a fleeting look of panic in her eyes but then she continues to look bored thereafter. "Are you going to say anything? Why are you so bitter and nasty, Mum? Why do you say those horrible things?"

"Stop being so dramatic, Lauren. I don't say horrible things. I state the truth, but you can't handle the truth."

So, there you have it. The truth, or at least, my mother's truth. She truly thinks I'm fat and disgusting and the only way I'll get a man is if I pay him.

"Dorothy... ENOUGH! That's not the truth. You hate her because she is a carbon copy of you. She reminds you so much of yourself that you cannot stand it. You despise her because she is happy with the things you could never accept about yourself. You hurt our girl to try and make yourself feel better about who you are." My dad has never, ever raised his voice in front of me before. He's never stood up for me before either. My mother's face is a picture as he finally finds his backbone and stands up to her.

He doesn't stop there, now he has found his gumption. Everything pours from him like lava from a volcano.

"This stops right now, Dorothy; you're hurting our daughter and we are going to lose her if you keep pushing her away. Lauren, my little lollipop, please forgive me. I will try to be a better man and, most importantly, a better dad."

My dad walks over to Tim and holds out his hand.

"Thank you, Tim. I couldn't have wished for better for my daughter. I know that you'll love her and look after her from the way you have just stood up for her and protected her. I hope in time I can change your opinion of me through my actions, too."

When Tim shakes his hand, hope flows from my heart right through my veins and throughout my whole body. It doesn't matter anymore what anyone thinks or says. With Tim on my team, I'll always have a home, right in his arms.

"So, you're getting married, Lollipop! Congratulations to both of you." My father's attempt at smoothing over what just happened is appreciated but it's not enough. My mother sits on the edge of her seat like she has a rod up her ass and purses her lips, making it look like she is chewing a wasp. While she passes no further comments about my appearance or unlikability, she also doesn't acknowledge that I am getting married either.

We sit uncomfortably for a few minutes, but when my dad offers to make tea, I stand and refuse. "We are hoping to set a date soon, and I would be happy to see you both there. But if keeping a civil tongue is too hard, I ask that you simply stay away." I hug my dad goodbye. "Your Christmas presents are in the bag in the hallway. I love you."

I walk away holding Tim's hand. In some ways, I feel relieved; this was long overdue. In other ways, I wonder if I ever get the blessing of a daughter, will I become as cold hearted and cruel as my mother?

When we reach the train station, Tim pulls me to him. "That was interesting. Let's not do that again in a rush." I smile at him, the man who has my heart and the first person to show me what unconditional love really looks and feels like.

With him, I have everything I will ever need.

~ Jamie ~

Christmas Eve arrives and today is the day I have been dreading: the day of Carl's wedding. However, Owen is coming with me, Billie and Jonty will be there and once we have stayed for an acceptable amount of time, we can leave, and Christmas will really start.

This will be our first Christmas, and we are going to spend the day at Billie's house. I asked Owen for this one thing, to celebrate Christmas with my family before we leave for New York, and he graciously agreed. It upsets me that next year I may be in a different country to my niece and nephew. Every Christmas since they were born is etched in my memory; I want this one to be spectacular.

Owen and I will be leaving for New York the day after New Year. Our tickets are booked, our bags are mostly packed and we discussed booking a suite until we signed for our apartment, which all came as part of Owen's resettlement package. However, it turned out to be unnecessary since the apartment, our new home together, is ready and waiting for us. I am still having trouble believing this is happening.

When Owen asked me to go to New York with him, I could think of a million reasons why I shouldn't or couldn't, but I instantly said yes anyway. I really love him and want to take this chance. I don't want to live a life of regret, a life filled with what ifs.

The following day, I marched into the CEO's office and demanded a transfer... I was amazed that they agreed to a temporary contract. I later found out that Owen had been trying to secure my job for me, too, and that made me so happy because it confirmed that he didn't just ask me to move with him on a whim, but that he truly wants me by his side.

Owen is dressed in an expensive suit and groans when he sees me in my dress. "You're not meant to show the bride up, Jamie. You look out of this world, babe," he tells me as he appreciates the effort I have made. As I fix his tie, I catch a glimpse of us in the mirror and smile. We look perfect together. "Why are you smiling?" he asks me with a look of amusement on his face.

"I just saw us together in the mirror, and we look so good." He kisses the top of my head and holds me close to him. My body instantly starts to flame with desire, and the feel of him hardening against me confirms he feels the same, too. "Come on, let's get this done and then we can have some fun."

Carl's wedding reception is at the Alexander Palace. I am hoping for two hours of toffee-nosed mingling at a maximum and then we can leave. Who gets married on Christmas Eve? It's a major pain in the ass. At least we don't have to suffer through the service and wedding breakfast, too.

Trepidation starts to fill me as we get closer to the venue. All these people will know that this marriage came from Carl cheating on me, and it makes me embarrassed and self-conscious.

The venue looks over the top but beautiful. Guests are greeted with flutes of champagne and a brass band. Carl and Francesca stand near the doors shaking hands and embracing their guests as they arrive. "Jamie, I'm so glad you came." Carl seems to look at me with genuine affection, and when he turns to Owen and extends his hand to him, I think this night might actually be okay.

"You look beautiful, Francesca. Congratulations." She gives me a tight smile, and I leave it at that. I quickly spot Billie and Jonty but groan when I realise they are sitting at a table with my father and stepmother.

"Jamie. I didn't think you would show. You're looking well. And who is this?" My father, a man of many words but they are all generic, non-committal words. The last time I saw him was when I broke things off with Carl and my dad visited me to instruct me 'to not make a scene'.

"Hi, Dad, this is Owen, my boyfriend. Owen, this is my Dad, Ted, and his wife, Marceline." My Dad continues to make standard small talk as we take our seats.

"We are surprised you actually came. I told Francesca we didn't know you had a boyfriend, and we were shocked to hear you were bringing someone. It's a bit trashy, Jamie!" Marceline comments, without invitation

"I'm sorry, what's a bit trashy? She was invited with a plus one. Francesca calling her trashy is hilarious, she's marrying the man she stole from Jamie, for fuck's sake." Anger flares in Billie's eyes as she protests on my behalf. Jonty winks at me; he'll calm her before it gets out of hand. Those two have always had my back.

"We contemplated that this man was an escort, but I'm sure I've seen you about before." My father has upped his jovial levels, trying to disguise his undertone of judgement.

"Yes, we've met before. Owen Matthews. I work with Jamie, and now we are together." Owen kisses my hand and heat bubbles in my tummy. "We are moving to New York next week, too, aren't we, babe?"

Marceline's eyes widen, "You're moving to New York? Oh, I get it, is this meant to be your 'look at me, I'm doing great' act? This is not the time nor the place to be making a scene, Jamie." Before I can reply to my stepmother, Billie does.

"Why don't you do us all a favour, Marceline, and fuck off. This has got fuck all to do with you." I love my sister; I love that she says exactly what she is thinking and has always completely had my back. Jonty simply touches her arm and Billie almost hisses at my dad and stepmother.

"This isn't an act. I'm in love with Owen. He got a promotion and is moving to New York, and we want to be together, so I am going, too. If you had bothered to contact me at all over the past five months you would know all this and a whole lot more. Why didn't you return my calls, Dad?"

My father has the good grace to look shamefaced, but I'm not falling for it. Not this time. He stayed away when I needed the people that loved me to support me. He actually sided with the man who cheated on me and humiliated me to save face with his business partner. There is no time like the present to clear things up. I am moving to New York next week and so God knows when I will see or hear from my father again.

"It made things a bit... awkward, you know, when you left Carl? It looks really bad on me, and I've been in business with Gerry for decades. So I thought it best to give you some time and space to sort your head and life out."

"I left Carl because I found him in bed screwing Francesca behind my back. My life fell apart because he cheated on me, and you treated me like I'd done something wrong." With anger firing up inside me, I continue to give my father a piece of my mind. "You ought to be ashamed of yourself... You call yourself my dad? You're no dad. That's my dad right there."

I stand up and point to Jonty.

"That's the man who has raised me and looked out for me. The two of them right there are my parents; they have done everything you failed to do, and I am proud to consider them my parents and as the people who raised me."

My sister beams at me with pride. I mean every single word I say.

"I am your daughter, and you let a man humiliate me and let me down." I slowly clap my dad as I stand up. "Well done. But don't worry, *Dad*, I want to thank you. Thank you for showing me exactly how to not be a parent. It was a hard lesson, but a valuable one all the same. I know if I do the absolute opposite of you when I have children then I'll be halfway decent. Thank you for showing me how not to do it. Come on, Owen."

"Jamie, wait..." My sister and Jonty join us. "Don't leave us here with this shower of shite. Let's go and have our family Christmas."

As I walk away, I am happy and content to draw that chapter of my life to a close.

CHAPTER FIFTEEN

~ Tim ~

After the debacle with Lauren's parents, I want to wrap her in cotton wool. No one will ever hurt her again if I have anything to do with it. I am furious about her mother; she is so vile and hateful. She is the opposite of my Lauren. I want to hate them both for hurting my delicate flower and for making her doubt herself.

I have always taken sanctuary in my family. My father passed away when I was a young man and my mother died just before Celeste was born. Felicity and I have each other and that is important. I look after her and she looks after me. Lauren has never had that, but she will now. My love will have a family with me, and we will cherish her and love her and eventually, she will learn to love herself.

"I want to move in together and set a date for our wedding, Flower." She rests her head on my shoulder and agrees that is what she wants, too. "Where shall we live? I quite like your apartment."

"I'd love to stay in my apartment, at least for now, Tim. Will you move in with me, please?" I kiss her as I agree, and inside I'm really happy that she asked me this time. My Lauren is becoming more secure and vocal in our relationship, and I love it. I want her to know this is what love looks and feels like. I wholly love her without limitation and not based on stupid conditions.

We are staying at my sister's house for the holidays. It's Christmas Eve, and Fliss is in slow labour. She is determined to wait until Christmas morning before she goes to hospital because she wants to see the children opening their presents. I am giddy in anticipation of becoming an uncle again and it has me thinking of the future.

"I want a baby," I tell Lauren bluntly, and she flashes her dimples at me as she smiles. She told me last night that she wants a baby and it completely threw me.

"Are you sure? You seemed scared shitless last night, Tim," she teases me as I kiss down her neck to her clavicle. "You know it could take a while, with my condition."

She explained to me last night that she has Polycystic Ovarian Syndrome and that we may have trouble conceiving, but I just told her that we will have a lot more sex to double our chances. On a more serious note, I added that we would face every obstacle together and if she wants to start trying, I am ready for that, too.

My silly sister ends up giving birth at home in the early hours of Christmas morning. I see things no man should see until his wife is giving him his own child. There is blood and guts and gore and a lot of crying… and that is just me!

On the bathroom floor, while holding onto her partner's hand and with her future sister-in-law helping to guide her baby's head into the world, my sister blessed me with another niece who she named Ivy.

Lauren and I are in awe of her, the tiny, little bundle of joy who yawns and falls into a deep slumber soon after being born. "I really want one now, Flower. She is so cute. I can just imagine our very own little one with gorgeous green eyes and big dimples just like her mummy."

When she looks back at me, still covered in blood and other strange fluids, her eyes blaze with passion and love. "I'm so glad we're going to try. You'll be an amazing dad, Tim."

"Merry Christmas, Lauren. Here is to many more, and who knows, this time next year that could be our baby you hold in your arms."

The midwife and paramedics arrive and after checking over mother and baby, they declare them both fit and well. They stay until the sun rises again to take some observations, but they then leave us to celebrate Christmas as a family.

We all drag our presents into Fliss and Marie's bedroom, and while Fliss nurses her newborn daughter in the middle of the bed, we all open our presents and toast with mimosas.

Lyndon looks crest-fallen when he realises he has another sister. "I'm stuck in a house with four girls now, Uncle Tim." But I assure him that as the only male, he is technically the man of the house and that seems to cheer him up somewhat.

I shower Lauren with presents. I love to treat her, but I am particularly looking forward to giving her the last present. It is a framed photo of us kissing at Tables & Fables and etched into the frame are the words: 'Our Only Christmas as an Unmarried Couple'.

"Thank you, Tim. It's perfect; everything is perfect."

~ Owen ~

I am not looking forward to going to Carl's wedding, but I want to support Jamie through this. I think this will be the ideal time for her to demonstrate that she has moved on and is happy.

I never expected the day to go as it does. Jamie obviously already told me about her strained relationship with her stepmother and from the few times she mentioned her father, I know she feels disappointed and let down by him. What actually happens at the wedding is far better and much more satisfying than I anticipated.

Seeing her stand up to her father and stepmother fills me with immense pride. My feisty and strong Jamie is back, firing on all cylinders, and she won't take any shit. It is such a turn on seeing her defending herself and paying tribute to Billie and Jonty. The way she keeps her temper, the heat rising on her cheeks, and her eloquence and grace leave me astounded.

I have loved her for a long time, even when I didn't know I did and now she is finally mine.

We all leave the Alexander Palace together and as soon as we hit the pavement, we all look at each other and burst out laughing.

"Did you see the look on Marceline's face? She looked like she'd swallowed a wasp," Jamie says, which sets off another round of laughter.

"The best part was when Billie told her to do us all a favour and fuck off. Her head wobbled. I nearly choked trying not to laugh," Jonty adds as he kisses his wife with pride. "Thank you for what you said in there, Jamie. It's been a pleasure being your pseudo-dad. We're going to miss you so much when you go to New York, but we are already planning a visit out very soon."

We part ways, getting into separate taxis after Jamie reassures them we will be at their house tonight. We are just going back to mine to collect our stuff. Billie raises her eyebrows at us. "What is it with you young ones and your euphemisms? You're running back to the privacy of your bedroom because that was totally hot, let's get it right!"

I don't disagree with her, but Jamie groans and covers her face that is red from blushing so much, which has us all laughing again.

When we get back to my apartment, I tell Jamie how proud of her I am, and she bursts into tears. "What's wrong, sweetheart? You did amazing; you told him and his wife exactly what you thought of them, but you kept your dignity and grace. You showed everyone that you still have fight and fire inside you. Plus, I heard the whispers, everyone was saying how beautiful you looked. They're not wrong, Jamie, you are the most magnificent woman I have ever met."

She smiles back at me with tears still in her eyes. "I'm just hormonal after starting the pill, but God, it felt good to get that all off my chest because I feel like I have tied up all my loose ends here. I can walk away now and not wonder if it was me or if I could have done things differently. It's done and I'm happy about it. Now it's time for the next chapter, for our new beginning."

She pushes me down on the settee and hitches up her long gown so she can straddle me.

"I can't wait for our next chapter, Jamie. You complete my life. I never thought life could be this good, and then I met you."

Her eyes are filled with passion and longing. "You're all I want in my stockings this year, Owen, and every year after. I love you so much. Merry Christmas," she whispers against my ear as she kisses down my neck and pulls my tie off. She unbuttons my shirt, kissing all the way down my chest, stopping only to kiss my tattoos. I lift my shirt off and throw it to one side and shiver from the sensation of my girl nestled on my lap and in my arms.

We kiss for a long time, lazily, hungrily and then finally more demandingly. I unzip her gown from the back and tug it up over her head, and when her body is finally free for me to see, I groan with longing for her. She sits still astride me in just a pair of French knickers. I kiss down her chest to her little bee stings, my wonderful mouthfuls of pure pleasure. Her exhale tells me this is how she likes it.

Jamie kisses me back, all down my own chest and lower still. As she unbuckles my belt, I lift my hips while she undresses me, briefs and pants both at once. "I want to suck you until you blow... Would that be okay, Owen?" I nod to her, not trusting my voice at this moment.

Jamie slips down between my legs, kissing every part of me until she reaches my dick. She playfully licks me, in featherlight strokes using the top and underside of her little pink tongue to caress me into a crazed state of need. "Suck me, beautiful, take me all in." I grip my dick still for her, and with a little smile, she places a small kiss on the tip before swirling her tongue around the tip and finally taking me all the way in her mouth, as far as she can. The little noises she makes drive me wild, and it doesn't take long for me to reach my climax. I haven't even touched her yet, but she just has the power to spell bind me and captivate me.

"I'm going to blow, babe. I'm so close." She bobs her head up and down faster until I cannot stand the pleasure any longer and release. Jamie's face is full of triumph as my cum fills her mouth and throat. I can't seem to stop.

"Baby, that was amazing... but I think it's my turn now!" I tell her as I get her to stand so I can help her out of her wet French knickers.

I lift her onto my face and use my hands to show her how to move so her pussy grazes my nose and tongue. She whimpers as she rubs herself against my hot, greedy mouth, slowly edging towards fulfilment. My nose is jammed right in against her clit and my tongue darts inside her and then back out to explore her folds. She doesn't need to tell me when she starts to cum. I sense it; I feel it. She becomes slippery and wet and her thighs tense as her movements become more erratic. I ravenously lick up all her honey as she quivers and shudders her way to satisfaction.

Afterwards, I make love to her, slowly and sweetly, and whisper all the love words I know. She is the light in my life, the love of my life and the greatest thing to ever happen to me. I know I am a lucky man.

As the bells ring out to indicate it's Christmas Day, we make our way back for a family Christmas at Billie and Jonty's house. Life doesn't get any better than this.

~ Billie ~

Christmas has been amazing, probably the best I have ever known, and I know that it comes down to having a better life balance. A little bit of what you fancy will always make you feel happier and more content. The children seem happier and my Jonty appears to have his spark back.

My little sister is finally settled in her life, too, and it is heart-warming to see her in love with a decent man. Owen is a cracking fella, and I know from the way he treats Jamie and from the way he looks at her that he loves her a whole lot and will take care of her when they move out to the States together. I am going to miss her more than I can express but I am also internally cheering her on from the side lines: 'Go on Jamie, this is your time now'. I am both proud and happy for her. I don't think we will be waiting long to hear their wedding bells.

Yesterday, Jonty and I sat down and spoke about our experimental Christmas present to one another and our thoughts. I initiated this experiment, but I am happy that he feels able to approach me so we could do the post-mortem together. For me, the greatest outcome from our experiment is that our home life, our vanilla sex life and our regular, mundane marriage all seems so much better now.

"Bilbo, I've got to be honest, I feel twenty years younger. I feel happier, content and satisfied. I know this has been non-stop intense but we had to go all out for the sake of the time span we set. I think this past month has been spectacular. I don't want to lose that side of our relationship again. What are your thoughts?" He waits with bated breath for my reply.

"I love you; I fancy you, and I have enjoyed every moment we have shared, Jonty. I want to keep that side of our relationship, too, albeit at a less intense pace. Just to keep the passion going and to keep our more varied preferences sated. I only want that with you. You're the man who owns my heart and fulfils my every fantasy."

We have settled on partaking in a bit of spice once a month, and I feel this is a better compromise. We can always reassess and change if this doesn't suit us. We are in complete synchronicity now and the future has never seemed brighter.

Tonight is New Year's Eve and we have a massive night planned. It's Open Mic Night at Tables & Fables and it's our first ticketed event. I managed to secure a reading from a really popular author, and she has a massive readership who have jumped on the opportunity to see their favourite author recite a passage from her newest book.

I am fixing the booth outside, I have a man on security for the first time ever; he's in charge of the guest list. Around his booth is a banner announcing our special guest. "LIVE: Best Selling Author: Melody Tyden". It's going to be a spectacular night.

On top of it being New Year, tonight is also a joint party for Jamie and Owen leaving and Tim and Lol getting engaged. It's all-hands-on-deck; even Jonty is having to work tonight which is hilarious. I don't think my husband has ever done a menial job. The thought of Jonty wearing an apron trying to make a latte macchiato is just too sweet.

Both Lol and Tim are performing tonight, too. I am delighted that reading for Lol last week boosted her confidence and readership enough that she feels worthy of taking the stage now. I always knew she had talent, and now this new year will see every dream fall into place for her. As for Tim, who knew he was so adorable? He is going to be playing his guitar and singing a Beatles song. He says it's for Lol and I have the distinct impression that everything he does will be for Lol now. He is completely devoted to her and a better matched couple, I would struggle to find.

We have a mixed bag of regular and new customers booked in tonight. One of the locals who has missed out on tickets stops when she sees the sign. "Is Melody Tyden really going to read live here tonight?" And when I tell her yes, she groans in frustration at missing out on such a treat. "This is my card. If she comes back to read again, call me, please. I love her work."

The children will be with us tonight. Oscar, the grouch, has set up his new PlayStation in Jamie's apartment and plans to play FIFA all night. My little Glow-worm, Chloe, has a miniature matching apron and will be helping us with the cakes and biscuits. She is more excited about working in the café than she has ever been about Christmas.

I have reserved a booth for Melody, who arrives before the allotted time with her husband and daughter and a small group of friends. I am starstruck when I finally meet her, and I tell her all about Lol and how talented I think she is. "She'll be reading a passage from her new book just before you, please check her out. She is so amazing and she just doesn't realise it yet."

Melody is modest and tells me she definitely will do. "It's usually the quiet ones who are brilliant. I'm looking forward to listening to her work."

The place is jam-packed and I know now that I will be asking Dana to join me as my partner here. Tables & Fables has taken on a life of its own and has become bigger than I had ever dreamed about. Who would have thought a little book café could become the epicentre of creative types?

Jamie and Owen have a date first but will be coming here, too; it is partly their leaving party after all. Jamie has graciously let us use her apartment for tonight in case the children became tired or anti-social in Oscar's case. She has moved most of her stuff to storage now anyway and stays at Owen's most nights.

I turn on the mic and announce that there is a full itinerary for tonight but if anyone else wants to perform they should come and speak to me straight away. The first performer takes the stage and the crowd seems to swell with excitement. After an hour or so, Lol takes to the stage and we all cheer for her. Her words sound so much better coming from her mouth; she can deliver them in the way she intended. I watch my friend with pride. She will find success this year; I can feel it. This feeling is compounded when I look at Melody Tyden and notice the impressed look on her face as she listens closely to Lol's reading.

Melody takes to the stage to do her reading and the crowd that have come to see her erupt into life. They encourage her so well; she has awesome supporters. She takes her time and then also answers a couple of questions from the crowd. Her fans, already armed with her newest paperback, swamp her to ask for signatures and she is generous to them and doesn't take their loyalty for granted. I watch from afar as Melody makes a beeline for Lol. I wonder what they are talking about.

The queue for the counter is becoming larger by the second and I hope Jonty hasn't broken the card machine again. The man is a disaster! When I check on him, I see him deep in conversation with a gorgeous couple, so I have to go and prompt him back to work.

The closer I get, the better this couple look, there is something very special about them alright. The woman has long dark hair, but it is evident she is a natural blonde just like me. She is beautiful. If only she was a little older… or I was a little younger. Her boyfriend is incredibly handsome; he has an air of authority about him. He reminds me so much of Jonty when he was younger.

Jonty looks engrossed and excited, and when he points to the ring on the man's finger, I get it. It's the same ring Jonty is wearing: a token of our kink. No wonder they appear special! Our 'kind' seem to attract each other like magnets.

I can't help but feel flattered when I compliment the young woman and her boyfriend looks at me admiringly, telling me he is game for fun. Maybe another time, another place, but right now it's the biggest night at Tables & Fables and if I slope off, so will my staff.

The surprise performance of the night has got to be Tim. He looks so different in his casual clothes with his guitar in his hands and the mic close to his lips. "This song is for my beautiful fiancée. You all know her as Lol Outloud but to me she is my

Flower, my Lauren. I love you." He blows a kiss to Lol and the crowd is in raptures. As he sings 'Dig a Pony' directly to her, Lol cries, in fact I think we all do. Tim is a talented showman and the song, although not as widely known as some of The Beatles other hits, is absolutely perfect.

Jamie and Owen return shortly before midnight and while I help to serve the last customers before the countdown starts, she gathers the children together so we can do the countdown as usual, as a family. "Here is to a new year, a new chapter and new beginnings. I hope the happiness we found at the end of this year continues into the next," Owen says as he clinks glasses with Jamie. They are so loved up; I couldn't have wished for better for my little sister.

I pick up my little Chloe as we do the countdown. Jonty holds on to Oscar by the shoulders so he doesn't scarper back to his PlayStation. Jamie and Owen are already kissing.

"Happy New Year, everyone..." I shout as the bells of Big Ben chime throughout the whole city.

"Happy New Year, Bilbo," Jonty murmurs into my ear before kissing me sweetly.

"Happy New Year, my sexy silver fox."

The worst part about being the boss is that you can't slack. This morning as I open the Café, I am already yawning and my body screams for its bed. My day is brightened when the young, handsome man with the kink ring that we met last night shows up asking for a word in private.

I take him into the back office and thankfully, due to hangovers and lack of sleep, no one takes any notice of us. "I wanted to approach you about a dynamic. My girl, Liv, has never been with a woman before but would like to explore it. I immediately thought of you. I know you are interested. I can tell you know what you're doing and that you can be trusted. This is my card if you are interested in the four of us meeting in the future."

I take his card and tell him I will discuss it with Jonty. Trying to be discreet, I take a peek at the name on his card.

Noah Stamer
Stamer Luxury Hotels Group.

Oh my! I can't keep my surprise in. "*The* Noah Stamer?"

He nods to me, self assured and confident.

"Ok, Noah Stamer. I will definitely discuss this with my husband. Are you sure your girl is up for this?"

"Trust me, Liv and I are completely on the same page."

I give him two Tables & Fables mugs as he leaves and he smiles as he looks down at them.

"We'll both have no option but to think of you now when we drink our coffee."

The thought sends a thrill through me.

~ The End ~

Bonus Chapter

~ Jamie ~

As I settle in my seat in business class, Owen checks the brochure. "I want to get you a massive Toblerone," he tells me, pointing out the various sizes and choices.

"You ate the last one, Owen, don't you mean you're getting yourself a massive Toblerone?" He laughs at my retort; we both enjoyed sharing the Toblerone that I bought on our way to Copenhagen. I am looking forward to sharing this one with him, too.

I expected to feel nervous, but because I am here on this flight with Owen, I don't. Now, I'm not miraculously cured, I still hate flying but Owen has the ability to make me forget.

The plane starts to move slowly, and I am both excited to start this new adventure with Owen and sad to leave my family and friends behind.

"Don't cry, babe. We will be back in six weeks for Tim's wedding," Owen tells me as tears well up in my eyes. "Besides, moving to New York means that you're getting closer to where my family is located. I can't wait to introduce you to my mom."

Owen grew up in Kingston, Ontario and it's not too far from New York. After speaking on the phone with his mom, I am eager to meet her, too. In fact, I am looking forward to getting to know his whole family. Owen has a younger sister, and two older brothers and a handful of nieces and nephews. Hopefully next weekend, once we have settled into our new apartment, we are going to drive up. I know Owen is itching to see them all.

When the flight attendant comes to offer us a drink, Owen orders tea and biscuits. "We always have to have tea and cookies when we fly because it helps calm her nerves." He holds my hand and winks at me when he explains our order. God, I love him. I am so blessed to have found my true love, and he was right under my nose the whole time.

My life has changed immeasurably, and yet Owen and I are about to embark on another exciting adventure.

I'll always be grateful for my Festive Fling.

Coming Soon: The Spinoff of Festive Flings

EMMA LEE-JOHNSON

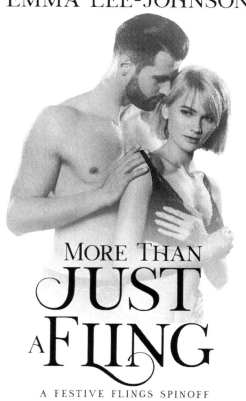

MORE THAN
JUST
A FLING

A FESTIVE FLINGS SPINOFF

More Than Just a Fling

Synopsis

Owen Matthews believes he is the luckiest man on this earth. He is young, successful, rich, good-looking and now, he has landed the woman he has secretly been in love with for years. With Jamie right beside him, he is moving from London to New York City after being promoted to a lucrative job with lots of perks.

Life couldn't get any better!

But as life often goes, when one thing falls into place, something else falls apart. Being in New York means being closer to his family in Ontario, and with that comes the baggage of the past. Is Owen *really* ready to commit to Jamie, or is there someone else lurking in the past who still shines a torch for him?

Owen's family are delighted that he is practically back on home soil; after all, New York isn't so far away. Will their expectations and plans for him match up to what his heart wants and needs?

Jamie loves her new life in New York, but she misses her family and friends... and then she starts to miss Owen too. What was the point in being here if she never sees him outside of work? She makes new friends and starts to find a life outside her relationship with Owen, making her wonder if this is even what she wants anymore?

With both being pulled in opposite directions... one question remains...

Is this More than just a Fling?

Expected: Late September 2022

Acknowledgement

There are many people I would like to thank. First and foremost, my husband and sons, for supporting me. I know I'm a pain, but you four are my world. Thank you for all the cups of tea, biscuits and for always having my back. I love you all.

Tables & Fables Book Café in Greenwich sadly does not exist. I wish it did. I promise, if writing doesn't work out, I will be opening my own Book Café with Open Mic Nights!

The café may not be real, but the guest author who featured on New Year's Eve, most definitely is. Melody Tyden is my very dear friend and an idol of mine; you can find her work on Amazon and Patreon. Thank you so, so much for everything, Melody, your friendship means the world to me.

Noah and Liv, who also made a guest appearance on New Year's Eve are characters from Melody's book, Tinsel Temptation. We made our smutty Christmas romance journey together over Christmas 2021. If you have enjoyed my book, then I would highly recommend not only Tinsel Temptation but the other three books in the Christmas in the City series.

The most important part of being an independent author is your support network. I am blessed to have a fantastic group that has my back. My broomies, we ride at sundown lol! Steph, Chicken, Emm, Brandi, M Jayy, T. Nikki, Char, Scar, Itchay, CassyDoll, Sara, Sahra, CK Marissa, Feather, Yra and Isi are just a select few who continually support and encourage me.

To my faithful readers, Emma's Angels with Attitude, thank you for sticking by me and supporting me as I attempt to make all my dreams a reality. I hope you enjoy the books as much as I enjoy writing them.

Last but by no means least, I would like to make special acknowledgement to a few extraordinary ladies who have helped me beyond measure. M J Espinosa, I got your back girl, and I am so grateful you came into my life. Steph C, I hope this is just the beginning, thank you for the invaluable support. Tanja, for helping me find all the A-Holes (if you know, you know).

Finally, you meet people in life that you just know are your people, I consider this woman to be one of my closest friends and allies, she has boosted me and buoyed me, and has kicked me up the butt when I have wanted to give up. She has shared my tears and my hollers of joy, and I couldn't ask for a better person in my corner. Mariarosa, from the bottom of my heart, thank you for everything you do for me, my little gem.

Books By This Author

The Alpha's Property

Eva: I used to dream about love at first sight and being swept off my feet. Instead, I have a husband who constantly humiliates me and puts me down, and has literally left me stranded at the side of the road. Life seems pretty grim until I walk into the car dealership and the most handsome man I've ever met tells me I belong to him.

Aiden: I've been waiting a long time to meet my mate, and I could never have imagined it would be someone like Eva. She's human, for a start, and she's already married. But dammit, the moment I laid eyes on her I knew I needed her. If there's even a chance for us to be together, I'll do whatever it takes to make her mine.

When Eva and Aiden's worlds collide, it's more than just their relationship at stake: there's Preston, Aiden's Beta, whose mate refuses to commit; Amber, Aiden's sister, whose trust issues prevent her from embracing the happiness her mate bond could bring; Salma, Eva's best friend and a Mafia princess who's being pushed into a marriage to keep her position; Alejandro, Salma's intended who wants a lot more from her than to share her throne; Melanie, whose eyes are gradually opened to the kind of man her lover is; and Ryan, Eva's husband who doesn't want her but doesn't want anyone else to have her too.

Lives intertwine and secrets are revealed as Eva comes to terms with Aiden's claim on her heart and soul: is she really ready to be The Alpha's Property?

Disclaimer: This book contains material of an adult nature and is intended for those aged 18 years and over.

The Alpha's Heir

Eva should be on cloud nine. Her abusive ex-husband is out of her life for good and she's mated to Alpha Aiden, a man who adores her. Things are never that easy, though, not when the truth about her father brings up a whole new set of challenges. She's got to face the past before moving forward, but how far can she bend without breaking?

Meanwhile, Aiden's attention is needed everywhere. He wants to support Eva and her transition to being his Luna, but he also must support his sister, Amber, as she faces trial. On top of that, there's the mystery about their mother and why she disappeared from their lives. It's a lot for any man to deal with.

He could ask for help from his Beta, Preston, but he has problems of his own, while Salma continues to search for the people responsible for poisoning her papa and her mysterious half-brother. Can she and Alejandro take the reins of their Mafia territory, or have they already been compromised?

Secrets and schemes combine in a perfect storm that threatens to tear apart the fragile happiness that's started to grow. With everyone facing their own demons, can they all pull through this together?

~*~ Trigger Warnings ~*~
The content in this book is of an adult nature, intended for adults over the age of 18 years.

It contains scenes of a sexual nature, violence and pregnancy loss.

Emma Lee-Johnson

Romance Author

My pen-name is Emma. I am a proud scouser and if you are not from the U.K, that means, I was born and bred in Liverpool, the birthplace of the Beatles and of course, the best football team in the world: Liverpool Football Club.

I am a happily married mother to three handsome sons. I love to read, write, bake and thrift. I have always wanted to write, but lacked confidence. I had a stack of pretty notebooks filled with ideas, plotlines, characters and dialogue, but I kept them hidden, fearing I was not good enough. I decided to take the plunge, after having a house fire, that me and my family were lucky to escape and I began to share my writing online.

I previously worked as a Mental Health Nurse. My passions are mental health awareness because of my work and Autism Awareness and Acceptance, the latter because two of my boys are diagnosed with Autism and I have had to work my ass off to get them the support and acceptance they have.

I decided that I wanted to explore the independent publishing route, I wanted to retain the rights to my own work and hold a physical copy of my writing. Less than a year after I first started sharing my writing I self-published my novel, The Alpha's Property, which is now joined by it sequel: The Alpha's Heir.

I have a few projects in the pipeline, including my Flings Series and another paranormal romance novel.

Keep In touch:

@emmaleejohnson | Linktree

Amazon Author Profile (Follow me for more updates and information.)

Website

Facebook Profile

Tiktok

Instagram

Emma's Angels with Attitude FB group A group for my readers and supporters, lots of fun, games and giveaways.

My Ko-fi Page Signed books and merch and blog posts too!

Printed in Great Britain
by Amazon

29291153R00167